OVERKILT

Books by Kaitlyn Dunnett

Liss MacCrimmon Mysteries:

Kilt Dead
Scone Cold Dead
A Wee Christmas Homicide
The Corpse Wore Tartan
Scotched
Bagpipes, Brides, and Homicides
Vampires, Bones, and Treacle Scones
Ho-Ho-Homicide
The Scottie Barked at Midnight
Kilt at the Highland Games
X Marks the Scot
Overkilt

Deadly Edits Mysteries:

Crime & Punctuation

Published by Kensington Publishing Corp.

OVERKILT

KAITLYN DUNNETT

KENSINGTON BOOKS
www.kensingtonbooks.com

KENSINGTON BOOKS are published by

Kensington Publishing Corp.
119 West 40th Street
New York, NY 10018

Library of Congress Card Catalogue Number: 2018944164

Kensington and the K logo Reg. U.S. Pat. & TM Off.

ISBN-13: 978-1-4967-1262-2
ISBN-10: 1-4967-1262-5
First Kensington Hardcover Edition: November 2018

eISBN-13: 978-1-4967-1264-6
eISBN-10: 1-4967-1264-1
Kensington Electronic Edition: November 2018

10 9 8 7 6 5 4 3 2 1

Printed in the United States of America

OVERKILT

Chapter One

The sight of two women in long-sleeved, high-necked, floor-length, pale purple cotton dresses, standing in front of the check-in desk at The Spruces, stopped Liss MacCrimmon Ruskin in her tracks. It wasn't because they didn't fit in with the rest of the décor. They were, in fact, more in keeping with their milieu than someone clad in baggy shorts or a wild Hawaiian-print shirt. Liss had seen guests wearing those fashion choices on more than one occasion.

The Spruces dated from the Victorian era, when the outfits these women had on were common in rural Maine, if not in these particular surroundings. Even on holiday in the late nineteenth century, the typical female staying at a luxury hotel in the western Maine mountains would have been tightly corseted and burdened with a bustle.

Ten years ago, when The Spruces had reopened after renovations had restored it to its former glory, all the amenities twenty-first century guests would expect had been added, but the most elaborate and expensive aspects of the past had been retained. The lobby Liss crossed boasted polished wooden floors, a high ceiling carved with animals and flowers, tall white pillars, and large area rugs that, when combined with plush seating, created cozy and intimate nooks where one could chat with friends in relative privacy.

The centerpiece of the room was an enormous fireplace, situated directly across from the main entrance. A fire had already been laid, although it would not be lit until September turned into October and the temperature dropped a few more degrees. Even without a warming blaze lighting the tile-lined hearth, it was quite a sight, boasting an ornate mantel with a beveled mirror above it. In summer, Joe Ruskin, Liss's father-in-law and the hotel's proprietor, substituted fresh flowers for kindling and logs.

Since she was on her way to meet her husband in the hotel bar, Liss's path took her close to the enormous nineteenth-century check-in desk. Curiosity had her slowing her steps and veering a bit nearer to Joe and the oddly dressed people who were talking to him. She knew Dan wasn't expecting her at any particular time. In fact, he was probably going to be too busy to talk to her. He'd been recruited by his father to work a shift for a bartender who'd called in sick.

If the tableau at the desk struck her as being odd at a distance, it became downright bizarre when viewed from only a few feet away. The two women, who wore their hair in braids that had been wrapped around their heads in a style long out of fashion, stood with eyes downcast. Their hands were loosely clasped at waist level. The man conversing in low tones with Joe Ruskin across the expanse of a gleaming mahogany check-in desk was equally unusual. He wore a shabby black suit and his hair and beard badly needed a trim. On closer inspection, Liss picked out a number of details that made him look even more out of place.

In one hand he held a plain black hat. On the strength of having watched way too many British sitcoms on the local PBS station, she identified it as a derby. This headgear stood out all the more when most men she knew, if they wore hats at all, went with ball caps with logos on the front. In winter, the ball caps were lined and often had ear flaps for additional warmth.

When the man turned slightly, she saw that his white shirt was collarless and his trousers were held up with suspenders. Like the two women, he looked like someone who'd just stepped out of an Amish costume drama on the Hallmark Channel.

Giving up any pretense of disinterest, Liss took advantage of the fact that she was a member of the owner's family and let herself into the area behind the desk. She could always pretend that she was checking the wall full of old-fashioned cubbyholes that had once held room keys and were still used to sort messages for guests.

When she sidled up to her father-in-law, Joe's sideways glance held equal parts of amusement—her interest in what was going on was less-than-subtle—and irritation. The latter emotion, Liss devoutly hoped, was aimed not at her but at the gentleman in black.

To her disappointment, the conversation appeared to have ended. The stranger turned away, using a curt gesture to indicate that the two women should follow him out of the hotel. They fell into step behind him, heads still bowed, and all three departed without another word.

"Who on earth was that?" Liss asked. "I know we used to have a couple of Shaker communities here in Maine but I thought they'd all died out."

Joe gave a derisive snort. "They aren't Shakers. Or Amish. They don't belong to any reputable group. They call themselves the New Age Pilgrims. You never ran into them before?"

Liss shook her head and eased onto the high stool behind the check-in desk. This had the makings of a long story.

"I guess I'm not surprised. They keep themselves to themselves . . . for the most part."

"In a place as small as Moosetookalook, there aren't many people I haven't met."

"This crowd lives over to Lower Mooseside." Joe named another of the four villages that made up the town. "They raise cattle, grow their own crops, and in general are pretty self-sufficient. So long as they don't bother anyone, no one pays them any mind."

"Are they a religious sect?"

Joe shrugged. "You couldn't prove it by me. That man who just left, fellow by the name of Hadley Spinner, calls himself a preacher, but if he's ever been to a theology school, it was the fly-by-night mail-order variety. Anyway, maybe fifteen years ago he showed up in the area with a couple of friends and bought some land. About a dozen more people have moved in with them since then."

"That sounds suspiciously like a commune," Liss said. "Or a cult."

"To hear them tell it, they just like to keep to older, simpler ways." Joe rolled his eyes as he shared this information.

"So what did he want with you? It looked as if you two were arguing about something."

"Tempest in a teapot," Joe said.

"More than that, I think."

"Maybe on his side, but that's his own fault for creating so many rules and regulations." Joe's mouth twitched, a clear signal that he was more amused than disgruntled now that he was looking back on the disagreement.

"What kind of rules and regulations?" Liss asked.

"I don't suppose you'll think it's funny, being such an independent sort of woman yourself, but the New Age Pilgrims supplement their income by having the womenfolk—Patsy down to the coffee shop calls them the lavender ladies—hire themselves out to do housework."

Liss made a moue of distaste. "*Just* the women?"

"What can I say? It's a patriarchal setup out there, as if you couldn't tell that from the way they dress. It's a wonder those gals don't keep their hair covered, too—wear bonnets or something. Anyway, when they take on a cleaning job, it's on the condition, set by Spinner, that the householder keep all male persons off the premises for the duration. No one of the opposite sex is allowed to remain in the home, not even boy babies."

"Okay," Liss said, stretching out the word's two syllables. She was still unclear about what this policy had to do with the odd little scene she'd just witnessed.

Joe's hint of a smile blossomed into a full-scale grin. "Spinner thinks I should add some of his people to the housekeeping staff at The Spruces."

Liss waited a beat before asking, "What did he expect you to do? Shoo away all the men staying at the hotel so the lavender ladies can change the bedding and towels and scrub the toilets?"

"That's exactly what he was proposing and he was somewhat put out when I explained how impossible it would be to do any such thing."

"Good grief! Suddenly I'm very glad Spinner and his followers have never come into Moosetookalook Scottish Emporium. Normal customers can be trying enough to deal with. I hate having to cope with crackpots."

"You showed up at exactly the right time," Joe said. "Spinner is so stubborn that he'd have belabored his point till the cows came home, even knowing he doesn't have a prayer of convincing me to do what he wants."

"You think I scared him off?"

Joe shrugged. "I've got a feeling he only likes to carry on in front of an audience when he's sure of winning."

Liss laughed. "More likely he was afraid the sight of me would corrupt his charges."

Since it was a warm early-autumn evening, her outfit provided a stark contrast to the clothing of Skinner's companions. Instead of a skirt, long or otherwise, she wore jeans. Her dressy, scallop-neck T-shirt was not overly tight, but it did fit snugly, flattering the few curves she possessed. As for her hair, she wore her dark brown locks long and hanging loose down her back, held away from her face by a jaunty emerald green scarf. Since she'd always liked bright colors, the pattern on the T-shirt was a wild mix of green, pink, and orange flowers.

"Whatever drove him away, I'm glad of it," Joe said. "I don't suppose he's much worse than any other run-of-the mill eccentric, and Lord knows we've got plenty of those in this part of the world, but he sure is a pain in the behind. Now get along with you and go keep your husband company. Tell him how much I appreciate him filling in at the last minute like this."

"No problem." Liss slid off the stool but lingered behind the check-in desk long enough to step close to Joe and plant a light kiss on his cheek. "We're family."

Liss did not give Hadley Spinner another thought as September segued into October and the first weeks of that month passed with their usual swiftness. She had no occasion to spend much time at The Spruces during that period until the evening before her thirty-eighth birthday, when

Dan insisted upon taking her out for a celebratory meal in the hotel dining room.

"You didn't have to dress up," Liss said as they waited to be shown to their table.

Although many similar establishments insisted that male guests wear jackets and ties and were prepared with loaners for anyone who showed up without, The Spruces had never adhered to a dress code. When he'd reopened the hotel, Joe had wanted it to be welcoming to everyone. Forcing someone into borrowed clothing wasn't his idea of friendly. As long as the patrons weren't barefoot or bare-chested, they were allowed to eat in late nineteenth-century splendor—linen tablecloths and napkins, fine china, crystal, real silverware, and the best food the hotel's chef could provide.

Despite the lack of rules and regulations, Dan had made the supreme sacrifice of wearing his one good suit and a brand-new tie. His black dress shoes were polished to a high shine and the white handkerchief in his breast pocket was freshly ironed. He'd even splashed on a little of the expensive men's cologne his sister had given him for Christmas. Liss appreciated all the little touches, all the more so because they gave her the excuse, rare in their everyday lives, to deck herself out in an outfit that was equally dressy.

For the occasion, she had chosen a bright red cocktail dress that flattered her coloring. She'd felt quite glamorous when she'd added an antique gold bracelet and matching necklace. She eschewed earrings, since her ears had never been pierced and clip-ons pinched. Besides, her hair would have hidden them anyway. Without a scarf, it fell forward to frame her face.

Only when she'd had to squeeze her feet into the three-inch heels that had been dyed to match her dress had she hesitated, tempted to substitute plain black ballet flats, but she'd told herself that this was a special occasion. She was glad now that she'd made the decision to choose style over comfort. It was nice, for once, to stand nearly eye-to-eye with Dan. At five-foot-nine, Liss was tall, but her husband stretched all the way up to six-foot-two.

When they were ensconced at a table for two in a quiet corner of the dining room, he sent her a smile that had her heart tripping and her lips curving upward. It didn't matter if he was covered in sawdust from his full-time job as a custom woodworker, or dressed to the nines as he was now, Dan Ruskin was one good-looking man. Years working for the family construction company, back before Joe bought the hotel and Dan went into business for himself, had given all the Ruskin men impressive physiques. Liss loved the way Dan's sandy brown hair was always a little mussed and the twinkle in his molasses brown eyes. And yet it was what was in her husband's heart that was most important to her. He was, plain and simple, a good man. Best of all, although she was not always the easiest person to live with, he loved her anyway.

"Happy birthday, Liss."

Dan produced a small jeweler's box from his jacket pocket and slid it across the table.

"It isn't my actual birthday yet," Liss protested. "I have a whole day to go before I'm officially a year older."

"Open it now anyway."

She flipped up the lid, looked inside, and started to laugh even before she investigated further. Instead of a ring or some other small piece of jewelry, the case contained a slip of paper. Slowly, drawing out the moment, Liss unfolded it and read what Dan had written in his semi-illegible hand: *"Good for one solid week of meal prep and housecleaning, and a good wash of every window in the house."*

"I love it," she said. "Thank you."

"You're sure? It's not too late to get you flowers or chocolate."

"This is a much better present and you know it. Chocolate would go straight to my hips and the cats would eat the flowers."

The last time she'd brought a floral arrangement into the house, the vase had been knocked over and the blossoms had been scattered all over the room within five minutes. Besides, she hated doing housework and was an unenthusiastic cook, which was why she and Dan usually shared the chores. She was delighted by the prospect of letting him handle everything for the next week.

"I thought I'd do the windows tomorrow morning," he said.

"There's no rush."

"Well, actually, there is." He started to say more but was interrupted by the arrival of their waiter.

Liss's eyes narrowed at the look of relief that flashed across his face. The windows might be sadly in need of that "good wash" but there was something else behind this determination to get the chore done right away. Something she was *not* going to be happy about. As soon as they'd ordered their meal—coquilles St. Jacques for her, and a sirloin steak, medium rare, for him—Liss put her elbows on the table, rested her chin on her fists, and leveled a stern look in her husband's direction.

"Spill."

"I'm not supposed to say anything."

"I don't like the sound of that."

His internal debate didn't last long. He knew her too well to think she'd stop nagging until she had an answer.

"I guess you'd rather be warned than taken by surprise. It's your mother."

Liss closed her eyes and bit back a groan. "Let me guess— she's planned something special for my birthday tomorrow."

"I'm afraid so. I'm sorry, Liss, but I couldn't talk her out of it. You know how determined Vi is when she gets one of her brilliant ideas."

Unfortunately, Liss did know. Ever since her parents had left Arizona and returned to Maine to live, Violet MacCrimmon had embraced one new enthusiasm after another. Most of these led her to try to recruit reluctant members of her family to help out, and to clashes and hurt feelings when Liss had to remind her that not everyone was retired with lots of free time on their hands.

Liss toyed with her fork. "I thought I had the perfect solution for keeping Mom out of my hair when I convinced her that I needed *her* help and got her to take over the chairmanship of the Halloween committee." Liss had been in charge of the festivities for more years than she liked to count and had been relieved when Vi agreed to organize the costume parade and trick-or-treating.

"You know your mother. She's good at multitasking."

"Halloween is still a week away. She ought to be up to her neck in those plans and not have any time left over to fuss at me." Struck by a singularly unpleasant thought, Liss lost her grip on her fork. It fell to the tabletop with a dull thump. "Please tell me she isn't planning a party that involves costumes and masks."

Dan grinned. "You used to love those costumed birthday parties when you were a kid."

"My mother loved them. I endured them."

His eyebrows lifted at that. "I'd never have guessed, but you can relax. You dodged that bullet. No costumes."

"But there is going to be a party?"

"I'm afraid so. She's invited about fifty people to help you celebrate. They'll be waiting at our house when you get home from work tomorrow."

"Hiding behind the furniture ready to leap out and yell, 'Surprise!'"

"That's the plan."

"Oh, goodie."

It could be worse, she supposed. Thanks to Dan's warning, she could freshen up and change into nicer clothes before she left the Emporium. But *fifty* people? The house would be full to bursting and she couldn't imagine how her mother expected to sneak everyone in, given that Liss could see both the front and side of their house from her store windows.

"I'm not going to think about this right now." This time, she was the one who welcomed the sight of their waiter. "Tonight is for us."

"Works for me," Dan said as their salads were set in front of them. "We deserve a nice romantic evening."

They had just finished dessert when Dan's father materialized beside their table. He clapped one hand on his son's shoulder and sent a smile winging Liss's way. "How's my favorite daughter-in-law?"

"I'm just fine, but you'd better not let June hear you call me that."

"When it's her birthday, *she'll* be my favorite," Joe said.

Liss knew that June, who was married to Dan's older brother Sam, would see the humor in Joe's logic. The whole Ruskin family was remarkably easygoing. She envied them their ability to take things in stride, especially on those occasions when she had to deal with her mother.

"You look cheerful, Dad," Dan said. "Business must be good."

"Business is excellent." Joe beamed at them. "The Thanksgiving Special is a big hit."

For the first few years after The Spruces opened, profits had been slim to none, but slowly word had spread, customers had come, and the hotel had acquired a reputation for excellence that drew even more guests. Anything to do with tourism was still a chancy proposition, but Joe seemed to have found a formula that worked.

"Lots of bookings?" Dan asked.

"More than we hoped for when Tricia dreamed up this promotion. We should be able to fill all those rooms that are usually empty during the stretch between leaf-peeper season and ski season. Even though Thanksgiving is still a bit more than a month away, reservations have us almost at capacity already."

Liss was pleased but not surprised to hear that Tricia Lynd had taken to her current job like a duck to water. By the time Joe hired that young woman to replace Liss's aunt, Margaret MacCrimmon Boyd, as events coordinator, Tricia had worked just about every other job in the hotel. She'd started out as an intern eight years earlier, a sort of Jill-of-all-trades, and had paid her dues with long hours waiting tables in the dining room, tending bar, running the gift shop, working at the front desk, serving as concierge, and even taking a turn in the housekeeping department.

"Are you okay for staff?" Dan asked. "I won't be able to spare many hours to help out." While it might be off-season for hotels in the area, November was a busy time of year for Dan's custom woodworking business and for Liss's shop, Moosetookalook Scottish Emporium.

"I'm all set," Joe assured him. "In fact, it's uncanny how smoothly everything is going." He chuckled. "The only flies in the ointment are the Pills." He smiled at Liss's puzzled look. "Remember that crackpot who was in here a month or so ago, name of Hadley Spinner? The leading light of the New Age Pilgrims?"

Light dawned. "The Pilgrims are the Pills?"

"You got it. Spinner showed up again the other day to inform me that, in his narrow-minded opinion, the Thanksgiving Special is an affront to family values. Can you believe that? He called the promotion an abomination and wanted me to cancel it."

"What on earth is he upset about?" Liss asked. "Don't tell me that a group named after the Pilgrims is against Thanksgiving."

"Oh, he has nothing against the holiday. He's all for it, in fact. What has him hot under the collar is that our promotion is designed to attract a niche clientele—childless couples who *don't* want to celebrate Thanksgiving with their families."

"Sounds like a great idea to me."

Liss winced when she realized Joe might take her words the wrong way. Ever since their marriage, she and Dan had spent every Thanksgiving with the Ruskins. When she spoke, she had been thinking of long-ago Thanksgiving dinners, meals presided over by Violet MacCrimmon. As a child. Liss had loved the idea of having both sets of grandparents come to the house to share a meal, but the reality of those gatherings had never quite lived up to her expectations. Conversations had always been stilted and everyone had looked uncomfortable throughout. They'd left just as soon as they could without giving offense.

"It *is* a great idea," Joe said.

"So what exactly is Spinner's beef?" Dan asked.

"He's got it into his head that most of the guests taking advantage of the Thanksgiving Special are unmarried or same-sex couples. According to him, I'm encouraging immorality."

Liss just stared at him. There was so much wrong with Spinner's complaint that she hardly knew where to begin.

"How did he come up with that notion?" Dan asked. "It's not like you're even allowed to ask for people's marital status or sexual orientation when they book a room."

"I wouldn't share any information I did have, but not much stays private these days. I'm guessing Spinner or one of his followers has been reading the comments on the hotel's Facebook page."

"I wouldn't have thought Spinner and his group held with computers," Liss said, "but that's neither here nor there. What business is it of his how other people conduct their lives?"

"He's a bigot and a blowhard who only sees his own point of view." Joe shrugged. "And I suspect he's still ticked off at me for refusing to put the lavender ladies on my payroll. Oh, well. With any luck, now that he's delivered his sermon on the subject of my business practices, he'll move on to annoying someone else. You two enjoy the rest of your evening. Liss, you don't look a day over thirty."

Chuckling at her look of chagrin, he went on his way. Liss lost no time dismissing the odious Hadley Spinner from her thoughts. Even better, implementing Dan's plan for part two of her birthday celebration, a plan which commenced as soon as they got home from dinner, succeeded in distracting her from worrying about the gathering her mother had organized. She managed to forget, until she awoke the next morning, just how much she hated surprise parties.

Liss took a deep breath as she climbed the steps to her front porch and prepared to open the door. She'd been a fool to think her mother would be too busy with the Halloween festival to remember her birthday. Belatedly, she realized that she should have made a preemptive strike and suggested that she and Dan and her parents go out to eat, or maybe take in a movie in honor of the occasion. Parties, surprise or otherwise, might be fun for kids, but even when she was younger, Liss had felt overwhelmed by all the fuss. Now that she was pushing forty, she liked being the center of attention even less. She preferred to avoid situations that threw her into the limelight.

This time there was no help for it. She had to go in and she had to pretend to be surprised and pleased by what awaited her. *Grin and bear it,* she told herself.

She opened the door.

Relatives, friends, and acquaintances seemed to explode out of every nook and cranny. The noise of their shouted "Surprise!" was deafening. Liss hadn't really believed Dan when he'd said her mother had invited fifty guests, but she couldn't deny the proof when it was right in front of her eyes. People were packed wall-to-wall in the living and dining rooms and in the kitchen, too.

Dan's brother and sister and their families were among the revelers. Liss's parents, Violet and Mac, and Aunt Margaret were in the thick of things, handing out punch and cookies. As soon as she spotted Liss, Margaret set her tray aside to greet her niece.

"Happy birthday, my dear."

She gave Liss an enthusiastic hug, briefly exposing her

to the perfume of the day. Liss didn't try to identify the light scent. Her aunt loved to experiment with little-known fragrances. In slim black slacks and a pale mauve tunic, her light gray hair newly styled in a sleek bob, she radiated vivaciousness. Retirement suited her. She looked younger and more energetic every time Liss saw her.

"Ed sends his love," Margaret added. Her grandson was away at college.

"I'll bet he was heartbroken to have to miss the party."

Margaret frowned, catching the sarcasm. "You know your mother means well, Liss."

"I know." But that didn't make dealing with her any easier.

Retrieving the abandoned serving tray, Margaret began to circulate once more. Her departure signaled the start of a barrage of well wishes accompanied by hugs, kisses, and witty quips along the lines of, "How does it feel to join the ranks of the old and decrepit?"

Sherri Campbell, one of Liss's closest friends, gave her husband a thump on the arm for that one. Although he had the solid, square build of a linebacker and she was even more petite than Liss's mother, he winced and rubbed the spot. Sherri was tougher than she looked. She had to be. She was Moosetookalook's chief of police.

"Liss and I are the same age," she reminded Pete. "You're the one getting on in years."

"Not compared to most of these folks."

When Liss took another look around, she realized he was right. Although there were younger faces, and even a few children, her mother had invited all the business owners who had shops facing the town square. With the exception of Sandy and Zara, Liss's next-door neighbors, who had once been her fellow performers in a professional Scottish dance company, most of them were at least ten years older than she was and many were past retirement age, even if they did still go to work every day.

Dolores Mayfield, Moosetookalook's formidable librarian, was the next to elbow her way through the crowd to offer her best wishes. She grabbed Liss's elbow with bony fingers and had to raise her voice to be heard above the racket of dozens of people all yakking at the same time.

"I'd have brought you a present," she bellowed, "but Vi said not to."

"Good grief, no," Liss said. "Just having you here is enough. Thank you so much for coming."

Dolores adjusted the glasses perched on her long, thin nose. "Roger would have been here, but he's feeling poorly."

Translation: Roger "Moose" Mayfield was too drunk to walk the few blocks from their house to hers.

"What a shame," Liss murmured.

She chatted with Dolores for a few more minutes before the librarian excused herself and left the party to go home and make supper for her spouse. By that time, Liss's jaw ached from the effort of holding a smile in place. She brightened when she spotted Dan plowing a trench through the assembled company. He couldn't rescue her, but once he was standing beside her, she felt less vulnerable.

He handed her the cup of punch he'd brought with him. He'd thoughtfully spiked it. Although the courage liquor provided might be false, at this point she welcomed anything that could bolster the belief that she'd survive the evening.

Without warning, her mother popped up next to them. Violet MacCrimmon had to stand on tiptoe to kiss her daughter's cheek. A slender five-foot-four, she kept herself in good shape and looked far younger than she was. Her hair was the same color as her daughter's, but where Liss's was natural, Vi's needed assistance to keep the gray from showing.

"Happy birthday, darling. Were you surprised?"

"That's putting it mildly. However did you manage to sneak all these people in here? I never saw a thing from the window at the Emporium."

Violet MacCrimmon's pale blue eyes sparkled behind her stylish glasses. "It took some planning," she admitted. "I knew it wouldn't be easy to fool you, so I told everyone to park on High Street or in the lot at the grocery store and cut across the Farleys' yard to your back door."

Note to self for tomorrow, Liss thought. *Apologize to the Farleys for all the people who trampled their lawn.*

The couple in question were on the far side of the living room, deep in conversation with Audrey Greenwood, the tall, blond vet who took care of their poodle, Margaret's Scottish terriers, and Liss's two Maine Coon cats. At the thought of her pets, Liss's breath caught. She grasped her mother's forearm.

"Mom, where are the cats?" Glenora, the smaller and younger of the two, was coal black and could easily make herself invisible, most often by perching atop the highest piece of furniture in the room, but Lumpkin, large and yellow, was hard to miss.

"Not to worry. I locked them in your guest room, the one Mac soundproofed back when we lived here."

That certainly explained why she didn't hear Lumpkin howling in protest. Her father had undertaken that particular DIY project after the neighbors they'd had back then complained about the racket he made when he practiced playing his bagpipes in the house.

"Isn't it wonderful how many friends you have?" Vi's

enthusiastic gesture encompassed the entire gathering. "Everyone I invited came except your father-in-law. He had to work."

"Wonderful," Liss echoed, straining to keep her lips curved upward. Some people had all the luck!

It *was* lovely that they'd turned up in her honor, but she couldn't help but wish that her mother hadn't asked them to come in the first place. This gathering felt more like a home invasion than a celebration. She took another swallow of the spiked punch and reminded herself that Violet hadn't deliberately set out to make her only child uncomfortable. She never did.

"Where did Dad get to?" she asked.

Liss felt certain that Dan hadn't been the only one who'd tried to talk Vi out of this party. Liss's father was well aware that his daughter preferred small gatherings to large ones. Then again, Mac MacCrimmon had a long history of folding in the face of his wife's determination. Violet had always been high-handed and she never listened to anyone else's advice. Liss wondered, not for the first time, whose idea it had been to move back to Maine. So far, neither of her parents had given her a good reason for their decision.

"He's in the kitchen refilling the snack trays." Mini quiches, pigs in blankets, and crackers with a dab of herbed cheese on top had joined several varieties of cookies making the rounds.

As bodies ebbed and flowed around them, quite a few pausing long enough to congratulate Liss on being another year older, Vi kept up a cheerful patter. She was in her element. It wasn't until there was a break in the litany of good wishes that Liss became aware that her mother had stopped speaking. Had she asked a question?

"Sorry. I was distracted."

Vi's censorious look instantly put her on the defensive.

"Give me a break, Mom. I was busy being gracious and charming to your guests."

Her mother's brows drew together, a sure warning of storm clouds ahead.

Be the grown-up, Liss told herself. *That jibe was uncalled for.*

Ever since her parents had returned to Maine, she had been struggling to learn the fine art of getting along with the one person who had always been able to push her buttons. The middle of a party was no time to start an argument with her mother. Taking care to keep her voice pleasant, she tried again.

"Did you just ask me a question?"

"No. I said that it's too bad Joe couldn't be here, but I suppose he has his hands full with all the trouble at the hotel."

"What trouble?" Joe had been in high spirits the previous evening. Liss couldn't imagine how that could have changed in less than twenty-four hours.

"That man Spinner," said Vi. "He's been posting on social media, trying to get tourists to boycott The Spruces, claiming that the hotel discriminates against families."

The sudden queasy feeling in the pit of Liss's stomach had nothing to do with the drink in her hand or the press of people around them. "That's ridiculous."

Angry on Joe's behalf, Liss spoke more loudly than she'd intended. Heads turned their way. The owner of Patsy's Coffee House, one of the major way stations for the Moosetookalook grapevine, had been working her way toward the door to the hall. Reversing course, she called out, "Spinner's wasting his time. No one will believe anything that nutcase says."

"I'm surprised they have a computer out at Pilgrim Farm," Stu Burroughs said from behind Patsy, who was blocking his path to the exit. "They're so backward that they don't even use lightweight modern snowshoes."

"No sale, huh?" Liss's face relaxed into a smile as she tried to imagine Spinner and a couple of his lavender ladies wandering through Stu's Ski Shop, the store right next door to Moosetookalook Scottish Emporium.

"I can live with that." Stu's face, what Liss could see of it around a bristly gray beard, went from pink to red in a heartbeat, casting doubt on his claim.

At five-foot-two, Stu was even shorter than Liss's mother, but where her build was petite, his was chunky. That he wore a bright orange shirt only emphasized his resemblance to a pumpkin.

"That's not the first time you've had a go-round with Spinner," Patsy reminded him.

The physical contrast between Stu and Patsy could not have been more pronounced. Not only was her skin as pale as new-fallen snow, but she was tall and almost cadaverously thin. Liss had never been able to figure out why Patsy didn't gain weight. She spent hours every day baking the most delicious breads, buns, doughnuts, muffins, pastries, and cookies known to man and selling them in her combination coffee house and café. Since this establishment was located just at the end of the street, Liss was a regular patron. The pounds would have piled on had she not regularly worked out at the dance studio Sandy and Zara owned.

"You should talk, Patsy," Stu shot back.

Patsy's grimace spoke louder than words, making it clear that she, too, had at some point exchanged heated words with Hadley Spinner. She and Stu continued sniping at each other as they left the party.

After they'd gone, Liss turned back to her mother, only to find that Vi's attention had shifted to her sister-in-law.

"I hope she doesn't get involved."

"Margaret? Why should she? She no longer works at the hotel."

"Because it's Hadley Spinner, of course." And with that enigmatic statement, Violet MacCrimmon wandered off, working the crowd with a casual style that Liss couldn't help but envy.

Now that she was tuned into the subject, Liss realized that Spinner's vendetta against The Spruces was *the* topic of the evening. As she tried to follow her mother's example and mingle, she overheard more bits and pieces of conversation.

"Any publicity is good publicity," someone said.

Liss had her doubts about the truth of that old saying, but she was heartened to discover that most people agreed with Patsy's opinion that no one in their right mind would pay any attention to a screwball like Hadley Spinner. He'd annoyed more than a few of her guests, although the run-ins they recounted didn't seem to amount to much. Spinner's pattern was to make impossible demands, provoke arguments, and get into a snit when he was refused. As far as she could tell, he'd never sued anyone and his quarrel with Joe appeared to be the first time that he'd gone after someone online.

"He's like a kid with a new toy," Margaret declared. "He'll get tired of it soon enough."

Since the crowd had thinned out to the point where Liss was able to have a private word with her aunt, she attempted to satisfy her curiosity. "You sound as if you have personal experience with him."

Margaret stared off into space for a moment, looking un-characteristically pensive. "Nothing I care to remember," she said. "In fact, I think it's time for a change of subject. Who wants to waste time talking about unpleasant subjects, especially when we've gathered together for a celebration?" She lifted her rum and cola and raised her voice. "A toast to the birthday girl!"

The party improved from then on. By the time the last straggler left and Liss was alone with Dan, she'd reluctantly admitted that, for the most part, she'd enjoyed herself.

Chapter Two

Since Halloween fell on a Tuesday, the powers-that-be in Moosetookalook had decreed that the costume parade and trick-or-treating should be held a few days earlier, on Saturday. With no school schedules to interfere, activities could start at noon and everyone would be safely back home, or at a community-sponsored party, by the time it got dark. In western Maine at the end of October, that was shortly after five-thirty.

The sun cooperated by beaming brightly down on the proceedings, but it did not deliver much in the way of warmth. Liss bundled up in a wool coat and added gloves, a scarf, and a hat to protect herself from the wind before she ventured out onto the porch of Moosetookalook Scottish Emporium to watch laughing, chattering children gather in the town square across the street.

At this time of year, the square did not look its best. The flowers in the beds planted on both sides of the paths had gone by, the trees had lost their spectacular fall foliage, and the grass had the look of dirty straw. The only bright colors to be seen were in the Halloween costumes and on the bandstand. Painted a gleaming white, it was festooned with orange and black bunting and balloons.

The town square was a comfortably large expanse of grass, paths, and flower beds, and contained all the features typical of New England towns. In addition to the bandstand, there was a flagpole, the stars and stripes fluttering from the top. On this day meant for merriment, the monument to the Civil War dead, a statue of a Union soldier with a plaque beneath that listed the local men who had died between 1861 and 1865, was largely ignored, but the playground, furnished with a jungle gym, slide, small merry-go-round, and swings, was crowded with masked youngsters.

Paved walking paths crisscrossed the entire area. Unless she was in a hurry, it took Liss several minutes to walk from the Emporium to the municipal building. Today she didn't intend to go farther afield than this porch. She was content to watch the spectacle from a distance. To be honest, she felt a deep sense of relief that she was not responsible for making sure everything ran smoothly.

From her vantage point, she spotted other shopkeepers doing the same thing she was. The Emporium was one of a number of businesses that surrounded the town square. It stood in the middle on Pine Street with Stu's Ski Shop on one side and Carrabassett County Wood Crafts on the other. Stu was sitting on his front steps, keeping an eye on the proceedings.

The post office, with the Clip and Curl in the back half of the structure, was located at the corner of Pine and Ash. After she waved to the postmaster, Liss's gaze moved north along Ash Street, lingering for a moment on a jewelry store that specialized in pieces made with Maine gemstones, especially tourmaline and garnet, before continuing on to the local history museum that occupied the corner of Ash and Main Street. Once upon a time, it had been a funeral home. The docent was standing in the doorway, shading her eyes against the sun.

Main Street was directly across the square from Pine. Liss didn't see anyone on the porch at Angie's Books, but there were several people in front of the redbrick municipal building that housed the town office, the police station, the garage for the fire truck, and the library. In an upstairs window, she could just make out Dolores Mayfield's silhouette as the librarian looked down on the scene from her domain.

Patsy's Coffee House completed the trio of buildings on Main Street. At the corner, Birch Street began, running along the east side of the town square. There were two private homes on Birch, the Farleys' on the corner and Liss and Dan's house in the middle of the block, but even they were commercial to some extent. John Farley offered accounting and tax services from the comfort of his living room and Dan's woodworking shop was situated behind their home in what had once been a carriage house.

The building at the corner of Birch and Pine housed Zara and Sandy's dance studio on the first floor and their apartment above. There were apartments above most of the businesses. Stu lived over his shop, and so did the couple who owned the jewelry store. Liss's aunt, who had owned Moosetookalook Scottish Emporium before Liss bought it from her, still occupied the rooms above the store, while the apartments above Carrabassett County Wood Crafts and the post office were rental units.

As if thinking about her had been a cue for her to enter the scene, Margaret Boyd emerged from between the buildings. She'd used the external stairs instead of the ones that came out behind Liss's sales counter. Spotting her niece, she called out a greeting but kept going, crossing the street to enter the square.

Liss saw many other familiar faces among the people milling about, but Zara's red hair made her stand out. She had her two carrot-topped children with her. They were dressed as characters from the Harry Potter books. So were several other children who lived in the immediate area.

Early on, Liss's mother had divided the town into districts, recruiting group leaders from among the moms living in each. Then she'd assigned a theme to each group. The half-dozen kids and one adult closest to Liss's side of the square carried a sign that read MAPLE STREET ZOO. She recognized a lion, a tiger, and a monkey, but the other animals were not so easy to identify.

The outlying villages of Lower Mooseside, Little Moose, and Ripley were represented as well. The "Ripley Superheroes" took up a position next to the zoo creatures. Superman, Batman, Ironman, and the Hulk were warmly dressed in costumes that covered their arms and legs, but Wonder Woman's outfit was considerably more skimpy. A girl of no more than ten had to wrap herself in her cape—fortunately a long one—in an effort to keep warm. Even from a distance, Liss could see the goosebumps on her bare legs. What on earth had her parents been thinking? A pair of flesh-colored tights wouldn't have made that much difference in the way the costume looked.

Her gaze left the superheroes to pass over other clusters of colorfully costumed children. It wasn't until a pocket of darkness caught her eye that she paused and stared. For a moment she assumed she was looking at Goths, or perhaps children dressed as vampires, but she knew that couldn't be right. Although she had listened with only half an ear when her mother was sharing her plans, she remembered that Vi had said, multiple times, that she was assigning only upbeat themes to the participating groups. This Halloween there would be no motorcycle gangs, no characters from horror movies, and no fangs dripping blood.

By narrowing her eyes, Liss was able to make out more. One of the black-clad figures held a sign of the same size and shape as the other groups but she was too far away to make out what it said. What she could see was that the people in this dreary little cluster weren't children at all. She was looking at a delegation of men from the New Age Pilgrims. Their somber black suits were a blight on the otherwise cheerful gathering.

When Vi began to shepherd everyone into neat lines, Liss lost sight of Hadley Spinner and his followers. She put them out of her mind as well. For the next quarter of an hour, she gave herself over to her enjoyment of the Halloween parade.

Interspersed between groups of costumed children were several floats, the local high school band and color guard, a drum and bugle corps, and Liss's father with his bagpipes. Once they formed up, they set off from the corner of Birch and Pine, passed the Emporium, and continued around the perimeter of the square until they were headed east on Main Street. Their route would take them to High Street, which ran south and eventually connected with the far end of Pine, which would bring them back to the town square. They'd then be released to go trick-or-treating. Later, everyone would gather at the gazebo-style bandstand where the winners of the best-costume awards would be announced.

When the music had faded into the distance, Liss left the porch for the welcome warmth of the Emporium. She stripped off her outer garments as she crossed to the counter, rubbing her icy hands together to restore circulation. Mittens would have been better than gloves for keeping out the cold.

Liss didn't expect to have many customers during the celebrations. Foot traffic was slow most days and she relied on online and mail-order sales to stay in the black. If her aunt hadn't owned the building, the overhead would probably have forced her to close the brick-and-mortar store altogether, but Moosetookalook Scottish Emporium had been founded in this location in 1955 by her grandfather and it went against the grain to shut it down. Besides, she did have bursts of walk-in business, especially in November, when most people did their Christmas shopping.

Promotional efforts the town had undertaken a few years earlier had resulted in an uptick in business. There were now several "shoppers' specials" bus tours that came to Moosetookalook on a regular basis. In addition to the Emporium, which featured Scottish imports and Scottish-themed gift items, and the other specialty shops around the town square, several more stores of interest to tourists were within easy walking distance.

Liss had just deposited her coat in the stockroom and was making herself a fresh mug of coffee when the bell over the front door jangled and Sherri Campbell called out a greeting.

"I'll be right out," Liss called back. "Do you want coffee?"

"Any more coffee and I'll float away," Sherri said from the doorway.

Liss turned, unsurprised to see that her friend was in uniform, her long blond hair neatly pulled back in a single braid. As Moosetookalook's chief of police, Sherri was always on call, even when she was off-duty and despite the fact that she was also a mother with three children, two of them still quite young. The smile that had started to form on Liss's lips dissolved the moment she caught sight of Sherri's expression.

"What's wrong?"

"Have you seen these flyers?" Sherri held out a folded sheet of plain multipurpose white paper.

Before she accepted the offering, Liss took a fortifying slurp of her coffee. Then she abandoned her mug on the worktable, grabbed hold of the flyer, and unfolded it. The bold black words leapt out at her:

JOIN WITH US TO DEFEND FAMILY VALUES
THE ONLY LAWFUL CONNECTION IS THE
MARRIAGE BED
Show Your Support
Saturday, November 4
10 AM
Moosetookalook Town Square
Boycott All Businesses With Ties To The Spruces

"I don't believe this," Liss muttered.

In a line across the bottom of the page was a list of the three businesses that were specific targets of the protest. Ruskin Construction, the family enterprise run by Sam Ruskin, came first, then Moosetookalook Scottish Emporium, and finally Dan's jigsaw-puzzle-table-making operation. One more line, in even smaller print, consisted of phone numbers. When Liss recognized the one for Ruskin Construction she stopped reading. From the look of this, she was going to have to start letting the answering machine screen all calls to the Emporium.

"Where did you get this?" she asked.

"The New Age Pilgrims were passing them out. They

also applied for, and were granted, a permit to hold a rally in the town square."

"Can't you *un*grant it?"

"It's not up to me. By the time I heard about it, it was a done deal." Sherri held both hands up, palms out. "Don't shoot the messenger."

"What idiot thought it was a good idea to let them protest against legitimate businesses?"

"That would be my mother-in-law, the selectwoman. I don't suppose Hadley Spinner's rhetoric goes over any better with Thea than it does with us, but she had no grounds to deny their request."

Thea Campbell had been on Moosetookalook's board of selectpersons for years and had a hand in everything that went on in the four villages that made up the town.

"As citizens of our little community," Sherri went on, "they have the right to express themselves, even if the ideas they advocate are offensive to you and me. Sad to say, some people will probably support them. This area isn't exactly a hotbed of liberal ideas."

Much as Liss disliked the idea of a demonstration right in front of her shop, especially one targeting her business, she couldn't argue with the group's right to free speech. She was considering the possibility of mounting a counter-demonstration when yet another appalling thought occurred to her.

"Oh, no! Sherri, we can't have people picketing in Moosetookalook this coming weekend. We have a busful of shoppers scheduled. These are people ready and willing to spend money on unique Christmas gifts. They aren't going to appreciate it if they have to cross a picket line."

"They won't need to cross anything. The demonstration

is confined to the square. I'll put extra men on and we'll make sure everyone obeys the law. And I do mean everyone."

But Liss was shaking her head. "It will still be disruptive."

"I think that's the idea." Sherri's tone was as dry as a pile of dead leaves.

"The other merchants are going to be fit to be tied."

"I'm sorry, Liss, but they'll just have to lump it. Spinner's done everything by the book."

"Maybe I can reason with him. Get him to change his mind."

Sherri's eyebrows shot up. "Have you met this guy?"

Liss pictured Spinner as she had seen him harassing Joe at the hotel. "We haven't been formally introduced."

"Consider yourself lucky. My advice is to ignore the New Age Pilgrims. They'll make a nuisance of themselves for a bit, realize they aren't convincing very many local people to agree with them, and go away."

"I don't know, Sherri. I've got a bad feeling about this."

Liss had always prided herself on being open-minded about other people's beliefs, respecting them even when they differed from her own, but for that very reason she objected to any one group trying to force an opinion down her throat. What Joe had said about Spinner's complaints was borne out by the flyer she held crumpled in her fist. Spinner saw the hotel's promotion as an attack on family values because his own definition of family was so narrow.

"How much do *you* know about the New Age Pilgrims?" she asked.

"Not a lot." Sherri toyed with a roll of packing tape. "There are a dozen or so individuals living on Spinner's farm. Except for occasionally annoying people they disagree with, they keep to themselves and stay out of trouble. And before you ask, being obnoxious isn't a crime."

"Does Spinner have a wife? Kids? Are the other people who live in that community married couples?"

"Huh," Sherri said. "I hadn't thought about it. If there are any children living on the property, they're being home-schooled. As for marital status, what difference does it make?"

"Quite a bit, given Spinner's objection to unmarried and same-sex couples taking advantage of Joe's promotion. That's why he's claiming the hotel is opposed to family values and should be boycotted."

"Well, that's one of the stupidest things I've ever heard. Anyone with any sense can see he has no basis for such a claim."

"Of course he doesn't. Joe's promotion just specified couples. Besides, even if he wanted to, he couldn't tell unmarried people or gay or lesbian couples that they couldn't participate because of their marital status or sexual orientation. He'd be breaking the law if he did."

"Agreed." Sherri replaced the tape and picked up a stapler. "The thing is, Spinner doesn't live in the same century as the rest of us."

"That's his problem, not ours." Liss sighed. "I get that he has every right to hold this rally, but are you sure we don't have anything to worry about?"

"He can spew all the vitriol he wants. I expect people will just ignore his ranting, the same way they always do." Sherri cocked her head to better hear the faint strains of "The Stars and Stripes Forever" as played by the high school marching band. The Halloween parade was almost back to where it had started. "I've got to go."

She was halfway across the shop when Liss called after

her, "Do you really need that stapler when you have a gun and pepper spray?"

"Oops. Sorry." With a laugh, she tossed it in Liss's direction. "I forgot I was holding it."

Catching the stapler one-handed, Liss carried it with her to the plate-glass display window that faced the town square. The view was almost identical to that from the porch but much warmer. Liss watched Sherri cross the street, then looked around for the New Age Pilgrims. They were nowhere in sight. She supposed it was too much to hope for that they'd stay gone, but it gave her a fleeting sense of satisfaction to throw their crumpled flyer into the wastepaper basket.

After that, she was too busy to worry about the coming demonstration or Spinner's campaign against the Ruskins. She had to rush to get out the baskets of candy she'd prepared before the first swarm of trick-or-treaters descended.

Despite her resolution not to worry about Hadley Spinner's campaign to ruin her business and those of Dan, Sam, and Joe Ruskin, Liss couldn't ignore what the leader of the New Age Pilgrims had planned. In the spirit of "know your enemy," she made a point of reading every one of Spinner's venom-laced online posts. The responses his followers posted were almost as disconcerting, but she consoled herself with the belief that these exchanges would go largely unnoticed in the greater cyber world. From what she'd observed, unless the person posting was a celebrity, traffic on any one account on any given day tended to be low. Not many more people than the ones who left comments were even aware of the exchange.

On Tuesday morning, the real Halloween, Liss's attempts

at rationalizing came crashing down. With a slowly dawning sense of horror, she saw that one of Spinner's nastiest posts had gone viral.

She stared at the numbers, unable to believe what she was seeing. Hadley Spinner's words had been read and liked by nearly half a million people. Hundreds had shared the post. Over a thousand people had left comments, and the majority appeared to support Spinner's hateful rhetoric and bigoted sentiments.

This was bad. Very bad. The most vitriolic of the comments didn't pull any punches. They wanted Joe and his entire family tarred and feathered . . . and worse. What was *wrong* with these people?

When the phone at Liss's elbow rang, she jumped a foot. She checked the caller ID and when it showed an unfamiliar number, she let it ring. The caller hung up rather than leave a message.

Liss sighed. Lost sale or wacko? It was impossible to tell. She was contemplating punching in the number to see who would answer when the door opened to admit a burst of chilly end-of-October air and a harried-looking Tricia Lynd.

The events coordinator for The Spruces was a woman in her late twenties with snapping black eyes and short hair that hugged her scalp. This week it was the color of a fine aged Burgundy. Lithe and energetic, she normally radiated vitality and enthusiasm. At the moment, both were noticeably absent.

"Do you know where Margaret is?" Tricia blurted out. "I've been knocking on her outside door but she doesn't answer."

Hearing the edge of panic in Tricia's voice, Liss wasn't

about to send her out looking. Margaret had taken the dogs for a walk. They could be anywhere in the village. Instead, she came out from behind the sales counter and deftly steered Tricia into the shop's "cozy corner," where two comfortable armchairs and a coffee table were arranged to allow customers to browse the Scottish-themed books offered for sale on a nearby shelf. The area was also an ideal spot for the owner to take the occasional break.

"Come and sit down while you wait for her. Would you like a cup of tea?"

Tricia gave a shaky laugh. "Margaret's cure-all? I don't think it will help."

"Good. Because my selection is limited."

She fixed them two mugs of coffee instead, inhaling the fragrant steam as she carried them out to the cozy corner. Tricia appeared to be a bit calmer by the time she'd taken a few sips, but she was still visibly upset.

"I could sure use Margaret's advice," she said. "She did such a wonderful job as events coordinator. She left me big shoes to fill."

Liss smiled, thinking of her aunt's size six feet, but she knew what Tricia meant. "She should be back soon, but if it would help to talk to me in the meantime, feel free. Is this about the New Age Pilgrims?"

"Our Couples Weekend is a public relations disaster." Tears welled up in Tricia's eyes.

"I'm sure that people who chose to stay at The Spruces will know better than to believe the nonsense Spinner spouts."

"You'd think, but there have already been cancellations and not just individual reservations either. One entire event, a wedding, just pulled out."

Liss's heart sank. Apparently, the power of social media was greater than she'd imagined.

"Did they say this smear campaign was the reason? Maybe the cancellations are just a coincidence."

Tricia took another sip of coffee before she answered. "The reservations were cancelled online, so maybe you're right, but I talked to the mother of the bride myself. She was very explicit about why she didn't want to do business with us. I tried to explain that there was no foundation for the claims Spinner is making, but she wasn't willing to listen."

"Her loss, then."

They heard Margaret and the two Scotties arrive home a few minutes later and Liss sent Tricia up the interior stairs behind the sales counter to talk to her. When she was alone again, she booted up her computer. She hesitated, but only long enough to find the right words. Then she posted a comment on Spinner's rant, one she hoped would convince at least a few people that they were being deceived by his outrageous claims.

An hour later, she took a break from unpacking and shelving new stock to check her e-mail. Along with a couple of customer queries and an obvious example of phishing, she found a message so vicious that she felt the color drain from her face. Just reading the words made her skin crawl.

Her first impulse was to delete it, but common sense stopped her before she could consign it to the virtual trash bin. It would be foolish to destroy evidence. Difficult as it was to believe, she had just received a death threat.

Liss wasn't afraid. Not exactly. She didn't believe that the anonymous sender really intended to come to Moosetookalook and do to her all the despicable things he'd listed in his e-mail. Chances were good that he didn't even live in the same state. But just to be safe, she forwarded the message to Sherri. This was something the police could look into.

Since it was obvious that the person who had sent her that e-mail had read her comment on Spinner's post, she braced herself and checked for other responses on his page. She swallowed convulsively when she saw how many there were. Even before she began to read, she knew that most of them would be negative, but she didn't expect them to range from the merely crude all the way to vicious and threatening. The threats weren't just against her person either. If these angry comments were anything to go by, Spinner's call to boycott Moosetookalook businesses connected to the hotel had widespread support.

Liss told herself that these were not people who would ever order merchandise from her in the first place. The loss of their nonexistent business would have no effect on her bottom line. All the same, by the time she exited her social media account she felt thoroughly uneasy. Her spirits sank even lower when she saw that there were no online orders waiting to be filled.

What if the boycott was working? From what she'd read during the past hour, it was painfully obvious that some people would believe anything they saw on the Internet.

Cut it out, she told herself. It wouldn't do any good to fall into a depression.

Moping around was not her natural response to bad news. She was too much of an optimist. She cheered herself up with the thought that Spinner's attempt to damage the reputation of local businesses would probably fizzle out. His online campaign was an overreaction to a non-issue, as was the upcoming demonstration.

It's overkill, she thought, and then had to fight a smile as an even better word occurred to her. Given the business she was in, Spinner's campaign against Moosetookalook Scottish Emporium was best described as "over*kilt.*"

"There's not much I can do," Sherri said an hour later as she and Liss ate cookies and sipped coffee in the Emporium's cozy corner. "I don't have the resources to find out who sent you that e-mail, and even if I could discover his identity, he's probably protected by his right to freedom of speech."

"Even when he says such horrible things?" Liss already knew the answer, but she felt compelled to ask.

"If you could identify him, and if you could prove that he presents a real threat to you, you might be able to get a restraining order to keep him away, but frankly those aren't worth the paper they're printed on. Unless he tries to carry out one of his threats, he's just mouthing off."

Liss's hands clenched more tightly around her coffee mug. "So if he attacks me, assuming I survive, *then* you can arrest him?"

"That's about the size of it. It stinks when you're the potential victim, but look at it from the other side. Say you lose your temper with a customer and blurt out a threat. Not anything you'd actually do, but the person is disruptive and you really, really want him to leave."

"Get out of here or I'll kill you?"

"Exactly. In the heat of anger, we've all said things we didn't mean."

Liss had to smile at the absurd notion that such a situation could ever arise at the Emporium, but at the same time she understood the point Sherri was trying to make. "Maybe you're right and this guy is just letting off steam. I hope so.

But I can't help but be concerned about the rally Spinner has planned for Saturday."

"It won't amount to anything. Remember that protest a few years back, when some society or other objected to that historical reenactment at the Scottish festival?"

"How could I forget? Because of that brouhaha, my father ended up being a suspect in a homicide."

"Not for long," Sherri reminded her, "and my point is that having picketers outside the grounds of The Spruces back then didn't amount to a hill of beans."

"This is different. Besides, the hotel itself wasn't the target that time. The Spruces was just the venue for the reenactment. What Spinner has spawned appears to have a much broader base, and he seems determined to damage my business, and Dan's, and Sam's, as well as Joe's."

"Seriously, Liss? Just how many people do you think are going to make the trek to tiny little Moosetookalook, Maine, because some blowhard sounded off on social media?"

"I don't think we should underestimate the power of the Internet."

"Oh, believe me, I don't. But I can't see this drawing much of a crowd." She held up one hand in the universal "stop" signal. The other held a half-eaten chocolate chip cookie from Patsy's Coffee House. "I'm not dismissing your concerns. My entire police force will be on duty on Saturday, plus a few officers borrowed from the sheriff's department, just to make sure there's no trouble."

Liss felt a little better hearing that. Sherri didn't have a large department but her officers were well trained, and the deputies would undoubtedly include Pete Campbell, Sherri's husband, a Moosetookalook native respected by the entire community. Still, the whole situation was worrisome.

"What if Spinner is able to pull in hotheads from away?"

Sherri dusted cookie crumbs off the front of her uniform and stood. "Don't worry," she said as she headed for the door. "I'll keep an eye on Spinner's posts and the responses he gets. In the meantime, don't add any more comments of your own. The best way to deal with Internet trolls is to ignore them."

Chapter Three

Two days later, Liss's morning began in the usual way. She got up, got dressed, fed Lumpkin and Glenora, and shared a light breakfast of coffee, orange juice, and whole wheat toast with Dan. When he headed out the back door to his woodworking shop, she left by the front and walked the short distance to Moosetookalook Scottish Emporium. It promised to be a gorgeous day, and warm for the beginning of November. She wore a jacket but she doubted she'd need one if she went outside again later.

She was halfway to her destination before she realized that something was wrong. At first it was only an impression of dark slashes across lighter-colored wood, but that was enough to make her stomach clench. She sped up until she was nearly running by the time she reached her store. Her legs trembled as she stepped up onto the porch and read the words that had been crudely printed on the door in bold black paint. During the night, someone had left a message aimed at Liss's customers: DO NOT SUPPORT A BUSINESS THAT SUPPORTS SIN.

The paint had run a little on some of the letters. Even though the dribbles were not red, they made Liss think of blood. She shuddered. For a moment, her mind went blank.

She couldn't look away from the words defacing her place of business but she couldn't think what to do about them, either.

"You, too, eh?"

Liss's entire body jerked at the sound of Maud Dennison's voice. She hadn't noticed the older woman arriving at Carrabassett County Wood Crafts, the co-op Dan had established with fellow woodworkers in the building next door to Moosetookalook Scottish Emporium.

"Me, too?" she asked, confused.

Maud's steely gaze matched her iron gray hair. For many years, those eyes had looked down a decidedly hooked nose to intimidate rambunctious seventh-graders. Like Liss's mother, who had taught history to teenagers for well over three decades, Maud had been a force to be reckoned with in the classroom. Liss took an involuntary step away from her.

"They painted CHILDREN OF THE DEVIL on the door of the craft shop," Maud said.

"Good grief."

"I can't imagine why the people in the apartment over the shop didn't hear them."

"Oh, my God! Margaret!"

Her hands made clumsy by anxiety, Liss fumbled with the lock on the Emporium's door. If her aunt had become aware of someone on the porch, she'd have come downstairs to investigate. What if they'd forced their way in and hurt her?

When she finally managed to get inside, she barely glanced at the shop as she rushed through. She didn't notice anything out of place, but she wasn't about to stop for a closer look. She was too anxious about Margaret's safety.

She'd climbed only a few steps toward her aunt's apartment before Margaret's two Scottish terriers, Dandy and Dondi, started to bark. The sound of Margaret's voice calling out to them to be quiet and then ordering them to sit and stay was music to Liss's ears.

She hurried the rest of the way upstairs, no longer in a panic but still concerned. She didn't realize that Maud was right behind her until they both stood on the tiny landing in front of Margaret's door and Margaret, still in her bathrobe, was peering out at them in bewilderment. The two dogs held their positions behind her, but they were vibrating with their need to greet the newcomers.

Margaret took one look at the expression on her niece's face and asked, "What's wrong?"

"A plague of vandals, that's what." Maud had never been one to mince words. Once they were inside the apartment, she extracted a cell phone from the pocket of her slacks. "I'm calling the police."

"Someone defaced the entrances to the Emporium and the craft shop." Liss told her aunt what the painted messages said.

"This has gotten out of hand." More angry than shocked, Margaret steered Liss and Maud into the kitchen. Since she preferred tea to coffee, the water in the kettle was already boiling. Arbitrarily deciding that this situation called for chamomile, she made three cups of the herbal brew. Liss accepted hers without enthusiasm.

"Sherri will be here as soon as she can," Maud said. She'd made a succinct report on the vandalism over the phone. She glanced at her watch, and nodded to herself. "She was still at home, but it shouldn't take her more than ten minutes."

A quarter of an hour later they were still waiting. Margaret had poured more tea without giving either Maud or

Liss the option of turning it down. Another five minutes passed before Sherri knocked on the door.

"Sorry it took me so long to get here," she apologized, "but your businesses weren't the only ones that were vandalized last night. Someone painted the word *prevert* on the door of Patsy's Coffee House."

"Prevert?" Liss wasn't sure she'd heard correctly.

Sherri's expression was wry. "We appear to have a vandal who can't spell. I assume he meant pervert."

"That still doesn't make any sense. Why—?" She broke off when she caught Margaret and Maud exchanging a look. "What?"

"I guess you didn't know," Margaret said. "Patsy is gay."

"No!"

Margaret chuckled. "Close your mouth. You'll catch flies."

Maud looked offended by Liss's reaction. "Do you have a problem with lesbians?"

Taken aback by the censure in the words, Liss struggled not to sound defensive. "Of course not. I was just surprised. Margaret's right. I didn't know. Why would I? I don't go around asking people about their sexual orientation. That's not something that matters to me."

She thought about adding that she had many LGBTQ friends from her days on tour with the dance company, but that just sounded lame. Maud would have to take her word for it that her automatic "no" had not been a negative reaction. Knowing Patsy was gay didn't make a bit of difference in the way Liss felt about her.

"You weren't living in Moosetookalook when Patsy was with Louise," Margaret said.

"They were partners for about eight years. If the law had been different back then, they'd have married."

"Where is Louise now?" Liss asked.

"She died. Cancer. One of the fast-moving kinds. Patsy was devastated. She's never shown any interest in anyone else since."

Maud nodded in agreement. "It's as if, after she lost Louise, she decided she'd rather be alone."

Sherri cleared her throat. "So whoever wrote *prevert* on Patsy's door must have known about Louise."

"That doesn't narrow things down much." Margaret placed a mug of coffee in front of Sherri.

The smell had Liss sitting up straighter and wondering why her friend rated special treatment. True, it wasn't very good coffee, but even instant was better than the chamomile she'd forced herself to choke down.

"I'd say most people who were living in Moosetookalook fifteen or so years ago knew that Patsy and Louise were in what used to be called a Boston marriage," Margaret said. "No one thought much about it then and I don't see why they should now."

Liss stopped trying to inhale caffeine fumes. "Fifteen years? Isn't that how long Hadley Spinner has been living in this area?"

"I don't think there's much question about the identity of our vandal," Maud said. "It has to be one of Spinner's people. Why else would they target two shops with Ruskin connections and one owned by a lesbian? They're all bigots out there at Pilgrim Farm."

"That may be the logical conclusion," Sherri agreed, "but it's going to be difficult to prove. If anyone had seen the culprit, they'd already have reported him." She shook her head. "He was darned lucky not to be caught. It took some time to paint messages on all three doors, and it couldn't have been done in total darkness. He must have had a flashlight or a lantern."

"How long does it take to spray paint a few words?" Margaret began to clear away cups and saucers. She gave her niece a disapproving look when she saw that Liss had taken only a few sips of her second cup of tea and had let the rest go cold.

"That's just it," Sherri said. "The messages weren't sprayed on. They were neatly printed using a paintbrush. Furthermore, whoever did it must have worn disposable gloves because I couldn't find any fingerprints."

"Spinner has to be behind it," Liss said. "You need to question him and his people. Maybe one of them will let something slip."

"I'll pay a visit to Spinner's farm," Sherri promised, "but I doubt he'll tell me much, and the rest of them barely speak at all."

"The New Age Pilgrims are beginning to sound more like a cult than a sect." Liss folded a napkin, the only thing Margaret had left on the table, and continued to smooth the soft fabric between her fingers as she asked, "Do you think they're dangerous?"

"I don't think Spinner is a Charles Manson or a Jim Jones, if that's what you mean."

"As near as I can tell," Margaret said, "with the rare exception, members of the group have never been more than a tad eccentric until recently. They were occasionally annoying, what with all that Bible thumping, but they weren't belligerent and they didn't go around filing lawsuits against their neighbors or threatening boycotts."

"That's right," Maud said. "Spinner has always been a chauvinist and a homophobic bigot, but for the most part he kept his opinions to himself."

"What about his followers? Any signs of brainwashing?" Liss's mind was still on cults.

"I'm pretty sure they were all like-minded to start with," Maud said. "Spinner's entire congregation is white and straight. The women act subservient, but nobody appears to be forcing them to behave that way. If they want to leave, they surely can."

Margaret looked as if she wanted to object to this last statement, but Sherri spoke again before Liss's aunt could get a word in.

"Do you know if they are a recognized church?" she asked. "Is Spinner ordained as a minister?"

"I've always assumed he is." Maud frowned. "Doesn't take much, does it? You can get certified by taking a mail-order course."

"He performs marriages for the couples who live out at his farm," Margaret said.

"In this state, any notary public can do that much." Sherri made a note in the little spiral-bound notebook she'd taken out of a pocket.

"What do the other Pilgrims call him?" Liss asked. "Pastor? Reverend?" She hoped it wasn't something like "The Master."

Once again, Maud was the one with the answer. "They're formal with each other, at least when they're out in public. He's Mr. Spinner to his congregation and he uses the same form of address with them."

"Mr. and Mrs.?" Liss felt certain he wouldn't tolerate the use of Ms.

Maud cracked a smile. "Not quite. They prefer to address women as Mistress. That's the old-fashioned, all-purpose version that covers both married and unmarried females. The husbands even address their wives that way, like they do in nineteenth-century novels."

Liss found herself smiling in return. She could just imagine Dan's reaction if she started saying things like "Your supper is ready, Mr. Ruskin," or "Come to bed, Mr. Ruskin."

It took a while for Sherri to process all three crime scenes. Once she was done, and Patsy's, the Emporium, and the craft shop were permitted to open, Liss asked Margaret to mind the store for a bit so that she could cut across the square and talk to their fellow victim. For one thing, she wanted to apologize. Patsy should never have been included in Spinner's vendetta against the Ruskins.

After taking a moment to scowl at the nasty word painted on the door, Liss went inside. Except for old Alex Permutter, ensconced in his favorite spot by the window and absorbed in his newspaper, the place was empty. The seating area that flanked the counter was small, boasting only three booths and two tables, although there were five stools at the counter itself. The clientele was a mix of those who came in for take-out and those who sat a spell, gossiping with their neighbors while they enjoyed the fruits of Patsy's labors.

A chalkboard on one wall advertised the day's specials and listed the coffee blends available. The latter could be purchased by the cup for consumption on the premises or off, or by the pound. Bins full of coffee beans flanked self-serve grinders for those who wanted to take some roasted goodness home with them.

As Liss looked around for Patsy, she inhaled deeply. Air redolent of coffee and baked goods had her mouth watering and her stomach growling. With a sense of shock, she realized that she'd lost the entire morning to the vandalism and that it was nearly lunchtime. If she wanted to talk to Patsy before the soup-and-sandwich crowd started to trickle in, she'd better get to it.

She found the skinny-as-a-rail baker in her kitchen, just taking an enormous pan of brownies out of the oven. Several loaves of bread were stacked next to a cutting board and two apple pies were cooling on racks. The remains of Patsy's early-morning baking—sticky buns, blueberry muffins, and Boston cream doughnuts—had already been relegated to a series of covered dishes on the counter.

"What, no whoopie pies?" Liss asked.

"Tomorrow," Patsy promised. "You here for a meal?"

"Maybe, but the real reason I came is to tell you how sorry I am that you were targeted this morning. Hadley Spinner's quarrel is with Joe, and by extension with the rest of the Ruskin family, but there was no reason to attack you."

"Don't worry about it, hon," Patsy said. "It's not your fault."

"But you're an innocent bystander. He should have left you out of it."

Patsy snorted at that. "Hardly innocent, and Spinner's dislike of me goes way back."

Having set the brownies aside to cool, she seized a serrated knife and began to slice the bread. She worked with deadly speed and precision and if she made her cuts with just a little more force than necessary, Liss could scarcely blame her.

Patsy's Coffee House had been around since Liss was a child, thriving even in a small town like this one because Patsy was a genius in the kitchen. She had little tolerance for fools, but like any successful business owner, she knew how to put on a friendly face for her customers. Moosetookalook as a whole, or so Liss had always believed, was a tolerant if conservative community, firmly believing in "live and let live."

"Did you do something lately to set him off?"

The blade paused in midair and Patsy sent her a narrow-eyed look. "I'm a lesbian. I exist. That's enough."

"But how does he even know that? I mean, I didn't until today and I've been in and out of this place all my life."

"It isn't a secret." Patsy frowned. "I suppose the subject just never came up when you were around."

"Exactly! Not that it would have made any difference to me if I had known. I don't choose my friends according to race or religion or sexual preference."

"*Spinner* does."

From behind her, Liss heard the faint sound of a door opening and closing. Patsy glanced through the service window and Liss's gaze followed hers. No one had come in. What they'd heard was old man Permutter leaving.

"This isn't a story I'd tell anyone," Patsy said when the bread was sliced and stacked. "It still leaves a bad taste in my mouth, and some sorrow, too. But here's how Spinner found out I was gay."

She leaned against the kitchen counter and folded her arms across her chest. A faraway look came into her eyes.

"Spinner was one of my regular customers when he first arrived in the area. He loved my whole wheat bread and he ate lunch here sometimes. One of those times, there was a stranger eating here, too. He was a good-lookin' fella, the kind who thinks he's God's gift to women. I wasn't bad-looking myself in those days, but Louise—you know who Louise was?"

Liss nodded.

"Louise was a real stunner. All the years we were together, I cooked and she waitressed. That day, this man kept hitting on her, telling her what a good time he could show her. He didn't listen when she said she wasn't interested. Finally, to get rid of him, she called me out of the kitchen and introduced me as her lover. The guy didn't believe her, which really ticked Louise off. She had quite a temper." Patsy's smile was fond. "To her mind, there was only one way to convince him she was telling the truth, so she grabbed me and laid one on me." The smile broadened. "That was some kiss, all right. I mean, the whole world faded away for a minute there. By the time we came up for air, the stranger had slapped down a twenty to pay his bill and left. We never even heard him go."

Liss would have smiled, too, but she had a sick feeling that she knew what had happened next. "I suppose Spinner witnessed the entire incident."

"Got it in one. He was some startled, let me tell you. Then he went ballistic. He claimed he finally understood why he always felt so uncomfortable patronizing my place. What a load of cow flops! Before that day, he never once had a bit of trouble scarfing down my homemade blueberry muffins or eating my corn chowder."

When Patsy was upset, her Maine accent became much more pronounced. *Never* and *chowder* came out as *nevah* and *chowdah*.

"Calm down, Patsy," Liss said. "Don't upset yourself over Hadley Spinner. He's not worth it."

"Thinks he's so wicked smart," Patsy muttered. "Throwing all those big words around. He called Louise a pernicious influence and said both of us were evil, unnatural women. Then he stormed out of the place, vowing never to come back. Well, that was fine with me!" She picked up the bread knife she'd been using and slammed it back into its slot with enough force to make the entire knife rack wobble.

"If you haven't done anything recently to provoke him, why would he go after you?"

"Because he's meaner than a rattlesnake and convinced that his way of thinking is the only *right* way." Patsy's hands flew as she started preparations for Moosetookalook's version of a lunch crowd, putting bacon in the oven for BLTs and getting lettuce out of the refrigerator to wash. "That man's got a warped sense of morality, the kind that dictates that everyone who is different is full of sin and fit only to be shunned if they won't see the evil of their ways. Ever hear of conversion therapy? He promotes it. He thinks sexual identity is a matter of choice. If he had his way, I'd be institutionalized, beaten, and subjected to electric shock treatments until I turned straight."

"That's barbaric."

"Also ineffective. Like trying to use dye or bleach to change the color of your skin."

Patsy's assertions worried Liss. Spinner was sounding more and more like a whack job with every story she heard about him. By defacing the doors to the craft shop and the coffee house, he'd already added new targets. Who knew what, or who, he or his followers would attack next?

"Spinner is still trying to get people to boycott all the Ruskin businesses because Joe's couples promotion at The Spruces violates his concept of family values," Liss said. "Now he's got a rally planned for the town square on Saturday."

"I heard," Patsy said. "That man's a menace."

"After what happened to your door, I'm afraid the protest may expand to cover much more than the hotel's Thanksgiving special."

Patsy picked up two pies and carried them through the

swinging door. Liss caught up with her as she placed them in the pie safe on the counter.

"Sherri says there's nothing we can do to prevent the demonstration. Spinner has all the necessary permits. And there's that free speech thing."

Patsy opened her mouth, then closed it again, looking thoughtful. "I was about to tell you to ignore them. That's how I've dealt with Spinner all these years and what I planned to keep on doing. Now I'm not so sure that will work any longer." She crossed the café to bus the table where Alex Permutter had been sitting. "I'm young enough that I just missed the era of protests that Margaret and your parents and Joe Ruskin lived through—civil rights and Vietnam and women's liberation and all that—but I'm beginning to understand what motivated the activists."

Liss followed her. "I'm not sure we want to provoke—"

"Why not?" She gave the table a swipe with a damp cloth. "They've been trying to provoke us. Besides, I doubt Spinner will stop at objecting to gay couples and unmarried straight couples. Next he'll go after divorced single parents like Angie. I bet you anything he thinks she's going straight to hell for her sins. He'll go out of his way to tell her so, and say so in front of her kids, too. And then he'll start bad-mouthing the bookstore, just the way he's slinging mud at your place and mine."

Patsy paused, dirty dishes in hand, to stare through her window at the town square where Saturday's demonstration was to take place. She paid no attention when the door opened to admit Pete Campbell, even though a big man wearing the distinctive brown uniform of a deputy sheriff was hard to ignore. His steps faltered when he caught sight of the expression on Patsy's face. Shifting his gaze to Liss, his eyebrows lifted in a question.

She shook her head at him, indicating that it would be best if he didn't ask it aloud. With a shrug, he made his way to the corner booth he favored and slid onto the bench seat. It was only when the couple who owned the jewelry store came in to claim a table that Patsy snapped out of her reverie.

"Someone," she said, not troubling to lower her voice as she stalked to the counter to dispose of the dishes, "needs to stop Hadley Spinner before he does any more damage." Without missing a beat, she turned and whipped out her order pad. "What can I get you folks today? The special is a BLT with a cup of clam chowdah and a choice of apple pie or a double chocolate brownie for dessert."

After she left Patsy's Coffee House, Liss went home and made lunch for herself and Dan. While they ate, she had to fend off Lumpkin's increasingly frantic demands for tidbits of leftover chicken. He went from his cute cat trick of begging while sitting up like a gopher to grabbing Liss's thigh with his claws extended. Throughout the meal, Dan fumed in silence, as upset as Liss was about the vandalism that had defaced three of the businesses in their small town.

His cell phone rang just as Liss began to clear away the plates and glasses. Dan hauled it out of his pocket and glanced at the number on the screen. "It's Sherri," he said, and answered the call. His side of the conversation consisted of one "uh-huh" after another with a final "okay then" before he disconnected.

"Well?"

"She says we can go ahead and clean the paint off the doors."

"Good. I hated that she made us leave it in place, but she

said someone higher up in law enforcement might want to take a first-hand look at it."

Dan nodded. "She thought this might qualify as a hate crime, but apparently not. To tell you the truth, Sherri sounded relieved about that. I guess she doesn't want some other department to take over her case." A layer of bitterness underscored his words.

"Have a little faith, Dan. You know Sherri's good at what she does."

"She is, but her hands are tied until that nut-job tries something worse than having one of his goons paint words on wood. I don't like waiting for the other shoe to drop."

"It's not like he's an ax murderer."

Her dry tone coaxed a reluctant smile out of him. "Are you sure? Who knows what goes on out at that farm of his."

Liss rolled her eyes. "I've got to get back to work."

She took an empty plate away from Lumpkin, who had leapt to the counter while her back was turned and licked it clean. Although there was nothing left but the floral design, he sent her a baleful look and then stomped off, tail swishing. A glance at the top of the refrigerator showed Liss that Glenora was in her usual spot. She'd watched them eat but couldn't be bothered to jump down and beg for scraps. It was beneath her dignity, Liss supposed.

Dan collected the cutlery and dropped it into the dishpan in the sink. After they'd eaten their supper, lunch dishes would be washed along with those used for their evening meal. Since it was just the two of them, neither Liss nor Dan had ever felt any need to own a dishwasher.

"I'll work on removing that paint this afternoon," Dan said.

"Do me a favor and start at Patsy's."

"I was planning to."

That settled, Liss went back to the Emporium. As soon as Margaret saw her coming, she let the two Scotties back inside. They'd spent the morning in their fenced-in yard behind the building and looked ready for a nap, but their owner was in no hurry to return to her apartment.

"You had a few walk-ins while you were out."

"Actual customers?" Liss knew she sounded skeptical.

She got out her feather duster, a soft cloth, and a spray bottle of lemon-scented furniture polish in preparation for resuming the one never-ending task of the shopkeeper. If she hoped to sell her Scottish-themed knickknacks, both they and the shelves they sat on had to gleam.

"Busybodies," Margaret admitted, reaching down to ruffle Dandy's fur. "Well, no. That's not quite accurate, but they did stop by out of curiosity."

"Let me guess." Liss studied the six-inch-high pewter figurine of a piper to make sure she'd wiped it clean of dust. When it passed muster, she put it back on the shelf. "Dolores Mayfield?"

"Of course." The librarian was the biggest gossip in town. She poked her long, thin nose into everybody's business.

"Julie Simpson?" As their postmaster, the brassy brunette with her loud, nasal voice and her New York accent was the person in charge of the other main stop on Moosetookalook's information train.

Margaret nodded. "She came in on her lunch hour."

Moosetookalook's post office was so tiny—the front half of the first floor of a small clapboard building—that Julie, since she was not only postmaster but also the sole employee at the facility, was authorized to close up shop from noon until one each day.

"A few other folks walked past and took pictures,"

Margaret continued, wandering over to the plate-glass display window to admire the view of the town square. "One of them was 'our intrepid staff reporter' from the *Daily Scoop*." Margaret meant Jerrilyn Jones, only child and beloved daughter of the editor and owner of their local online news source. "She took a picture."

Liss grimaced. "The sooner Dan cleans off that paint, the better."

"He appears to be finished with Patsy's door," Margaret reported, "and if I'm not mistaken, his path and Sherri's are about to intersect on our doorstep."

Hoping there was news, preferably of Spinner's arrest, Liss abandoned her cleaning supplies and scurried after her aunt, who had already gone out onto the front porch. Liss closed the door to keep the Scotties inside only a second before Dan exploded into speech.

"What do you mean you haven't talked to him yet?" he shouted.

Sherri glared at him, unimpressed by the display of temper. "Settle down, Dan. He's next on my list. It's not as if he's going anywhere, and I had a few other things to attend to first." She shifted her attention to Liss. "I thought you ought to know about one of them."

"What now?" Realizing that she was holding her breath, Liss let it out in a whoosh of air.

"A suspicious number of people from away have checked into the Day Lily Inn during the last twenty-four hours."

"That dump," Dan said before the significance hit him. When it did, his expression hardened. "Demonstrators. I guess they didn't have much choice about where to stay, since they're boycotting The Spruces."

"Be glad of it." Sherri glanced around, saw that they'd attracted the interest of a couple strolling through the town square and of the docent standing on the porch of the Historical Society Museum. "Let's take this inside."

"Who did Spinner recruit?" Margaret asked the moment they were in private. "Hell's Angels? Skinheads? Maybe members of the KKK?"

"Not funny, Margaret."

Liss sent her husband a startled look. It wasn't like him to snap at people. The only explanation was that he was more upset by Spinner's activities than she'd realized.

"I don't know who they are," Sherri said, "but they're a scruffy-looking bunch. No shaved heads. No leather jackets." She paused and looked thoughtful. "Now that I think about it, I have to wonder if Spinner recruited them from a homeless shelter."

"I wouldn't put it past him," Margaret said.

"The point is, there are more of them coming. Every room at the Day Lily is booked to the legal max—that's four to a room. The only logical explanation, just as Dan said, is that they're here to take part in the demonstration on Saturday. There may be more of them I don't know about, maybe staying in nearby towns and waiting to show up on that day."

"Can't you do anything?" Liss asked. "Evict them? Send them back where they came from?"

"On what grounds? They haven't done anything illegal." Sherri sounded as frustrated as Liss felt.

With a resounding thump, the cleaning equipment Dan had carried over from Patsy's hit the floor. "Maybe you can't do anything," he said, heading for the door, "but I can."

"Dan, wait!" Liss called. "Where are you going? What are you going to do?" The expression on his face alarmed her. He looked like a man who was spoiling for a fight.

"Margaret, can you—?"

"Go!"

Liss went.

Dan was already halfway to their house with Sherri right behind him. She'd been forced to run to keep up with his longer strides. By the time Liss caught up with them, Dan was already getting into his truck. She grabbed hold of the handle to prevent him from closing the door.

"Dan, stop. You shouldn't drive when you're this angry."

"Get out of the vehicle, Dan." Sherri used the authoritative voice she usually reserved for occasions when she was about to arrest someone.

He ignored them both, jerking the door free of Liss's grip with one hand and starting the engine with the other. Furious at his highhandedness and seriously rattled by the grimly determined expression on his face, Liss pounded on the window so hard that it made her knuckles throb. He ran it down just far enough for her to hear what he had to say.

"I'm going out to Pilgrim Farm and tell Spinner to call off his dogs." His head jerked around at the sound of the passenger side door opening.

Sherri heaved herself inside. "I was headed that way myself. You can give me a lift." Unspoken was the warning that with her along, he'd better keep his temper in check.

Liss stepped back, meaning to circle around the front of the truck and join the party, but Dan threw the vehicle into reverse and backed rapidly out of the driveway before she could reach the other side. Staring openmouthed, she watched her husband burn rubber as he drove away.

Uttering an expletive best deleted from polite conversation, Liss ran for her own car, thankful that it was parked at the curb in front of the house and that she had her keys in the pocket of her jeans. "Going to confront Hadley Spinner, are you, Dan?" she muttered under her breath. "Not without me, you're not."

She didn't have her driver's license with her, but she wasn't about to let that stop her. Sherri wasn't likely to hassle her about it. Not under these circumstances. As soon as the engine roared to life, she hit the gas and took off, tires squealing. There was a good reason why it was imperative that she catch up with Dan before he got very far. Without him to lead the way, she didn't have the slightest idea how to find Pilgrim Farm.

Chapter Four

There are no particular boundaries between Moosetookalook and Lower Mooseside. One village runs into the other along a two-lane country road dotted with farmhouses. Liss was especially glad she had someone to lead the way when Dan turned off onto a very narrow, extremely steep gravel road, the kind she avoided like the plague during the winter months. As she followed her husband's truck, it occurred to her to wonder how he knew where Spinner lived. Until that encounter with him at The Spruces back in September, she'd never even heard mention of the man's name.

At the top of the rise, a scattering of buildings came into view. They were well kept, freshly painted a glaring white, and surrounded by extensive, recently harvested fields and a fenced-in area where a dozen black and white cows were grazing. The house itself looked old but in good repair.

It was clear from the lack of a sidewalk leading up to it that the front door was rarely used. This was a common practice in many homes in rural Maine. Familiar with it, Dan pulled into the driveway and parked in the dooryard at the side of the house. Liss brought her car to a stop alongside his truck.

There were no other vehicles in sight, and no people, either. Reluctance slowing her movements, Liss got out and stood next to her car. Using the door to shield most of her body from anyone inside the building, she took a closer look at her surroundings.

Most of the outbuildings were easy to identify. She spotted a chicken coop—that was easy since there were free-range chickens scratching the ground in front of it. There was a sugar shack for boiling sap to make maple syrup. Another small building appeared to be a smokehouse. The only structure that puzzled her was a large building, square and squat, that sat off by itself at the edge of a cornfield.

In true northern New England fashion, the farmhouse was connected to several other buildings in sequence. It was a practical arrangement that spared the farmer the necessity of going outside on a cold winter morning to feed his livestock and milk his cows. That long section between the house and barn was the ell.

Liss shifted her gaze to the left, where a breezeway built at a right angle to the barn connected it to what looked like a garage. Before winter came, the Pilgrims would doubtless close in the open spaces with panels that matched the rest of the siding.

Having exited Dan's truck, Sherri was making a survey of her own. "We're being watched," she said, nodding in the direction of the house. In an upstairs window, a curtain twitched.

That accounts for one person, Liss thought, *but where are the other dozen or so?*

She looked more closely at the barn. The doors in the loft stood open. Hay had likely been hoisted through them in the not-too-distant past. That would make a good vantage point from which to check out uninvited visitors. The shadows within prevented her from seeing if anyone was watching them from up there, but she'd swear she could feel eyes tracking her every movement.

She almost jumped out of her skin when a door slammed. A solitary figure emerged from the door into the ell: Hadley Spinner. He was bareheaded, revealing wispy, straw-colored hair that was thinning on top. His scraggly beard was slightly darker in color. They framed a leathery, deeply lined, darkly tanned face. Having left off his suit coat, he had rolled the sleeves of his collarless white shirt to his elbows to reveal muscular arms. Working on a farm year-round had kept his body in good physical condition. Many a younger man would have envied him those broad shoulders.

Spinner stopped at a distance of a few feet to glower at them. His nostrils flared, as if there was an unpleasant smell coming from the intruders in his dooryard.

Dan took a step forward, his hands curling into fists at his sides. Before he could speak, Sherri caught his arm and hissed a few words of warning. Liss couldn't hear exactly what she said, but it convinced him to back down.

Satisfied that Dan would behave, Sherri addressed the man they'd come to see. "Mr. Spinner, I need to talk to your people. All of them."

"I answer for them."

"Not in this instance."

Out of the corner of her eye, Liss caught a small movement at the side of the breezeway. She turned her head just slightly, far enough to make out a bit of lavender skirt. When she shifted her gaze to the loft doors, she discovered that the space was no longer empty. Two men stood in the opening, staring down on the scene below. From their dark trousers held up by suspenders to their unkempt beards, they'd copied the look of their leader.

When they saw her watching them, they backed away. They emerged from the barn at ground level a minute or two later and went to stand behind Hadley Spinner. They made no threatening moves, but Liss couldn't help but feel uneasy. Her wariness increased as the other New Age Pilgrims drifted outside. In all there were eight men, eight women, and one young child, a girl dressed in a pale purple dress exactly like those the women wore. She sucked her thumb and stared, wide-eyed, at the three visitors. Liss wasn't good at guessing children's ages, having none herself, but she thought the girl must be two or three years old.

Having that many pairs of staring eyes fixed on her made Liss's palms sweat, but the creepiest thing about the assembled Pilgrims was the fact that they looked so eerily alike. There was some variety of shape and size among the women, but the men were almost identical in height and build and the resemblance was reinforced by their facial hair and clothing. She wondered if they were all related to Hadley Spinner. Maybe brothers or cousins? Her overactive imagination kicked in to suggest that they might be clones, a theory that made as much sense as any other, given the weirdness of this entire situation.

Sherri broke off her low-voiced dialogue with Spinner to count heads. "Is this everyone?" Spinner surveyed his troops, looking none-too-pleased to discover that his followers were standing in full view of strangers. Had he expected them to stay out of sight?

"Mistress Spinner, come here." He snapped out the command like a drill sergeant who expected instant obedience from the troops.

A woman stepped out of the ranks and approached him at a brisk pace. She was sturdily built and wore a pair of old-fashioned round, rimless spectacles perched on a snub nose. Like the other women, she wore a plain lavender gown, but she had pinned a small gold watch to the fabric above her left breast and had a half dozen keys suspended from the leather belt she wore at her waist. They clinked and rattled with every step she took.

"Mistress Spinner, did any woman under your supervision leave the house last night?"

"Certainly not, Mr. Spinner. I slept, as I always do, with my mattress blocking the only door."

"What about the window?" Sherri asked.

Mistress Spinner gestured toward the second floor of the house with one hand. "See for yourself."

Liss stared at the windows in the upstairs rooms in shock. Every one of them was barred. At night, while they slept, these women were little better off than prisoners in the county jail.

"I can myself vouch for my brethren in the New Age Pilgrims," Spinner said. "They spent the night in the barracks, as they always do, until we all rose at dawn to praise the Lord and begin our chores."

So that was what the square squat building housed.

"You have no cause to doubt my word and no right to question my people," Spinner declared.

"I have every right, Mr. Spinner. A crime has been committed, and given your recent activities, and those you have planned for the weekend, a member of your merry band is the most likely suspect."

"You *mock* me?" Outrage turned his face a mottled red.

The set of Sherri's jaw told Liss she wasn't about to apologize for that "merry band" crack. She was clearly fed up with Spinner's obstructionist attitude, as well as with his posturing.

"I am the duly appointed chief of police of the town of Moosetookalook, Mr. Spinner. It is my duty to pursue this matter, with or without your cooperation. I'd prefer to talk to each individual here at the farm but, if necessary, I will call in reinforcements and have everyone taken to the police station to be interviewed."

Liss had been watching the Pilgrims as Sherri spoke. At those words, she saw a pleased smile appear on the face of the young woman standing just behind Hadley Spinner. It disappeared when the man standing next to her clamped a hand over her right elbow. His response to the possibility of being questioned by the police was a ferocious scowl.

Curious, Liss searched the other faces for a reaction. She found only one. A man standing a little apart from the rest regarded their leader with an expression she could only describe as sly. He looked to be about Spinner's age— as much as a decade older than some of the rest of the group.

Her gaze came back to Spinner just as he spat on the dry ground, narrowly missing Sherri's shoes.

"Send in your troops, if you can raise them. We will defend our right to freedom from oppression."

A quick glance at the woman who had smiled, a blonde who wore her hair in two long braids that hung nearly to her waist, showed Liss an expression that was carefully blank.

"Mr. Spinner, your contempt for the law is making this situation far more complicated than it needs to be," Sherri said with more patience than Liss could have managed. "Why are you so determined to protect a vandal who defaced private property?"

Spinner smirked at her. "You have no evidence that one of my people did anything of the kind. We have already told you that no one left Pilgrim Farm last night. You can ask no more of us."

"I *could* ask you to cancel your rally in the town square."

"You would ask in vain. Sin must be exposed and eradicated."

"Oh, please," Liss muttered under her breath.

Either Spinner had extremely good hearing or she'd spoken more loudly than she'd intended. The look he sent her was so filled with venom that for a moment she stopped breathing. This was what it must feel like, she thought, to attract the attention of a boa constrictor. She had not a doubt in the world that Spinner would enjoy squeezing the life out of her.

"I know who you are." His words came out in a threatening rumble. "You're that *dancer*."

He flung the word at her like an accusation, his tone of voice calling up the image of a cheap dive, a scanty costume, and a pole. Liss hadn't danced professionally for ten years, but when she had earned her living that way, it had been as part of a troupe that put on a show called *Strathspey*. By way of explanation, Liss always told people to think *Riverdance*, only Scottish. There had been nothing sleazy, salacious, or sinful about their performances.

Although she knew it would be a waste of time to try to reason with a man like Hadley Spinner, Liss couldn't stop herself from blurting out a question: "What's wrong with dancing?"

"It inflames the passions. Women who dance seduce men by their obscene movements."

He didn't stop there. Liss felt her face blanch, then flame when he launched into a vitriolic rant that grew louder and more frightening with every insult he flung at her. She hunched her shoulders under the force of his verbal attack. Her heart pounded so loudly that she could barely make out the crude, vicious words. She was grateful for that, and even more grateful that she still stood in the shelter of her car door. She wanted more than anything to hop back inside, start the engine, and flee, but she found to her horror that she could neither move nor tear her gaze away from Spinner's hate-filled eyes. That they were so dark a brown as to appear black made them all the more frightening.

There was something seriously wrong with this man. To say he had no respect or regard for women was the least of it. Even Sherri, who was armed, had taken a step away from him. The Pilgrims, male and female, stood still as statues, as if mesmerized by his performance . . . or terrified that he would turn on them next.

An angry bellow broke the spell. Liss blinked, and when she opened her eyes again it was to see her husband going for Spinner's throat.

For a moment, no one else moved.

"Dan, stop!" Liss shouted, running toward the fray. She had never seen him so out of control. "You'll kill him!"

"I think that's the idea." Sherri's voice was grim as she caught hold of Dan's right arm and hauled at it.

Liss grabbed the left one. She kept shouting Dan's name, but she wasn't getting through to him. In a desperate bid for his attention, she delivered a swift kick to his leg, but it had no effect. He did not loosen his grip.

Spinner's arms flailed. His eyes bugged out. To judge by the color of his face, he was losing his battle to suck in air. The other, older Pilgrim finally intervened, but even his greater strength was not sufficient to pry Dan's hands away from Spinner's throat.

Liss still had a grip on her husband's arm, tugging for all

she was worth. Since he'd stripped down to a T-shirt to work on the defaced doors, there was bare skin level with her face. Unable to think of anything else to do, desperate to stop him before it was too late, she bit down as hard as she could—hard enough to draw blood and viciously enough to penetrate the blind rage that was driving him to strangle Hadley Spinner.

A cry of despair issued from Dan's throat as he flung the older man away from him. Liss and Sherri went flying, too, although they both managed to stay on their feet. The other Pilgrim beat a rapid retreat, ignoring his fallen leader.

Fists once again clenched at his sides, Dan backed away. Guilt and disbelief mingled in his expression. Abruptly, he turned and ran, stopping only when he reached his truck. He leaned against the hood of the cab and buried his head in his arms, shoulders shaking.

Liss wiped her mouth on her sleeve, but the metallic taste of blood lingered, making her stomach twist into knots. She could only imagine what Dan was feeling. He had to be furious at himself, and disgusted by what he had done in the heat of anger. Spinner was still red in the face, gasping and choking.

With hesitant steps, Mistress Spinner came forward to kneel beside her husband and inspect the damage to his throat. "He will recover," she said in an emotionless monotone. "You had best go now."

If looks could kill, Spinner's glare would have struck Dan dead on the spot. It was probably a good thing he had not yet regained his ability to speak.

When Sherri and Liss reached the parked vehicles, Sherri held out a hand. "Give me your keys. I'll drive your car back. You drive Dan's truck. He's in no condition to get behind the wheel."

"And I am?"

Sherri shot her a look. Liss relinquished her keys.

The ride home was accomplished in total silence. Liss's thoughts were jumbled. She didn't know what to say. When they were back in their own driveway, she sent a wary glance Dan's way. Even after she turned off the ignition, he continued to stare straight ahead, refusing to look at her.

"You okay?"

"Would you be? Christ, Liss, I almost killed him."

"But you didn't. He's okay."

Dan rubbed his arm, still with his eyes averted. "Thanks to you."

Liss watched him with anxious eyes. What had happened at Pilgrim Farm had scared her. The calm, considerate Dan Ruskin she knew did not lose control. She could count on the fingers of one hand the number of times she'd seen him angry, and on none of those occasions had he resorted to physical violence.

"Something just snapped," he said in a low, choked voice. "I was already furious about the vandalism, but when he started insulting you, it got to the point where I couldn't stand to hear one more venomous word come out of his mouth. I had to make him shut up."

He stared at the hands resting on his knees, as if he couldn't believe he'd wrapped them around another human being's throat and nearly choked the life out of him.

"You wanted to throttle him," Liss said. "It's not like you were trying to kill him."

"I'm not so sure about that."

Liss opened her mouth, then closed it again. Spinner's rant against dancers, and against her in particular, had rapidly turned obscene. There had been no indication that he'd intended to stop spewing crude insults. Would he have attacked her with more than words if Dan hadn't gone after him first? There was no way to tell, but Liss was certain of one thing. If Spinner had been spouting vicious slanders against Dan, she could easily imagine herself reacting to the abuse in exactly the same way he had. The mental picture of her hands around Spinner's neck was at the same time deeply satisfying and extremely disturbing.

Sherri pulled into the driveway behind Dan's truck just as Liss and Dan began to climb the steps to the porch. In the village, front doors *were* used, unless there was a more convenient side entrance off a parking area. All three of them went inside together. They were greeted at the door by Lumpkin and Glenora, who seemed to know that their humans were in need of soothing. As soon as Liss and Dan were seated side by side on the sofa, one cat appropriated each lap. Sherri took the chair opposite and appeared to be gathering her thoughts.

"How much trouble am I in?" Dan asked.

"Are you going to arrest him?" Liss spoke at the same time.

Sherri glowered at them both. "I can't take you two anywhere, can I? Here's the thing. I just witnessed an altercation serious enough that I'm going to have to file an incident report with the district attorney."

Liss felt her stomach drop to her toes. She wanted this to be a bad dream, but the claws Lumpkin was rhythmically sinking into her thigh made it clear that everything was all too real.

"What happens then?" Dan's face was ashen.

Liss reached out to grasp his hand and give it a reassuring squeeze.

"I can have a private word with the D.A. to more fully

explain the circumstances, but it will be up to her to decide whether or not to issue a warrant for your arrest."

"What do you think she'll do?" Liss asked.

Sherri hesitated, then shrugged. "No guarantees, but once I repeat some of what Spinner said, and explain to her what's been going on with him, she'll probably be inclined to sympathize with you. She might still arrest you for something," she warned them, "but at least it won't be attempted murder."

"What about Spinner? Can he press charges if the D.A. doesn't?"

"Of course he can." She sounded annoyed. "Don't you think he has a case? He can certainly make one for assault, possibly even attempted murder, and there's no way you can deny what happened. The attack was witnessed by the entire New Age Pilgrim community *and* by the chief of police. What the hell were you thinking to go after him like that?"

"I *wasn't* thinking. I just wanted to stop the filth coming out of his mouth."

"It would have been smarter to walk away, but what's done is done and, amazingly, Spinner wasn't much damaged. The man has a neck like an ox." Sherri leaned toward them and looked Dan straight in the eye. "I want your promise that you'll stay far away from Spinner, his followers, and Pilgrim Farm. When they demonstrate on Saturday, you don't leave this house. Understood?"

Thunderclouds gathered in Dan's expression, but he nodded.

"I think I want to hear that promise out loud."

He raked the fingers of his right hand through hair that was still disheveled from the fight with Spinner. At his hesitation, Liss pinched his thigh. "Tell the nice lady what she wants to hear . . . and *mean* it."

"I'll stay out of their way."

"Good. I've never heard that Spinner was litigious, but if he decides to sue, he could certainly win a civil case. Don't give him any provocation."

Liss bit back a groan. If Spinner sued for damages, he could bankrupt them.

"I'll keep you in the loop," Sherri promised as she stood. "Meanwhile, the best thing you two can do is to go on as usual and stay out of trouble. Oh, and take care of that bite on your arm. Puncture wounds can be nasty."

When she'd gone, Liss sent her husband a bleak look. "This is not going to end well."

"Will you bake me a cake with a file in it when I'm in prison?"

"That's not funny, Dan." She could feel tears welling up in her eyes and turned away before he could see them. The cats fled.

Behind her, she heard a deep sigh. "I know it's not." His hands gently cupped her shoulders, turning her until her cheek was nestled against his collarbone. "No matter what happens, we'll deal with it. We'll get through it. We'll survive." He gave a wry chuckle. "Maybe we'll get lucky and someone will push that pompous jackass off a cliff before he has a chance to bring charges against me."

Liss didn't return to work that afternoon. It was the next day before she saw her aunt again, at which time she recounted the whole sordid story of their encounter with Hadley Spinner.

"I'm a little surprised you haven't already heard all the details," she said when she'd finished. "The Moosetookalook grapevine is usually more efficient."

"The folks out at Pilgrim Farm keep themselves to themselves," Margaret reminded her.

"I guess I should be grateful for small favors."

Liss kept her hands busy while they talked, packing orders to be shipped out later in the day. Spinner's campaign didn't seem to be affecting the mail-order end of the business. In fact, the number of purchases made through the Emporium's Web site was up slightly from the same time the previous year.

"And for the big one, too," Margaret said.

"Big favor? What big favor?" Liss affixed a label and added the box, which contained a stuffed Loch Ness monster, to the take-to-the-post-office pile.

"If Spinner was going to take legal action, he'd have done it already. He's never been one to waste time." Beside her at the worktable, Margaret wound more bubble wrap around the highly breakable bisque figurine of a Scottish dancer.

Liss reached for the next packing slip. "Maybe he's saving that piece of nastiness for a time when it will have more impact."

Margaret shook her head, setting light gray locks bouncing. "Think about it, Liss. If he sues, he opens the New Age Pilgrims up to public scrutiny. You can't imagine that he wants a lot of attention focused on Pilgrim Farm. Not the way his people live. It's one thing to stage this protest and mouth off about the sins of others but quite another to have a magnifying glass focused on your own lifestyle."

Liss hoped her aunt was right, but she didn't trust Spinner to use common sense. He didn't seem quite sane to her and she already knew he was capable of holding a grudge. Why would he pass up an opportunity for revenge . . . unless he had something more personal in mind? A shudder passed through her at the thought.

When the landline in the shop rang, Liss was glad of an excuse to escape the atmosphere of doom and gloom in the stockroom. She answered the phone with a bright and cheery "Good morning. Moosetookalook Scottish Emporium. How may I help you?"

"You can correct your damned Web site," said an annoyed female voice.

Liss held the receiver away from her ear and stared at it for a moment before she replied. "What on earth are you talking about?"

"Your phone number. It's wrong on your Web site."

Fingers busy, Liss had already called up the URL in question and scrolled down to the contact information. "I'm looking at it now." She was careful to keep her voice pleasant. "The phone number is correct."

"Five-oh-three-three?"

"That's right. Those are the last four digits of the number."

"Well, it's wrong somewhere." The woman sounded huffy. "I'm seven-oh-three-three and I've been getting calls for you all week and I am sick to death of being annoyed by morons."

With a sinking feeling in the pit of her stomach, Liss understood what must have happened. "These calls—" She had to clear her throat before she could continue. "I'm guessing they're not friendly."

"Not hardly. A couple of them yelled at me for being opposed to family values and I won't even repeat some of the things that one caller said."

"I am so sorry. I think they must have found the number on a flyer that was handed out at Halloween. I didn't have anything to do with it, but—"

"I don't care where their information came from, I just want these calls to stop. If they don't, I'll keep on doing what I did yesterday."

"Excuse me?"

"Well, I'd had enough, hadn't I? What do I care if one of the callers said she wanted to show support by placing an order?" Now the woman sounded snide, almost spiteful. "If she was too dumb to call the right number and too stubborn to believe me when I told her she had the wrong person, she deserved to be roundly cussed out for her stupidity." With a sound suspiciously like a snarl, she disconnected.

Numb, Liss cradled the receiver. Just what she needed—a new disaster in public relations. She could appreciate how annoying it must have been to get such nasty phone calls simply because her number and the Emporium's differed by one digit, but had it really been necessary to add to the damage Spinner's flyer had done?

Liss hadn't recognized her caller's voice, but the local phone number told her that the irate woman lived in the immediate area. Liss probably knew her, at least in passing. The calls she'd received must have come from local people as well. That was the only way they'd have gotten hold of one of Spinner's flyers with the incorrect number . . . unless he'd posted it online. The very thought triggered a pounding headache.

Margaret chose that moment to emerge from the stockroom. She took one look at Liss's face and demanded to know why she'd gone pale.

Recounting the details of the phone conversation and her thoughts on the matter proved to be good therapy. Margaret nodded sagely and assured her that the customer who'd wanted to order something was obviously a good person who would figure out how to contact the Emporium and follow through. Liss tried hard to believe her.

"I'd better go online and do damage control. I can add a note to our Web site to explain the mix-up."

"Good idea. While you do that I'll go brew a nice soothing cup of tea." Margaret headed for the stairs to her apartment, knowing full well how poor the selection in Liss's stockroom was.

"Anything but chamomile," Liss called after her.

She'd posted alerts on the Web site and all the shop's social media accounts by the time Margaret returned to hand her a plain ceramic mug full of hot liquid. Liss sniffed cautiously at the steaming brew but could not tell what it was.

Margaret smiled. "Green tea. I decided that under these circumstances a little caffeine couldn't hurt."

Liss appreciated the gesture, although she'd have preferred coffee, and carried the mug to the cozy corner. Margaret followed her, settling into the other comfortable chair. Liss had taken a few sips before she noticed the pensive expression on her aunt's face.

"What's wrong?"

Margaret shrugged. "Nothing anyone can do anything about now."

"Something to do with Spinner?" Liss thought that was a safe bet.

"Sadly, yes. Some years back, when you were on the road with your dance company, I got to know one of the lavender ladies. She was a delightful young woman, but clearly unhappy with the choice she'd made by joining the New Age Pilgrims."

Liss frowned at the way Margaret was twisting her hands together. She doubted her aunt was aware of what she was doing, which made the repetitive movement all the more disconcerting to watch.

"I encouraged her to leave Pilgrim Farm and I thought I'd convinced her to seek refuge in the women's shelter down to Fallstown, but I underestimated the peer pressure being brought to bear on her by Spinner and his followers. The last time I saw her, she told me it would be a sin to leave her husband."

"She was married to another Pilgrim?"

"They're all married out there. It's a requirement. Couples only."

"And yet they sleep apart," Liss murmured, shaking her head. What sense did that make?

"I felt at the time that she'd been browbeaten into staying. I should have done more to help her get away."

"Browbeaten? Or beaten?" Liss wouldn't put it past Spinner to favor corporal punishment for infractions by his flock, and domestic violence was a way of life in far too many families.

"I never saw any evidence of physical abuse, but she was definitely being manipulated by that bunch. She wanted to leave. After they coerced her into staying, she must have seen only one way out. When she drowned in the stock pond, it was ruled an accident, but I've always been convinced she took her own life."

Chapter Five

Liss left home and walked to work earlier than usual on Saturday morning, hoping to avoid coming to the attention of the crowd already gathering in the town square. Thanks to Dan's altercation with Hadley Spinner at Pilgrim Farm, Spinner's followers knew exactly what she looked like.

Her route took her along two sides of the square. When the volume of noise from the picketers suddenly dropped to near nothing, she knew she'd been recognized. Speeding up, she all but ran the last few feet to the Emporium. Catcalls followed her as she scurried up the porch steps, but at least no one shouted anything obscene.

Once inside, Liss tried to go about business as usual, all too aware that in a few hours a bus full of potential customers would roll into town. The tour company, which specialized in scenic shopping adventures, had worked well with Moosetookalook's Small Business Association for several years. The company scheduled five or six annual visits. All those who had shops on or near the town square had seen that same number of upticks in their profits.

When the time came to unlock the door and flip the CLOSED sign to OPEN, Liss drew in a deep breath and risked taking her first good look at the activity on the opposite side of Pine Street. The breath came back out in a whoosh as she felt her eyes widen. So much for a *small* rally!

The square was packed with placard-carrying demonstrators. Those in the distinctive black suits of the New Age Pilgrims were out in force, but they made up only a small fraction of the crowd. Sherri had warned them that there were people from away staying at the Day Lily Inn but Liss had never imagined there would be so many of them.

She didn't recognize anyone among those faces she could see clearly, but one thing was immediately obvious. There was not a single female among the demonstrators, nor were there any people of color.

"Bigots," Liss muttered as she released the dead bolt and turned the sign around. "Chauvinists."

The first old white guy who told her she should be at home, barefoot and pregnant, instead of running her own business, was going to get an earful. Liss didn't consider herself a feminist, but she *had* been raised by one.

She spotted several uniformed officers stationed at the edges of the crowd. Two wore the blue of the Moosetookalook Police Department while the others sported the tan slacks and brown shirts worn by Carrabassett County sheriff's deputies. The last thing Liss wanted was a clash between demonstrators and the police, but she was glad the cops were present to keep an eye on things. As long as the picketers stayed in the square, there was still a chance that shoppers would be able to visit Moosetookalook's businesses in peace.

Liss had been staring at the scene in the town square for several minutes before she realized that the protestors were not just milling about. The lines were a big scraggly, but they were moving in an orderly fashion along the paths, following a route that brought each individual close enough to the Emporium for her to read the sign he carried.

Several placards referenced Bible verses. Liss wasn't enough of a churchgoer to know what Genesis 13:13 said, or Matthew 19:4:4, or Hebrews 13:4, but she could make an educated guess based upon the messages printed on other signs. One said PROTECT FAMILY VALUES and another, DO NOT LIVE IN SIN. Bold black letters on one large placard proclaimed: DIVORCE, REMARRIAGE, AND SAME SEX MARRIAGE ARE ALL SIN.

Such narrow-mindedness is the real sin, Liss thought.

She was about to abandon her post and try to get some work done when she caught sight of a sign with a slightly different message. It read: PREVERTS WILL GO TO HELL. The man who carried it wore a black suit and a derby.

Liss fished her cell phone out of her pocket and used speed dial to contact the chief of police. "How common do you think it is to misspell *pervert?*" she asked when Sherri answered.

"Not common enough to ignore. I'm on the corner by Angie's Books."

"Then this guy is marching toward you. He's one of Spinner's lot."

"Not Spinner himself?"

"I don't think so, but you know how much they all look alike, especially at a distance."

Once she broke the connection, Liss craned her neck, hoping to see what happened on the far side of the square. Standing on tiptoe didn't help, either. The trees weren't an obstacle now that most of the branches were bare, but there were dozens of people between her vantage point and the spot where Sherri was most likely to intercept the Pilgrim who did not know how to spell.

What she could see was the tour bus. It had just passed Patsy's Coffee House and was about to stop in front of the municipal building. Before any of the passengers could disembark, a great shout went up from the demonstrators.

Liss ground her teeth together as she watched the protestors swarm the vehicle, waving their signs and shouting at the people inside. She'd been worried that shoppers would have to cross a picket line, but this was far worse. Anyone who exited the bus would be obliged to wade through the middle of a frenzied mob.

On leaden feet, Liss went out onto the Emporium's porch. Ignoring the chill in the air, she clenched the smooth wood of the railing so hard that it made her hands ache, and she leaned out in an effort to see more of what was going on.

Sherri and the other officers attempted to bring order to the chaos but their efforts met with little success. Spinner had amassed too many bodies. The demonstrators gave way only when the bus began to inch forward. Parting to let it through, they cheered when it drove away, taking potential customers for Moosetookalook's businesses with it.

"Before you ask," Sherri said as she stalked into the Emporium a couple of hours later, "I was not able to question the guy with the PREVERT sign."

She passed Liss and headed straight for the stockroom, emerging after a few minutes with a mug of coffee in one hand. She'd calmed down, but only a little. There was still an angry glint in her eyes.

Liss sent a sympathetic smile her way. "I know you did your best to find him."

It had taken Liss at least an hour to regain her equilibrium after watching Spinner's mob drive the tour bus away. Sherri hadn't had the privacy—a dubious advantage under the circumstances—to let off steam and come to terms with the wretched turn events had taken.

Picking up her own half-full mug from atop the sales counter, Liss joined Sherri in the cozy corner. "Are things quieting down any out there? I haven't dared look."

"Not so you'd notice." Sherri leaned her head against the back of the armchair and closed her eyes. "Those people are nuts, Liss. Complete and total loony tunes. The only thing they have going for them is that they aren't violent. Spinner's got them marching in a nice, organized formation."

"And chanting." Although she couldn't make out the words with her door and windows closed, Liss had been able to tell that much.

"And chanting," Sherri agreed. "They have a permit to demonstrate until dusk and it's obvious they mean to stay till the bitter end."

"Who are they trying to impress? There hasn't been any news coverage. Thank goodness!"

Sitting up straight again, Sherri grimaced. "As near as I can tell, their aim is to convince nearby shopkeepers to blame you for driving their business away."

Liss gave an unladylike snort. "Does he really think they're that stupid?"

"He knows they're upset. He's hoping they'll take it out on you and Dan and Sam and Joe."

"It won't work." She wanted to believe that was true, but she'd been wrong before. "And Spinner certainly isn't winning any friends by attacking Patsy. That PREVERT sign wasn't the only one expressing anti-LGBTQ sentiments."

Sherri drained the last of the coffee from her mug before speaking. "I was closing in on the guy with the sign when the bus arrived. His back was to me, so I couldn't get a look at his face. I don't know which of the Pilgrims it was and, unfortunately, Spinner himself caught sight of where I was headed. I could all but see the light bulb go on over his head. While I was distracted by the mob scene around the tour bus, he must have warned his follower to ditch the sign. A while later, I found it behind a bush. It was pretty well trampled, but I may still be able to lift an identifiable fingerprint or two. Until I have time to get to it, I've locked it in my office for safekeeping."

"Here's hoping you're successful." Liss lifted her mug in a toast before draining the last of the lukewarm coffee. Neither of them spoke while Sherri finished her drink. The only sound in the quiet shop was the steady chanting that filtered in from outside.

"I need to get back to work." Despite her words, Sherri made no effort to leave the chair.

"Take another five. You look like you need it."

"Oh, thank you very much." She managed a smile, but it was a paltry effort.

Too restless to sit still any longer, Liss rose and went to the window. Across the way, Patsy was watching the activity in the square from the small stoop at the front of the café. Liss took that as a sign that she didn't have any customers.

With a sigh, she shifted her attention back to the demonstrators and frowned. The crowd seemed larger than it had been earlier. After a moment, she realized why.

"Oh-oh."

"What?" Sherri was on her feet, hearing the alarm in her friend's voice.

Liss heard her crossing the shop but didn't take her eyes off the scene beyond the plate glass. "Some of the locals are facing off with Spinner's lot."

She recognized the couple from the jewelry store and Angie from Angie's Books and even Joe Ruskin, who should have been at the hotel. He had a decidedly hostile look on his face.

Stu Burroughs had left the ski shop to cross Pine Street and stand glaring at the protestors from the sidewalk. She could almost feel anger radiating from him in red hot waves. Stu was like a bantam rooster, easily riled and aggressive. In the usual way of things, he never completely lost his temper. He tended to retreat into his man cave and brood rather than do anything more violent than shout at the person who'd upset him.

Then again, Liss thought, she'd always believed Dan to be the epitome of self-control. She'd certainly been wrong there!

"Huh," Sherri said from beside her.

When Liss shot her a questioning look, Sherri simply pointed.

"I don't see—oh."

There, on the Birch Street side of the town square, right in front of Liss's house, were her parents. They appeared to be quarreling. Knowing her mother, Liss could guess that she wanted to wade into the fray and possibly beat Spinner over the head with his own placard. Her father, always more level-headed, would be arguing that to do so would only make things worse.

A movement nearer at hand caught Liss's attention as Margaret emerged from the side of the building. She had the two Scotties with her on their leashes. As if the picketers were beneath her notice, she crossed Pine Street and plunged into the swirling mass of humanity. The dogs, thinking this was a new game, darted this way and that, barking joyfully and causing more than one demonstrator to leap out of the way. After a moment, they were swallowed up by the crowd.

"Is there *anyone* who isn't out there?"

Although it had been a rhetorical question, Sherri responded. "*Dan* had better not be."

Liss turned, ready to snap at her friend, but before she could get a word out, Sherri had opened the door. Liss followed her as far as the porch, where they both stopped dead.

Demonstrators at the corner of Pine and Birch had scattered. The chanting had died away, replaced by shouts. It took Liss a moment to understand what had happened. Then she saw that two men were at the heart of the commotion. One was a figure in a black suit. The other was Stu Burroughs.

Following Sherri, Liss ran toward them. She was concerned on her neighbor's behalf. She had never known exactly how old Stu was, but Stu's Ski Shop, with its purple shutters and its life-sized skier on the sign mounted on the roof of the front porch, had been in the same location for as long as she could remember. When Stu had stopped dying his hair to a flat black a few years earlier and started growing a beard, both had come in as a match for the salt and pepper coloring of his bushy eyebrows. Whatever his age, he wasn't in good shape. He'd been roly-poly enough to play Santa Claus in the annual Christmas festivities for at least a decade and now his pudgy face had gone beet red and his breathing was ragged.

As she closed the distance, Liss recognized Stu's opponent. Hadley Spinner had clenched his right hand into a fist and drawn it back from his body, primed to throw a punch.

"Break it up, you two!" Sherri shouted,

Her command had no effect on either man, but with the help of another officer, she kept Stu and Spinner apart.

Liss hung back while Sherri talked them down, but despite having to hug herself for warmth, she didn't return to her shop. If Stu was marched off to the municipal building with its single small holding cell in the police station, she would have to bail him out.

Instead, Sherri released him. Liss watched Stu stomp back across Pine Street and up the steps to his shop. He went inside and slammed the door behind him. A moment later, the CLOSED sign appeared in the window.

"Crisis averted," Sherri said, returning to her friend's side.

Spinner had already disappeared into the crowd of demonstrators.

"What was that all about? Beyond the obvious."

"I have no idea. Any suggestions? You know Stu better than I do."

Liss shook her head. "When Stu was dissing Spinner at my birthday party, Patsy hinted that the bad blood between them went way back, but no one mentioned any details."

"Tempers are short on both sides." Sherri's voice was grim.

"I don't know what the demonstrators have to complain about," Liss said, "but the merchants who counted on the tourists on that bus spending money in Moosetookalook have every right to be upset."

"I've never seen Stu *that* angry. Maybe what's happening here today isn't the only thing he's mad about."

Liss gazed thoughtfully at the ski shop. As she watched, a curtain in an upstairs window was drawn back. Stu must have gone straight up to his apartment above the store. He held a can of beer in one hand and was scowling as he stared at the scene in the town square. If looks could kill, Liss thought, Hadley Spinner would be dead right now.

It was like watching a train wreck, or a ten car pileup on the interstate. No matter how much Liss wanted to look away from what was happening across the street, her gaze kept returning to the demonstration.

At some point during the early afternoon, every shop-keeper in the vicinity had come out to stare. Other towns-people, too, had gathered to watch and shake their heads. Liss had heard the occasional catcall, but there were no further confrontations. Hadley Spinner kept his troops under control, endlessly walking the paths in the town square and chanting. The altercation with Stu didn't seem to have slowed him down in the least.

Just when she thought that things might be winding down, the news van from Channel Six showed up. Liss watched in an agony of indecision as they interviewed Spinner. Should she go out and try to tell her side of the story, or hope Spinner would condemn himself by spouting his radical opinions? Close-up shots of a few of those placards ought to make it clear to viewers that he was just using his opposition to the hotel's Thanksgiving promotion to advance his own agenda.

In the end, Liss decided she was likely to do more harm than good if she tried to talk to a reporter. As worked up as she was, she'd come off sounding defensive, or end up making accusations against Spinner and his people. Since the New Age Pilgrims were a church of sorts, her words could all too easily be misinterpreted as an attack on religion. That Spinner had no tolerance for views other than his own was beside the point.

When the camera swung in her direction, she hastily backed away from the Emporium's window. There were no customers in the shop. There hadn't been a single one all day. As much to keep herself from going out as to prevent the camera crew from coming in, Liss locked the front door and flipped the OPEN sign around to read CLOSED. Then she retreated into the stockroom to focus on filling orders.

It helped to remember that if Spinner had been hoping to hurt her online business with his social media campaign, he had failed rather spectacularly. Several customers had added notes to their shopping carts to say that they sympathized with her situation.

Liss didn't usually work to music, but on this occasion she was moved to dig out the iPod her part-time summer employee, Angie's daughter Beth, had forgotten when she left for college in September. The earbuds effectively blocked out the chanting and most other sounds as well.

Listening to loud but unfamiliar tunes, Liss got busy. It was some time later when real-life pounding on the door of the shop conflicted with the beat of a drum solo and caught her attention. She chose to ignore the summons. After a few minutes, whoever wanted to get in gave up and went away.

Liss half expected the knocker to move on to the side door, which opened directly onto the driveway from the stockroom, and was glad she'd taken the precaution of locking it. Just to be on the safe side, she turned her back on the glass panel set into it and resumed unpacking new stock, but no one tried to get in that way. It was a bit later before it occurred to her that, from the street, the stock-room door was hidden from view by the stairs leading up to Margaret's second-floor apartment. No one unfamiliar with the building would know it existed.

After everything else was done, Liss busied herself doing some general tidying up. She had no idea how much time passed before she became aware of the gradual diminution of light that meant the sun was about to set. She had just removed the earbuds when someone rattled the doorknob.

Liss gave an involuntary start and relaxed only slightly when she recognized her mother on the other side of the glass panel. She didn't rush to let her in and was caught off guard when Vi staggered across the threshold. Her face was three shades paler than usual and her pupils were so large that they nearly obscured the blue of her eyes.

"What's wrong, Mom? You look like you've seen a ghost."

Vi closed her eyes and pressed one hand to her heart. Her breath soughed in and out in a harsh, disjointed fashion that was difficult to hear.

"You're shaking." Liss slung an arm around her much shorter mother's shoulders. "Come and sit down."

She tried to steer her toward one of the high stools beside the worktable but Vi resisted. When she'd disentangled herself, she headed straight for the coffeepot.

"I'll be fine in a minute. Can you heat hot water in that thing? I could do with a strong cup of tea. You do have tea, don't you? If not, we'd better go upstairs to Margaret's place. She always has tea."

Now she was babbling. Something was definitely wrong, but Liss knew better than to try to hurry along an explanation. Tea was probably a good idea. She opened a cupboard and pointed out a box of Earl Grey tea bags.

Vi made a disapproving sound when she saw that it was a store brand sold by a local grocery chain. "I suppose it will have to do."

She didn't say another word until the tea was brewed. By then her color was back to normal and so were her pupils. The pulse throbbing at her throat looked a bit erratic to Liss but she forbore to mention it.

Vi took her first sip, grimaced, and hoisted herself onto one of the stools before she took another. The hand that held the ceramic mug was almost steady.

Liss remained standing. "Now do you want to tell me what upset you?"

Vi glanced at the door and Liss followed her gaze. Darkness had fallen in earnest and yet there seemed to be a great deal of light out there. Some of that light was red and blue and flashing.

"What's going on, Mom?" Liss was relieved to see that both the hand tremor and the erratic pulse point had subsided.

Vi polished off the tea before she spoke. "Well, dear, while your father was having his teeth cleaned at the dentist's, I thought I'd walk back to the town square and see how the demonstration was going. The dentist's office on Elm Street is only a couple of blocks away. I was delighted to see that the crowd was breaking up for the night. Honestly, I can't believe we're having to re-fight the same old battles. It's the twenty-first century, for goodness' sake!"

"Mom, stick to the point. I know all about the progress advocates of equal rights and civil rights have made over the last five decades."

"Rights that can all too easily be lost!"

Liss cut Vi off before she could go off on a tangent by gesturing toward the glass panel in the stockroom door.

"Those red and blue lights belong to emergency vehicles. Something happened at the demonstration and from the state you were in when you got here, you were right in the middle of it. What else did you see when you got to the town square?"

Vi's shoulders slumped and she stared into her empty mug. "I've been trying not to think about that."

Liss waited. She didn't attempt to comfort her mother. She'd only be rebuffed. Vi wasn't a demonstrative person and she'd never liked to be hugged.

"In the gloaming. Such an evocative word for twilight." Vi drew in a deep breath, then another. "Dusk, but with overtones of something. . . ."

Her voice trailed off into silence. After a moment, she shook herself and met Liss's eyes. Hers had a haunted look.

"Just about everyone was gone, even the police who'd been keeping an eye on things, but they left a ton of litter behind. I started to pick up some of the bigger pieces, signs and such, although I'm not sure what I was going to do with them. It isn't as if there are any trash cans in the square. I really must talk to Thea Campbell about that."

"Mom!"

Vi put her hands over her ears. "You don't have to shout at me!"

Liss moderated her volume, if not her tone. "Stop evading my question. What did you see that upset you so badly?"

"The body, of course."

Liss sagged against the side of the worktable. Although her throat had constricted, she managed a whisper. "What body?"

"The one that was propped up on the merry-go-round.

I thought at first that he was just resting, but when I went closer I saw the knife sticking out of his back. Isn't it strange? He was killed in the middle of a crowd of his own supporters and no one noticed."

"His supporters?" Liss echoed. "Are you telling me the dead man is Hadley Spinner?"

"Well, I never met him when he was alive, but that's who Sherri said it was when she took a look at him." Vi shuddered. "He did not have a pleasant appearance, did he? That scruffy beard made him look like a tramp."

Chapter Six

Liss was unsurprised to find a state police detective at her door on Sunday morning, especially since that detective was someone she knew well and who knew her. She was prepared to do all she could to help the authorities discover who had killed Hadley Spinner. She hadn't liked the man, but no one deserved to have their life cut short by a vicious killer wielding a knife.

"Come in, Gordon. Coffee?"

As Gordon Tandy stepped over her threshold, Liss regarded him with critical eyes. She hadn't seen him for a while and he'd put on a few pounds in the interim. With a sense of shock, she realized he must be close to fifty by now. His reddish-brown hair, even worn as short as he kept it, was showing the first strands of gray. He still had the boyish good looks that had always made him appear to be younger than he was, but the years were starting to catch up to him.

"Coffee would be great. Thanks."

He sounded tired, as well he might. He'd probably been up all night working the case. She doubted that the extra hour they'd gained from the end of daylight savings time had helped. It only meant he'd been on the scene that much longer.

Liss had enjoyed a clear view of the crime scene from her bedroom windows. Portable lights had burned into the wee hours as technicians from the major-crimes unit gathered evidence.

Gordon followed her into the kitchen, watching her while she poured the coffee. He waited until after he'd taken his first sip to speak. "You were at work all day yesterday, right?"

"Right." She leaned back against the counter, braced for a barrage of questions.

"See anything suspicious?"

"I'd have reported it if I had. To tell you the truth, by the time Spinner was killed I was in the stockroom, trying very hard to ignore everything that was going on in the town square."

Gordon nodded, as if this confirmed what he'd already been told. Since Liss had talked to Sherri, albeit briefly, the previous evening, she assumed that her friend was the source of his information. She opened her mouth to ask a question and shut it again when she realized that his attention was no longer focused on her. He was staring through the window in the back door at the converted carriage house.

"Dan in his shop?"

"He's packing up an order that ships out tomorrow." She frowned when Gordon headed for the door, taking his coffee with him. "I thought you were here to question me."

"Your husband is the one who lit into Spinner the other day."

"Wait a minute! You can't think *Dan* had anything to do with that man's death. For one thing, he stayed inside all day yesterday, either in the shop or in the house. He was under orders from Sherri to keep out of Spinner's way."

The look Gordon sent back over his shoulder contained both sympathy and, more alarming, pity. "You can't be sure of that, Liss. You weren't here. And there was certainly bad blood between them. Dan had his hands around Spinner's throat, choking him. I've read the incident report."

"I know my husband. He's not capable of cold-blooded murder."

But Gordon was already out the door and on his way to Dan's woodworking shop. Liss stared after him, struggling to come to grips with the enormity of this turn of events. Gordon wasn't just interviewing people with a view of the crime scene. He considered Dan a serious suspect in a homicide investigation.

She started to follow him, then checked the movement. Neither man would thank her for interfering. Feeling helpless, a sensation she hated, she stood in the doorway, her eyes glued to the entrance to the shop, and concentrated all her will on making Gordon come back out quickly, satisfied of Dan's innocence.

He stayed in there far too long for Liss's peace of mind. The stony expression on his face when he exited was not reassuring, either. She tried to tell herself that she had nothing to worry about. Gordon hadn't brought Dan out in handcuffs. That was a plus.

Catching sight of her, Gordon headed her way, but he was not inclined to stop and chat. He handed her his empty mug and said only, "Thanks for the coffee." Then he avoided being trapped into answering her questions, or refusing to answer them, by heading down the driveway toward the street instead of passing through the house.

Liss took the alternate route through the kitchen, down the hallway, and out onto her front porch. She was about to call to Gordon to come back when she realized that he wasn't getting into his car. Instead, he was walking rapidly north along Birch Street, aiming straight for Patsy's Coffee House. Liss stared at the empty mug he'd returned to her. Surely he wasn't in need of more coffee.

Still watching Gordon's progress, Liss sat on the porch steps and tried to think like a cop. They'd have plenty of alibis to check. Spinner had not been well liked. Joe and Stu must be on Gordon's suspect list, too. But Patsy? Just because Spinner's people had singled her out to harass? That seemed a stretch.

Then she remembered Patsy's heated words after the paint incident, and that Deputy Pete Campbell had been right there to hear them. Although Patsy did have a clear view of the playground from the windows of the café, Liss had a feeling that Gordon wasn't just going to ask her if she'd seen anything suspicious the previous day.

Liss's hand tightened on Gordon's mug. Patsy could have reached the merry-go-round from her front stoop in a matter of seconds. She had access to a good supply of sharp knives, too. Liss could imagine her striking out in anger, but she could not conceive of any situation in which Patsy would stab someone in the back, not even a louse like Hadley Spinner.

She couldn't picture Dan doing such a thing either. Or Joe. Or Stu.

When Gordon came out of the café some twenty minutes later, Liss was still sitting on her front steps, waiting for him to pass the house on his way to his car.

A resigned look on his face, he came to a halt when he drew level with her. "If you're thinking about meddling in this case, forget it. You know me well enough to be certain I'm not going to railroad anybody. Let me do my job."

"I'd be delighted to, so long as you take a hard look at everyone out at Pilgrim Farm."

"Any particular reason why you think one of them would kill Spinner?"

Liss shrugged. "It seems to me that familiarity might breed contempt. Spinner was a petty tyrant. The rules and regulations he set up for his followers were harsh. Resentment is a pretty powerful motive."

"Thank you, Nancy Drew. I will keep your suggestions in mind."

She bristled at the mockery in his voice but held her tongue. It wouldn't help matters if she annoyed him more than she already had.

"I'm serious, Liss. Keep out of this. Have a little faith in the system."

"I'll try." It wasn't exactly a promise to butt out, but it was the best she could manage.

What confidence she had in Gordon's methods wavered when she saw him walk past his car and head for Stu's Ski Shop. She knew he had to conduct interviews. She understood why Stu had to be questioned as a suspect. She knew Gordon was an honest and thorough cop. But it was hard to watch him focus on people she felt certain were innocent.

Long before the demonstration in the town square and the murder of Hadley Spinner, Liss and Dan had made plans to have supper on that Sunday evening with her parents at the winterized camp where the MacCrimmons were living until they decided whether or not to move into the new senior citizens' housing being built on the outskirts of Moosetookalook village. It was after dark when they set out on the eight-mile drive. The last mile was over a rutted dirt access road where the headlights of Dan's truck provided the only illumination.

Most of the camps that lined the lakeside had already been closed up for the season. Even Patsy wouldn't use her place, right next door to the camp Mac and Vi were renting, once the snow flew. Aside from Liss's parents, only two hardy families intended to spend the winter months on the shores of Ledge Lake.

Staring out of the truck window at a bleak, shadowy landscape, Liss found herself dreading the hours ahead. Socializing with her mother was always something of a trial, since they so rarely agreed about anything, but tonight she was especially aware of looming conversational pitfalls. Dan had refused to talk about being questioned by Gordon, and Vi was sure to want to discuss the murder. She'd think she was entitled to speculate about it, since she'd been the one to discover the dead man on the merry-go-round.

There were other perils as well. Any time they were together, Vi managed to find one of Liss's hot buttons to push. It was an innate talent. At some point during the evening ahead, Liss was going to end up snapping at her mother.

These days, she tried very hard to be careful what she said and to let Vi's most opinionated statements go unanswered. She made a concerted effort not to upset her mother, even though Vi never returned the favor.

When her parents announced that they were returning to Moosetookalook for good, Liss's first thought had been that there was some health issue behind the move. Neither of them were spring chickens, but they both insisted they'd come back because they missed their old hometown and were tired of life in the sunbelt. They'd even, Vi claimed, missed Maine winters.

Although Liss wanted to believe them, she wasn't certain she should. Vi had lived with high blood pressure for years and Mac suffered from arthritis. His condition had been the reason they'd moved to Arizona to begin with. He'd had a number of joints replaced since then, to the point where he called himself the bionic man, but Liss knew his neck still bothered him, and his ankles, too. And Vi? Who could tell? Unlike most people her age, she never took the question "How are you?" literally.

The truck slowed to a crawl as they approached their destination. Liss kept her eyes peeled for the lights from the camp. When they reached a level area clear of shrubbery on the lake side of the dirt road, the beam of the headlights picked out the name MacCrimmon in bold red script on the small, hand-painted sign Liss's mother had nailed to a tree. Dan pulled in next to Mac and Vi's car with inches to spare. The slope dropped off steeply a foot in front of his bumper.

Just as Liss reached for the door handle, Dan spoke. "Before we go in, there's something I need to tell you."

Liss tensed as she swiveled around in the seat to face him. A full moon had risen and shed enough light into the interior of the cab to make out his solemn expression.

"A confession?"

Her ill-conceived attempt to lighten the mood sank into a deep, dark abyss. For a moment she thought Dan was going to tell her to get out so he could drive off somewhere alone. To her relief, he just shook his head and started again.

"Aside from what happened the other day, Gordon had another reason for talking to me. I don't know how he found out. Hardly anybody knows about it."

"Knows about what?" Liss's overactive imagination was already providing her with a frightening selection of possibilities. "Who else did you throttle?"

"Nothing like that." Dan gave her hand a squeeze. "And I need your promise that you won't mention this to Dad or Sam."

"I won't. But if it's something Gordon is aware of—"

Dan gave a short, humorless laugh. "If he arrests me, all bets are off, but since I didn't kill Spinner, I'm hoping that won't happen."

"Okay. So what's the big secret that I shouldn't share with your father or brother?"

Dan took a deep breath. "It was right after Spinner showed up in Moosetookalook. Fourteen or fifteen years ago. I was working with Dad and Sam at Ruskin Construction. My sister wasn't married yet."

Liss had been away, touring the country in Strathspey, and her parents had already left for Arizona. That had been a time in her life when she'd had zero interest in her old hometown. If she thought of Dan at all, it was as one of the many boys in her class in school. His father and siblings hadn't even registered on her radar.

"Go on. Is this about Mary?"

"Yeah." He ran his free hand through his hair, leaving it standing on end. "She was at loose ends. Kind of a rebel, if you can picture it."

Thinking of the woman Mary Ruskin Winchester was now, Liss couldn't, but the sinking sensation in the pit of her stomach told her she wouldn't like where this story was going.

"One of the men who came here with Spinner made a play for her. Next thing I knew, she was all set to join up with that bunch. When I found out about it, I went ballistic. I went out there and hauled her back home."

"Let me guess. You had to beat someone up to get her away?"

"There was an . . . altercation." He sounded sheepish. "As it turned out, though, Mary was already having second thoughts. She dragged me away before I could do any serious damage and made me promise not to say a word to Dad or Sam. I never have."

Liss mimed zipping her lips and her husband cracked a smile. "That explains how you knew the way to Pilgrim Farm."

"And why Gordon Tandy has taken such an interest in me. There wasn't much I could tell him about yesterday, though. I followed Sherri's orders and stayed in the workshop all day. I even went so far as to keep my earphones on, whether I was using power equipment or not, so I couldn't hear the noise from the demonstration."

"Great minds," Liss murmured, thinking of her earbuds.

"I think Tandy believed me, but who can tell?"

Before Liss could find the words to reassure him, a powerful outdoor light came on, blinding her until her eyes adjusted. "I guess they know we're here."

She and Dan got out of the truck. Her father waited at the door, a welcoming smile on his face. She managed a small one of her own and kissed his cheek, silently chanting her mantra for the evening: *Be the grown-up. Avoid conflict.*

Any hope of getting through the meal in peace disappeared less than fifteen minutes later.

Along with poultry and vegetables, Violet MacCrimmon served up her opinion of recent events.

"I've been keeping a close eye on what's been happening in town," she announced. "It seems to me that the only ones the police suspect are people who would never have resorted to murder."

"You don't know what the detectives are thinking." Liss

took a sip of a very fine white wine, hoping it would make her mother's opinions go down more smoothly.

"I know which people Gordon Tandy questioned."

"Besides me?" Dan asked.

"You, of course, Dan. Well, naturally they had to be suspicious of you after what happened out at Pilgrim Farm. And they talked to Joe because this whole smear campaign came about because of him. Stu was on the list after the incident at the demonstration and so was Patsy, because her place was vandalized right along with Liss's shop and Carrabassett County Wood Crafts. And I assume they talked to that young woman who took over Margaret's job, Tricia something."

"Tricia Lynd," Dan supplied. "I'm pretty sure she was working at the hotel all day yesterday. For that matter, so was my dad." He tucked into his salad, spearing a cherry tomato with his fork.

Vi shook her head. So far she hadn't touched her food. "Not all day, he wasn't. I saw him in town. As for this Tricia person, it wouldn't have taken her long to drive to the town square from The Spruces. It's easy walking distance, too. And then there's Margaret."

"What about Margaret?" Liss asked.

Resolutely, she continued eating, shoving another forkful of her mother's chicken parmesan into her mouth. If she was chewing, she couldn't argue. Not that she had any argument to voice. She'd seen Joe Ruskin in town, too. As for Tricia, although she'd always found her a pleasant and energetic young woman, Liss didn't know her very well.

"Margaret was questioned, too," Vi said.

Liss frowned. How had she missed that? Surely Gordon didn't think that Margaret had killed Spinner to avenge that friend she'd told Liss about? Her aunt might not believe that her friend's death was an accident, but she wasn't the sort of person to seek vigilante justice.

"What connection does Margaret have to Hadley Spinner?" Dan asked.

"None that we need to worry about," Liss's father said. "The cops are just covering all the bases. Eat up, Violet. Your food is getting cold." He applied himself to finishing his meal.

"My point," Vi said, after taking a few bites, "is that since no one has a perfect alibi, Gordon Tandy and the other police officers are going to waste a good deal of time looking at the wrong people."

"And I suppose you know who the right people are?" The challenging words came out of Liss's mouth before she could stop them.

She tried to throttle back her antagonism, but once again her mother had managed to trigger a response. It was one thing for Liss to have doubts about Gordon, but she didn't like hearing anyone else criticize him, especially someone who didn't know him as well as she did.

"Of course not," Vi said. "Don't be so sensitive. Besides, I'm certain you'll be able to discover who's guilty."

"Me? Oh, no. Don't bring me into this. I want nothing to do with investigating a murder."

"Not even when your own husband is under suspicion?"

Liss abruptly lost her appetite. She shoved her plate aside, feeling the weight of her mother's stare as she did so. Its force was not at all diminished by the fact that Vi's eyes were pale blue and half hidden by her glasses. Over the years, Vi had employed that look many times. Inevitably, it shook Liss's self-confidence. Her first instinct was to react in exactly the same way she had when she was twelve.

You're a grown woman, she reminded herself. *Do not let a simple difference of opinion deteriorate into a shouting match.*

Careful to keep her voice level, she said, "I'm staying out of it."

"A pity, since you're so good at solving crimes."

This rare maternal compliment took Liss aback. For a moment, she was at a loss for words, but she recovered quickly. "I don't know where you got that idea. In the past I've been wrong as often as I've been right, and more than once my mistakes put me and those I care for in danger."

"I got that idea from first-hand experience when we were here for your wedding, and from the letters Margaret has written to us over the years, and from the *Daily Scoop.* It was lovely being able to read all the Moosetookalook news online when we were living in Arizona."

"Mother—"

Vi talked right over her attempt at protest, giving examples, and she did so in the tone of voice guaranteed to set her daughter's teeth on edge. Liss could never put her finger on just why the sound of it had such a negative effect on her, but there was no denying that it did.

Do not let her walk all over you, Liss warned herself. *Do not let her pressure you into agreeing to do something you shouldn't, just to get her to stop nagging.*

"Enough!" Liss held up one hand, palm out, to reinforce the command.

To her surprise, Vi closed her mouth. Liss looked around for Dan and Mac. She'd been so focused on her mother that she hadn't noticed them leaving the table, or grabbing their jackets, or slipping outside through the sliding glass doors to the deck. Having learned the hard way to keep out of "discussions" between mother and daughter, the two men were leaning against the railing, watching the calm, dark waters of Ledge Lake and being very careful not to glance behind them.

"Mother, I appreciate that you think I'm clever enough to solve this crime." Liss was relieved to discover that her voice was level. "But I have been told not to meddle and I intend to obey that order."

"Piffle."

"What?"

"It means nonsense."

"I know what it means. What do *you* mean?"

"I mean that you *need* to be involved. You aren't going to be able to stay out of it if they arrest Dan. Don't you remember what I went through when your father was suspected of murdering someone?"

Liss sighed. "I remember very well. But no one's going to arrest Dan."

"Margaret, then. Or Joe. And if not one of the family, then Patsy or Stu."

"None of them will be arrested because none of them killed Spinner."

"You can't know that."

Liss struggled to hold her tongue. *Be conciliatory. Do not fight over this.*

"Whether they arrest someone you care about or not," Vi continued, "the police will waste far too much time investigating people you and I both know would never kill anyone. Think of the tremendous damage that investigation will do to local businesses, not to mention the harm it will cause individual reputations. It only makes sense that the one person who has proven herself adept at discovering the truth in similar situations should conduct her own search for the killer."

"I am not a detective." She enunciated each word distinctly. "Hire a professional if you're worried that the wrong person could be arrested."

"There is no need to bring in a private investigator when you are so obviously the best person for the job. You're certain to be successful . . . especially since I'm going to help you."

Liss stared at her mother in appalled silence.

Having said her piece, Vi abruptly stood and, with brisk efficiency, began to clear the table. She bustled about, moving at top speed. Liss grabbed the few remaining dishes and followed her mother into the kitchen. She had every intention of continuing the argument, but the words died on her lips when Vi swayed and had to grab the rim of the sink to steady herself. Her free hand went to the pulse point on her neck.

Anxiety shafted through Liss as she took Vi's arm and led her to a chair. If this was an act designed to quell her objections, it was a good one, but somehow she didn't think her mother was faking.

"Are you okay?"

"Just a little dizzy spell. Nothing that need concern you."

Liss didn't bother to hide her irritation. "Oh, of course not. Like you having a radical mastectomy a few years ago was none of my business? I'm not buying that argument. What caused the dizziness?"

"Beta blockers, if you must know." Vi sounded annoyed.

"I don't know what that means."

In an irritated tone of voice, Vi explained: "I've been taking a medication for my blood pressure that turns out to have been a bad choice for someone with a tiny little irregularity in her heart rhythm. It's nothing to worry about. The doctor I'm seeing here is very good. I've stopped taking that medicine and we're working on finding another that works as well."

Liss sent her a skeptical look. "What tiny little irregularity?"

Vi heaved a sigh. "It's just one of those odd little quirks some people are born with. I had a stress test two weeks ago, so you don't have to worry that I'm about to have a heart attack."

She had a stress test? Liss felt her frustration ratchet up a notch at this revelation of yet another thing Vi hadn't bothered to share with her only child.

"Anyway, what happens is that when I move too fast my heart rate slows way down instead of speeding up the way it would for most people. That makes me woozy, but only for a minute. Literally. The spells don't last any longer than that. I'm fine now."

As if to prove it, she bounced out of the chair, a smile on her face, and began to load the dishwasher.

Moosetookalook Scottish Emporium was closed on Mondays. On this particular Monday, Liss had nothing she needed to do and too much time to think. Her mother's expectations weighed heavily on her. It wasn't so much that she wanted to *please* Vi, she told herself. It was more that, on reflection, she could see the sense in what she'd proposed. As long as the police were focused on Liss's friends and family members, they weren't going to look very hard at the people out at Pilgrim Farm.

She wondered how many of them were mourning Hadley Spinner. She'd had the distinct impression, on her one visit to the place, that some of his followers were not all that fond of him. Then again, could the New Age Pilgrims survive without their leader? Would they want to? For all the police knew, the Pills might be about to scatter to the four winds, never to be heard from again . . . and never to be interviewed about Spinner's murder.

"Mother knows best," she muttered under her breath as she grabbed her car keys and headed out the door.

Someone needed to check on Spinner's widow and the rest of what Sherri had called his "merry band." Since Gordon Tandy appeared to have other priorities, she'd actually be doing him a favor by going out there to ask a few questions.

She was already in the driver's seat when common sense caught up with her. Liss sighed. It might not be such a smart idea to visit Pilgrim Farm on her own, *especially* if one of the Pilgrims was a murderer. Since she had no intention of inviting her mother to go along, and taking Dan with her was out of the question, she got out of the car and walked to the municipal building, circling around to the back door that led from the parking lot into a hallway.

The Moosetookalook Police Department was the first door she came to. As usual during the day, it was open. She passed through the waiting area with its worn plastic chairs and rapped lightly on the inner door.

Sherri looked up from her computer terminal, a frown on her face. The expression lightened when she caught sight of Liss. "Paperwork," she complained. "Even when everything is digital, there never seems to be an end to it."

"I'm looking for someone to ride shotgun," Liss said.

Sherri's eyes widened slightly. "Literally?"

"Maybe. I want to pay a condolence visit to Mrs. Spinner."

"Don't you mean *Mistress* Spinner?" There was the hint of a smile in her voice.

"Whatever."

"Why?"

"Do I need a reason?"

"Yes. Especially if you think you need an armed escort."

Liss shrugged. "That's just a precaution. They might not be too thrilled to see me after what happened the last time we were out there."

"Then why go?"

Liss wasn't about to admit that it was because her mother had told her to investigate. Instead she hemmed and hawed and finally went with guilt. "I feel as if I'm responsible somehow. If he hadn't been demonstrating against Ruskin businesses, he'd probably still be alive."

"Are you listening to yourself?" Sherri asked. "That makes no sense at all."

"Just humor me, okay? I want to go out there and talk to Spinner's widow in person and I don't think it would be smart to go alone."

After a short silence, Sherri stood. "You're snooping, aren't you? You think one of them did in the head honcho." She held up a hand, the palm aimed Liss's way. "Never mind denying it. It's as plain as the nose on your face."

"Remember when we were there before? There was one guy who had a sly look on his face when he twigged to the fact that you wanted to talk to all of them, not just Spinner."

"A sly look? Really? That's all you have to go on?"

"Don't get sarcastic with me. That's a closed society out there, and a strange one to boot. Who knows what jealousies and ambitions have been lurking under the surface. Has *Gordon* questioned them yet?"

"How would I know? The state police don't tell me anything."

Liss sent her a sympathetic look, knowing that this was one of the frustrations of being in local law enforcement. When a major crimes unit from the state took over, the first officer on the scene was pushed out of the loop. "It wouldn't be out of line for you to go out there to see how they're coping."

"That gives *me* an excuse," Sherri said. "What's yours?"

"Neighborly concern?"

A derisive snort told Liss what her friend thought of that suggestion.

"Sherri, Spinner's dead. They must be in chaos out there." The unlovely image of a chicken with its head cut off flashed through her mind. Release the body and it took off running, darting this way and that and around in circles until it finally collapsed. That was a scene she'd witnessed more than once when she'd visited a great-uncle's farm as a child. It had never failed to disturb her.

The sound of Sherri's fingers drumming on the desktop brought her back to the present. After a moment, she stood. "We go, but we take the patrol car."

"Fine with me."

That settled, they set off for Pilgrim Farm. They didn't talk on the drive. Noting Sherri's frown, Liss wondered if she was already regretting that she'd agreed to the plan. Liss felt her own doubts increase with every mile that passed. By the time they arrived at their destination, she had begun to second-guess herself. Had it been the height of foolishness to think she could accomplish anything by coming here? Even worse, if there was a killer at the farm, were she and Sherri walking straight into danger?

It was as quiet in the dooryard as it had been the last

time they'd visited. Liss wondered if everyone had left, or if it was just that the residents habitually took cover when strangers showed up.

Sherri got out of the cruiser, made a megaphone of her hands, and shouted, "Hello, the house. Is anyone at home?"

A pale, spectacled face appeared in the door into the ell. Mistress Spinner blinked at them, or perhaps at the brightness of the day, and then slowly drifted into the open. She wore a long white apron over her ankle-length skirt, and was twisting her hands in the fabric as she approached.

"Good morning, Mistress Spinner," Sherri said. "I just came out to see if there was any way I could be of help to you. I am so sorry for your loss."

"Mr. Spinner was a good man," Mistress Spinner said in pious tones.

I don't know about that, Liss thought.

"We have already prepared a burial site for him." She directed their attention to a small private cemetery Liss hadn't noticed on her earlier visit. "Do you know when the body will be released?"

"I'm sorry, I don't." That was another thing the local chief of police had no say in.

They walked with the widow to the stone wall that surrounded the graves. There were only a few. One, Liss supposed, belonged to Margaret's friend, the woman who had drowned in the stock pond.

"He'll be laid to rest there," Mistress Spinner said, pointing.

The hole had already been dug and a marker put in place. The simple wooden cross had the name Jasper Spinner painted on it.

Liss frowned. "Jasper? I thought Mr. Spinner's name was Hadley."

Brow furrowing in confusion, Mistress Spinner turned toward her.

Then an all-too-familiar male voice spoke from behind them. "Are you under the mistaken impression," Hadley Spinner asked, "that I am the one who was so foully murdered?"

Chapter Seven

"Did you know?"

"Of course I didn't." The tires on the police cruiser squealed as Sherri gunned the engine.

They'd beat a hasty retreat after Spinner's appearance, leaving before he could toss them off the property. The car had nearly gone off the road twice since then.

"I'm the one who identified him. I took one look at the clothes and the beard and I said, 'That's Hadley Spinner.' I mean, I couldn't think who else it would be. I didn't even go fishing in his pocket for ID. I just assumed . . . what a rookie mistake! We're never supposed to assume anything. We're supposed to look for the facts."

"Calm down, Sherri, or I'm going to be the one taking the keys away from you."

The vehicle slowed, but the litany of self-recrimination went on. Liss had never seen Sherri so rattled.

"Will you stop it!" she finally shouted, cutting off a rant in midsentence. "You came to the logical conclusion. How were you supposed to know that Spinner had a cousin who was almost a dead ringer for him?"

Hadley had told them that much before they left. He'd seemed more amused than angry at their mistake.

"I saw him," Sherri said. "Jasper, I mean. We both did the day Dan insisted on going out to the farm. I should have remembered that there was an especially strong resemblance between Hadley and one of his Pilgrims."

"But no one wanted to kill Jasper," Liss reminded her. "No one you knew of, anyway. Anyone with half a brain would look at that dead body, recall how many enemies Hadley has made, and come to the same conclusion."

"I wish I could believe that." Sherri's voice dropped into its normal register and she had stopped driving like a madwoman. "But cops *can't* assume. And after I did, everyone else took my word for it that the dead guy was Hadley Spinner."

Frowning, Liss stared through the windshield without seeing any of the passing countryside. Had they? Maybe so, but not for long. Jasper must have had a wallet on him and, at the least, it would have contained his driver's license. The state police must have discovered Sherri's mistake soon after they took over at the crime scene. *Gordon* definitely knew the truth by the time he started questioning suspects the next day.

"That low-down, sneaky snake in the grass," she whispered.

"What?" Startled, Sherri momentarily took her eyes off the road to give Liss a hard stare. "Who?"

"Gordon Tandy, that's who. He's deliberately let everyone go on thinking it was Hadley Spinner who was murdered. That's deceitful."

"Maybe he. . . . No. You're right. If not before, the state police would have learned Jasper's true identity when they went out to Pilgrim Farm to talk to Spinner's wife." She shook her head, a reluctant smile tugging at the corners of her mouth. "That's smart detective work. You were right when you said that no one wanted Jasper dead. He had to have been killed by mistake, so it makes sense to investigate as if Hadley was the victim."

"The killer got the wrong man," Liss agreed, but her annoyance at Gordon didn't decrease one iota.

Why hadn't he leveled with her? She'd thought they were friends, even if he and Dan weren't particularly fond of one another. She sighed. She should have been suspicious about Gordon's behavior right from the get-go. The initial story in the *Daily Scoop*, their local online daily newspaper, had reported that the victim's name was being withheld until next-of-kin could be notified. That was hogwash. It would have taken only a few minutes to drive out to Pilgrim Farm and talk to Mistress Spinner. If the victim *had* been Hadley Spinner, that identification would have been shared with the media as soon as the police broke the bad news. As for Jasper's next-of-kin, that was probably his wife, and that meant one of the lavender ladies. She'd have been equally easy to find. That the *Scoop*'s report had never been updated made Liss certain that the police were deliberately hiding the victim's identity. She wasn't sure why that made her so angry, but the fact remained that it did.

"How much trouble will I be in if I tell Dan and the other suspects that Spinner is still alive? They have a right to know the truth."

Sherri made the turn that would take them straight to the center of town. "Gordon won't be happy about it, but it won't matter much. Everyone will find out soon enough. The thing is, Liss, this won't change anything."

"What do you mean?"

"If Jasper died because the killer mistook him for Hadley, then the pool of suspects stays the same. The only people who can be eliminated are those who knew both men well enough to tell them apart."

"Damn," Liss muttered under her breath. Sherri was right. All this new development did was clear the Pilgrims and keep police attention focused on the people she knew were innocent—Dan, Joe, Margaret, Patsy, and Stu.

Sherri pulled into the parking lot behind the municipal building and killed the engine. "I don't suppose you'll listen to my advice, but I'll give it to you anyway. Let the state police handle the investigation."

"And if they arrest the wrong person?"

"Then start raising money for a defense fund." She got out of the cruiser.

Liss sat for a moment longer in the passenger seat, her emotions in turmoil. She was angry with Gordon for deceiving her and frightened for Dan because he had no one to back up his alibi. Were any of the others Gordon had questioned in the clear? To Liss's mind, there was only one way to find out. She needed to talk to each of them, and the sooner the better. She even had a good excuse for doing so—she could share the news that Hadley Spinner was still among the living.

Dan was the first person Liss told about the mix-up in the murder victim's identity. She found him in his workshop. Since it was Monday, he'd started work on a new custom-made jigsaw-puzzle table. Each one took the best part of a week to complete, with a day every once in a while set aside to mill a supply of table legs. He'd just shut off one of the saws when she opened the door and stepped into a haze of sawdust.

The smile that greeted her abruptly vanished when she broke the news.

"Damn shame."

"Dan!" She put one hand on his arm. "Be careful the wrong person doesn't hear you say that."

He shrugged. "I can't help how I feel. The world would have been a better place without Hadley Spinner in it."

She didn't want to argue. Going up on tiptoe to give him a peck on the cheek, she turned to leave.

His eyes narrowed. "Where are you off to now?"

"The other suspects have a right to know the truth of the situation."

"And you don't think telling them will be labeled meddling by Tandy and his fellow officers?"

"I do. I just don't *care*."

Dan opened his mouth, then closed it again. After a moment, he said, "Fine. I'll call Dad and fill him in."

"That's okay. I need to run out to the hotel anyway."

"I knew it. You're snooping. Please tell me you don't really believe my father is a murderer."

"Of course I don't, but I would like to ask him what he told Gordon. Maybe he's already been eliminated as a suspect."

Dan shook his head. "He hasn't. He was in town earlier that day and when he went back to the hotel he holed up in his office. No one can verify that he stayed there."

"Was he online? If so, there will be a record of it on his computer."

"He said he was working on the payroll."

"Then the time he saved his work will prove he was there."

"We already thought of that. He didn't finish till late. The computer stayed on but he could have gone out and come back again."

That was not what Liss wanted to hear, but Dan's information had saved her a trip out to The Spruces. When she left the workshop, she headed for Patsy's instead.

In contrast to the last time she'd gone to the coffee house to have a private word with Patsy, today the place was packed. Liss hesitated just inside the door, uncertain whether to continue on or retreat. It was only when she spotted Stu in one of the booths that a light bulb went on over her head. What better way to make certain that neither Patsy nor Stu was a murderer than to watch their reactions when she announced that Spinner was still alive. With a dozen witnesses, every facial nuance, every word they uttered, would be noticed and remarked upon. Even if she missed something, she'd hear about it later.

She surveyed the other customers, all locals, hesitating to go ahead with her plan only when she recognized the couple sitting in the booth behind Stu's. She hadn't expected to see her parents in town, but she didn't suppose it mattered that they were present. They'd hear about the mix-up in identities sooner or later anyway.

Stepping up to the counter, where Patsy waited in expectation of taking her lunch order, Liss cleared her throat. She'd learned how to project her voice during the years she'd spent touring, even though most of her performance had been dancing rather than acting. She used that training to make sure her words reached every corner of the café.

"May I have your attention? I have an announcement to make."

Heads swiveled her way. She saw recognition in most faces, followed closely by curiosity. Only her mother looked annoyed. Liss shifted slightly, enabling her to watch both Patsy and Stu.

"The man murdered in the town square on Saturday was not Hadley Spinner."

A chorus of "What?" and "How can that be?" greeted this news. Stu scowled. Patsy looked puzzled.

"Who was it then?" asked Audrey Greenwood, the local veterinarian.

"Jasper Spinner. All I know is that he was Hadley's cousin and that they looked very much alike. Enough so that it would have been easy to mistake one for the other."

Stu's response was profane.

Patsy was silent for a moment and then said, her voice laconic, "I guess there won't be dancing in the streets after all."

The buzz of conversation grew louder as Liss made her way to Stu's booth. She arrived just in time to keep him from escaping.

"Move," he said in a gruff voice. "I've got to get back to work."

"I only need a minute. Help me out, Stu. Did you stay in your apartment the rest of the afternoon on Saturday?"

"That's none of your damn business." The dark red stain creeping from his neck into his face gave visible proof that someone who was angry could be said to be "hot under the collar."

Since he looked ready to shove her out of the way if she didn't back up, Liss retreated a few steps, but she wasn't about to stop asking questions. "I'm trying to help you," she said in a low voice as he passed her.

He swung around, eyes flashing. "You're fishing to see if I have an alibi. Bad enough I had to put up with the police's questions. I don't have to say a damned word to you."

With that, he stormed out. The other customers didn't even pretend they weren't watching him go. As soon as the door slammed, they resumed speculating among themselves. Liss once again approached the lunch counter.

"I don't know what he's so het up about." Patsy gave an extra hard scrub to the Formica surface in front of her.

The smell of bleach made Liss's nose wrinkle, but it dissipated quickly, overpowered by the much more pleasant scents of cinnamon and cooked apples. Patsy had been baking pies.

The people seated on stools applied themselves to their food and tried to pretend they weren't listening. Liss knew them all—the postmaster, the town clerk, and Thea Campbell, Sherri's formidable mother-in-law and one of the town's select persons. Maybe this hadn't been such a brilliant idea after all, Liss thought, but it was too late to reverse course. She focused her attention on Patsy.

"Does that mean you're willing to tell me where you were at the time of the murder?"

Patsy shrugged her bony shoulders. "Might as well. I didn't go any closer to the town square than my own front stoop and I didn't see what happened on the merry-go-round. It wasn't until I saw the lights from the emergency vehicles that I had any clue there was something wrong."

"You'd have been closed by then, right?"

Patsy nodded.

"Did you look over that way when you locked up?"

"I did not. Do you think I wanted to see those morons marching around in the square? I secured the door and pulled the shade and went about my business. I may not have had many customers because of the demonstration, but I still had to clean up and get ready for the next morning. Sundays always get busy early. People like their treats both before and after church."

"Was anyone with you?"

Patsy's eyebrows shot up. "Since when can I afford help in this place? I work alone. I close up alone. Nobody's going to come forward to verify my alibi." She gave a bark of laughter. "Only one likely to have seen me running my mop around is the killer."

"I can't prove where I was at the time either," Liss told her.

"But you aren't one of the people the cops are taking a close look at, are you?" Patsy didn't sound as if she resented that fact. She was just pointing it out.

For the first time, Liss wondered about that. Why *wasn't* she a suspect? Spinner's vendetta had targeted her business, too. And she was the one he'd insulted, pushing Dan into attacking him.

Since Patsy had customers waiting to pay their bills, Liss drifted away from the counter. Belatedly, she remembered that her parents were sitting in one of the booths. Vi's lips were tightly pursed in disapproval as she watched her daughter walk toward them.

"Hi, Mom. Hi, Dad. I didn't expect to see you here."

"Obviously." There was a snap in Vi's voice.

Liss blinked at her. "You just got a chance to watch your daughter detect. I'd have thought you'd find that interesting."

"I found it disturbing, but that's beside the point." Vi toyed with her fork and avoided meeting Liss's eyes.

Sliding into the booth beside her father, Liss put her elbows on the table and her chin on her fists. "Okay. I'll bite. What *is* the point?"

"How did you find out that it wasn't Hadley?"

Liss squirmed a bit, finally twigging to what had upset her mother. "Sherri and I went out to Pilgrim Farm this morning."

"And you didn't stop to think that I might want to go along? I thought we were going to investigate this murder together."

Since Vi looked genuinely hurt by the oversight, Liss fought down her first impulse—to remind her that she'd never agreed to do any sleuthing in the first place, let alone to do so in partnership with her mother. The very idea of working that closely with Vi was enough to make her break out in hives.

"I was in a hurry," she excused herself. "I had an idea about the Pilgrims that I wanted to check out and I didn't want to delay doing it. The police might have been out there if I'd put off going and it would have taken too much time to get hold of you and then wait for you to drive into town from Ledge Lake."

This rambling explanation was full of holes, but Vi seemed to buy it. When she turned aside to fish for something in her oversized tote bag, Liss's father gave her a thumbs-up that brought a faint smile to her lips. She supposed it was too much to hope for that she was finally getting the hang of dealing with her mother.

She rapidly abandoned that notion when Vi found what she'd been searching for.

With a thunk, a small but deadly-looking gun landed on the table between them. That it was hot pink in color didn't make it any less alarming. Liss gaped, at first unable to find words to express the shock and dismay she was feeling. The term *pistol-packin' mama* was not supposed to refer to *her* mother.

"Don't worry," Vi said in a cheerful voice. "It's legal and licensed and in this state it's no problem anymore to carry concealed."

"Put it away, Vi," Mac said quietly. "I don't think Liss likes firearms. I know I don't."

Vi pouted. "I don't see what all the fuss is about. I learned to shoot when we were in Arizona. Snakes, you know. But this should work just as well to ward off two-legged vermin."

Their exchange had been low voiced but intense and had attracted the attention of other customers. Catching sight of the gun, Patsy bore down on them with a stern expression on her thin face.

"Put it away, Mom," Liss whispered. "You won't need it. Neither of us is going to do anything dangerous."

The weapon disappeared back into Vi's tote a moment before Patsy slapped the check down on their table. "Violet MacCrimmon," she declared. "You are a piece of work."

Liss couldn't have said it better herself.

Chapter Eight

Liss wanted to talk to her aunt next, but Margaret Boyd had left Moosetookalook early that morning, hours before Liss had come up with the bright idea to drive out to Pilgrim Farm. Margaret had been planning for weeks to attend a workshop put on by the Three Cities Genealogical Society. She was gone most of the day.

When Liss spotted Margaret's car and knew she was back home, she reached for the phone.

"Can you come over?" she asked. "We need to talk."

It was doubtful that Margaret had heard anything about the latest development in the murder case. Liss wanted to be the one to tell her. She was also looking forward to the opportunity to ask her aunt a few pointed questions.

"What has Violet done now?" Margaret asked. In the background, Liss could hear the sound of kibble being poured into dishes for Dandy and Dondi.

"You don't want to know." Ever since she'd left Patsy's, Liss had been trying to get the image of that pink gun out of her mind. The only thing worse than a loose cannon was one that was armed.

A few minutes later, a flurry of movement and the tapping of tiny toenails on Liss's back porch heralded Margaret's arrival. Liss supposed she should have expected that she'd bring the two Scottish terriers with her, since the dogs had been cooped up in the apartment for most of the day.

"Come on in," she called, and reached into an overhead cabinet for two dessert plates.

The Scotties made their usual circuit of the room as soon as Margaret let them off their leashes, sniffing every corner, intrigued by the scent of cat even though no felines were in sight. The first time Dandy had met Liss's large yellow Maine Coon cat, Lumpkin had let her know in no uncertain terms who ruled this particular roost. Liss thought he was upstairs, asleep on the bed, and hoped he'd stay there.

Glenora, unnoticed by the dogs, was curled up on the top of the refrigerator, her black fur making her almost invisible in the small space between it and the underside of another kitchen cabinet. She narrowed her green eyes until they were mere slits as she monitored the canine activity below her perch.

"What would you like to drink?" Liss didn't keep a many varieties of tea in the house, although she did have a better selection at home than in the stockroom at the shop.

Margaret inhaled and a blissful look came over her face. "With gingerbread? How about a glass of milk?"

She settled in at the table while Liss cut two generous squares of the freshly baked treat. She wasn't much of a cook, but she'd followed an old family recipe and the result did smell wonderful. Since it looked a bit burnt around the edges, she took both portions from the middle and topped them with generous dollops of whipped cream for good measure.

"Did you have a good meeting?" she asked when she'd placed the milk and gingerbread in front of her aunt.

Liss started to return to the kitchen counter for the second glass and plate and stopped short. Glenora had come down from her aerie and was sniffing delicately at the whipped cream. The two dogs sat on the floor directly below her, tongues hanging out and black eyes bright with interest.

Margaret chuckled. "Come here, you two."

Reluctantly, they trotted over to the table and sat beside Margaret's chair while Liss shooed Glenora off the counter. The cat jumped to the floor and sauntered over to the food and water bowls she shared with Lumpkin. After sniffing at the contents in each of the two sections of the food dish, she turned to Liss with an affronted look.

"What's wrong with what's already in there?"

Glenora's body language expressed utter disdain.

Margaret laughed. "Obviously, Her Highness wishes to see the menu."

"Her Highness is in for a disappointment." Liss joined her aunt at the table just as Margaret took her first bite of gingerbread. "What's the verdict?"

"Your baking skills are . . . improving."

"Damned with faint praise." She tasted a forkful for herself and grimaced. "What am I doing wrong? It never comes out as moist as it does when you make it."

"It could be your oven. Some run hotter than others."

It was a kind thing to say, but Liss knew it wasn't the stove that was at fault. She had years of culinary failures behind her, starting with a lamentable inability to bake scones. They came out as hard as rocks even when she used a box mix. She hastily scooped up her aunt's plate. "You don't have to eat it."

That Margaret didn't object to having her gingerbread whisked away and dumped into the garbage convinced

Liss that she ought to go back to buying all her desserts at Patsy's Coffee House.

It was only when she reached for the pan to throw the rest away that she realized that Glenora was once again on the counter. This time the cat was a good foot away from the open container of whipped cream, but a telltale white mustache stood out against the black fur on her face. Despite her exasperation, Liss couldn't help but smile. That expression vanished the instant Margaret spoke.

"Why did you really ask me to come over here?"

Liss took her time putting the lid on the whipped cream and returning it to the refrigerator. She didn't know why she was procrastinating. She certainly didn't believe her aunt could have killed anybody, but she turned so she could see Margaret's face when she made her announcement.

"Hadley Spinner isn't dead. It was his cousin Jasper who was murdered on Saturday."

Margaret looked mildly surprised, but neither shocked nor dismayed. "The Pilgrims do all look a lot alike," she said. "I can understand how one might be mistaken for the other."

"I saw you go into the park on Saturday."

"I took the dogs for their regular walk."

"When did you get back?"

Margaret smiled. "Are you asking me if I have an alibi for the time of the murder? Don't answer. Of course you are. I'd be amazed if you didn't ask."

"Well? Do you?" Liss rotated her shoulders to ease the mounting tension. The muscles of her neck felt equally cramped.

"Sadly, no. The dogs were with me in my apartment at the time, but no one else was."

"Did you know Jasper?"

"Slightly." She frowned. "If he's the one who was killed, that could explain why I came in for such intense questioning by your old beau, the state trooper."

Liss ignored the reference to Gordon's long-ago romantic interest in her. His courtship had been brief. They'd only gone out a few times before she'd realized that Dan, not Gordon, was the man with whom she wanted to spend the rest of her life.

"Why would Gordon think you had a motive to kill either Hadley or Jasper?"

Margaret sighed. "Do you remember that friend I told you about the other day?"

"The young woman at Pilgrim Farm? The one who drowned?"

"Yes. There's more to the story." As if to fortify herself, Margaret took a sip of milk. She looked as if she regretted not asking for a soothing cup of tea.

Leaning back against the counter, Liss was prepared to be a sympathetic listener.

"I made a huge fuss at the time," Margaret confessed. "I hoped to get the police to investigate the death as a homicide, but they refused to reopen the case. Perhaps Gordon feels I've been harboring a desire for revenge."

"That's the stupidest thing I've ever heard. That all took place years ago."

Margaret's lips twisted into a wry smile. "Isn't revenge supposed to be a dish best served cold?"

Liss rolled her eyes. "Aside from the fact that I can't imagine you killing anyone, not even Hadley Spinner, you aren't the type to hold a grudge. Am I to take it that Gordon led you to believe that Hadley Spinner was the victim?"

A thoughtful look on her face, Margaret considered the question. "He didn't correct any assumption I might have made, but in this case it wouldn't have made a bit of difference if he had told me it was Jasper. I was equally angry with both of them when Susan died." She stopped speaking to take another sip of the milk. There was a note of bitterness in her voice when she continued. "Jasper Spinner was Susan's husband. Even more than Hadley, he was responsible for convincing her she couldn't leave . . . not until death did them part."

Well, that was a new twist, Liss thought, and not one she liked. The two women sat in silence for a bit while Liss tried to think what else to ask her aunt. She gave a start when the two dogs, who had been lying next to the table, suddenly scrambled to their feet. She didn't have to look far for the reason they'd gone on alert. Lumpkin stood in the doorway from the hall, back arched and fur fluffed to make him look even bigger than he was.

Margaret grabbed Dandy and Dondi by their collars a split second before they could bolt toward the cat. They tried to wriggle out of her grasp, but when she ordered them to sit, they obeyed. Their eyes remained glued to the cat.

Lumpkin subsided. Sending one final contemptuous glare their way, he ignored the Scotties and waddled over to inspect his food and water bowls. As Glenora had earlier, he sniffed, rejected the contents, and sent Liss a look that clearly indicated that he expected to be offered something better.

Resigned, Liss collected the empty milk glasses and got to her feet. "When I opened that can this morning, they both thought it was the greatest thing since sliced bread. That lasted for about two bites. They are spoiled brats."

"Uh-huh," her aunt said, "and who is it who spoils them? You aren't getting a bit of sympathy from me."

Just as Liss reached the sink, Lumpkin let loose with a

demanding half-meow, half-yowl. She'd read somewhere that Maine Coons were supposed to chirp, but Lumpkin had never made that delicate a sound in his entire life.

"Your dish will have to be empty before I'll consider putting out more," she said over her shoulder. With her back to the cat, she busied herself rinsing out the glasses. "If you don't like that flavor, eat the crunchy stuff." The feeder on the far side of the water bowl was always filled with dry cat food.

Liss ran hot water into the now-empty gingerbread pan and added a squirt of dishwashing liquid, hoping that if she let it soak for an hour or so, what had burned onto the sides would be easier to clean off. She was also procrastinating by engaging in this domestic chore. She was reluctant to ask Margaret more questions about Susan and Jasper and Hadley. She was certain she wouldn't like the answers.

"Uh, Liss?"

The odd note in Margaret's voice caught her niece's attention. She sounded as if she was trying to stifle laughter. Then Liss heard a slurping sound.

She turned to find that Dandy had her face buried in the bowl full of canned cat food while Dondi made short work of the kibble. He was scarfing it up as fast as it flowed out of the feeder.

"Come here, Dandy. Come here, Dondi. Bad doggies." But Margaret's mirth-filled commands lacked force. Neither Scottie paid any attention to her.

"Oh, good grief!" Liss stomped across the kitchen and grabbed hold of their collars, hauling them away from the cat food. She kept tugging until she'd returned them to Margaret, who hastily clipped on their leashes.

"I'm so sorry," her aunt apologized. "My mind was on something else and, honestly, I didn't think they'd go for the cat food." Another sputter of laughter escaped her. "They've never done that before."

"Don't worry about it."

Liss picked up the bowls and the feeder and set them on the counter. She jumped back, her hand to her heart, when Glenora landed lightly right next to them. Liss had no idea where the little black cat had come from but when she sniffed at the empty bowls and then bumped her head against Liss's arm, Liss reached out to stroke her soft fur.

"Did you put Dandy and Dondi up to that trick just so you and Lumpkin could get a different flavor of cat food?"

Glenora's response was clear enough. She began to purr.

"Of course you didn't. What was I thinking?" She started toward the pantry where she kept the cat food, almost tripping over Lumpkin en route. Unfazed, he attempted to wind himself around her ankles the entire time she was getting a fresh can, opening it, and dividing the contents between the two sections of the clean cat food dish she took out of a cabinet. That done, she hoisted his considerable bulk onto the counter beside Glenora. He was too fat to leap up there by himself and she wasn't about to put more food on the floor while Margaret's two dogs were still in the vicinity.

Lumpkin took one bite and turned up his nose, rejecting the fresh offering.

"Suit yourself," Liss said, "but that's all you're getting for the rest of the day."

Margaret snickered. "I don't know why you expect him to believe that. You and Dan slip tidbits to him at every meal."

"Not when it's pizza," Liss defended herself. "Or lasagna. Or anything with tomato sauce."

She turned to find Margaret on the brink of departure.

Before she could ask any of her questions, her aunt waved good-bye and was gone.

The next morning, before Liss opened Moosetookalook Scottish Emporium for the day, she made a detour to Patsy's Coffee House. She closed her eyes and felt a blissful smile come over her features when she walked through the door and inhaled the mouthwatering aroma of freshly baked sticky buns. She had a weakness for these oversized cinnamon rolls lightly topped with luscious icing.

On her way to the counter, she glanced casually around to see who else was in the café and her good mood abruptly tanked. "What are you doing here?"

Gordon Tandy looked up from his coffee and a slice of banana bread with a puzzled expression on his face. "Having breakfast?"

"You've got a lot of nerve coming in here after the way you've been hounding Patsy and the other townspeople, not to mention the fact that you deceived everyone."

"Hold on," Patsy called from the kitchen area. "Don't run off a paying customer."

"If it's any consolation," Gordon said, "I'm no longer on her free-coffee-for-the-cops list."

"Good." Hands on hips, Liss glowered down at him. For a change, since he was seated, she had the advantage of height.

Gordon regarded her over the rim of his mug, his expression enigmatic. "I suppose I have you to thank for spreading the word that Hadley Spinner is still alive?"

"People had a right to know." Liss hated that she sounded defensive. "Besides, they'd have found out soon enough on their own. You can't have expected the Pills to keep quiet about it."

One eyebrow lifted slightly at her use of Joe Ruskin's nickname for the New Age Pilgrims. "I had hoped to keep word from getting out for a little longer."

"Why? So you could trick someone into admitting to a perfectly natural dislike of Hadley Spinner?"

The lighter flecks in Gordon's dark brown eyes glittered. "Sit down, Liss."

She was tempted to tell him she'd rather remain standing, but since that response would be both childish and churlish, she sat. Around them, normal conversation resumed. Until that moment, Liss had been oblivious to the fact that there were other customers in the café. The clatter of cutlery on china and the low hum of voices had her taking a quick look around.

Alex Permutter was at his usual table, this time with his wife. Liss's next-door neighbor, John Farley the accountant, was seated on a stool at the counter. Gloria Weir, who owned Ye Olde Hobbie Shoppe, was at another table and gave Liss a finger wave before going back to her juice and muffin. Two men she didn't know occupied a booth by the window and seemed inordinately interested in her. She avoided making eye contact.

"Reporters," Gordon said in a low voice. "Lewiston *Sun* and *Bangor Daily News*."

"Damn."

The door behind Liss opened and closed. Gordon glanced past her and grimaced. "And here's the young lady from the *Daily Scoop*. My day is complete."

Although his scowl was meant to ward off questions from Jerrilyn Jones, the online newspaper's only full-time employee, Liss also felt the impact of that look. Gordon Tandy was not a happy camper. She briefly considered apologizing for meddling in his case but decided against it. She wasn't in the mood for a lecture.

"I won't insult you by trying to tell you how to do your job," she said instead, "but there's something seriously out of whack about those people out at Pilgrim Farm."

Gordon said nothing.

"I wouldn't be surprised if my aunt was right about what happened to her friend."

"The friend who was married to the victim?" Gordon asked. "That connection doesn't make Margaret into any less like a person of interest to the police."

"You can't seriously believe—"

He lifted a hand to silence her. "I'm not telling you anything about the investigation except that you need to stay out of it. You have no way of knowing what might jeopardize our efforts to build a case. Spreading the word about Spinner may not have caused us any serious problems, but you couldn't have known that it wouldn't."

Giving her no opportunity for rebuttal, he stood, tossed a ten-dollar bill on the table, and headed for the door. He didn't exactly stalk out, but his dismissal could not have been any more obvious. Neither could the suggestion that he was taking a serious look at Margaret Boyd's motive.

Stay out of it? Let him railroad her aunt? Not a chance! Liss was more determined than ever to prove the innocence of all those she cared about. She purchased two sticky buns and a large coffee to go, made a brief stop at the town office to vote—it was an off-year, so there were only four state-wide yes-or-no questions on the ballot— and then opened the Emporium.

She told herself she was glad she had no customers. That meant she could start making lists of suspects and motives and alibis. Once she'd written down all she knew, she felt certain that some brilliant new avenue of investigation would occur to her.

"I've had a wonderful idea!" Violet MacCrimmon announced as she swanned into Moosetookalook Scottish Emporium just after lunch.

Liss braced herself. Her mother looked entirely too pleased about her latest brainstorm.

"What idea is that, Mom?" She hit the key to print out a newly received order for kilt hose and stepped away from the computer on the sales counter. She was prepared to listen. Her list making had yielded a big fat zero when it came to inspiration.

"Infiltrate." She heaved an exasperated sigh when she saw the blank expression on her daughter's face. "The New Age Pilgrims. The only way to find out which one of them tried to kill Hadley Spinner is to join up."

Liss burst out laughing. "You've got to be kidding!"

She crossed the shop to where her mother was fiddling with a display of tartan scarves, leaving them in disarray. Was she nervous? That surprised Liss. Her mother had nerves of steel, except for that one time when she'd just discovered a dead body on the merry-go-round.

"I am perfectly serious," Vi insisted. "What better way to glean information?"

"And just who did you have in mind as a spy? I'm pretty sure they wouldn't believe me if I tried to tell them I'd had an epiphany and wanted to mend my wicked ways."

Vi drew herself up straighter and abandoned the scarves. "I was thinking of myself. And your father, of course, since they only accept married couples."

Figuratively picking her jaw up off the floor and slamming it back into place, Liss stared at her mother. "And Daddy agreed to this?"

"Well, he hasn't yet, since I haven't told him about it, but I'm certain he will."

Liss barely managed not to blurt out the first thought that popped into her head—*He's not that crazy!* would not go over well. Vi could twist Mac MacCrimmon around her little finger most of the time, but this was different. For one thing, to do such a thing could be dangerous. Assuming that there *was* a murderer out at Pilgrim Farm, the killer wouldn't look kindly on anyone snooping around. Furthermore, if Margaret was right about her friend Susan, not one but two Pilgrims had fallen victim to foul play.

Realizing that she was pacing, Liss came to a halt with her back to the display window. "It won't work. One of them will realize you're related to me and they'll turn you away."

"I'll tell them we're estranged."

"We will be if you keep this up."

"Liss, dear, give me some credit. I was quite a good actress when I was younger. I'm sure I can convince Spinner and his followers of my sincerity."

"Maybe you can, but Daddy is much too easy to read. They'll throw the two of you out on your . . . ears before you're halfway through your pitch."

"Well, then, you have nothing to worry about, do you?"

Liss was ready to tear out clumps of her own hair from sheer frustration. "I can't believe how stubborn you're being about this."

"No, I don't suppose you can. Just as you never see that this is exactly the same reaction you provoke in other people when you doggedly pursue your own course against the counsel of friends, relatives, and members of the law enforcement community."

"What?" Liss could hardly believe what she was hearing.

"We're more alike than you want to admit."

Liss opened her mouth and closed it again. She didn't buy that comparison for a moment, but at the same time she had a feeling she'd be fighting a losing battle if she continued to try to talk her mother out of this foolhardy attempt to "help" the police solve Jasper Spinner's murder.

Calm down, she ordered herself. *Think.*

"You'd have to wear one of those long, unflattering dresses," she said aloud, "and twist your hair into an ugly bun or wear it in braids."

Vi had unbuttoned her coat but hadn't taken it off. Underneath she wore tailored cranberry-colored wool slacks and a knit top bordered with cream, green, and pale pink stripes. She glanced down at the ensemble but didn't miss a beat.

"I've worn dowdy costumes in the past. Did you know I played one of the leads in *The Crucible* in college?"

"Spinner will send you out to do housework."

"I've scrubbed floors before, too."

"Not recently, you haven't."

Vi had hired someone to come in once a week to clean the house when the MacCrimmons lived in Arizona. Before that, back when Liss was a girl, she'd assigned the chores she liked least to her daughter. It was no wonder that Liss had developed an aversion to washing windows. Ironing came in a close second on her never-do-again list.

Losing patience, Liss pulled out the big guns. "There's another reason why you shouldn't try to join up."

"What's that, dear?"

"Your health. Those dizzy spells."

"I haven't had another one. I'm fine."

"Haven't had another since the one I witnessed? Mom, that was only two days ago."

"This is exactly why I don't share my health issues with you. You worry too much. You *fuss*."

"*I* fuss?" Liss caught herself sputtering and pressed her lips tightly together.

"I know what I'm doing," Vi insisted.

"You're too old." Liss clamped both hands over her mouth. She hadn't meant to blurt that out, even if it was the truth.

Vi recoiled as if she'd been struck. All the vitality seemed to drain out of her. "That's a terrible thing to say," she whispered. "A person is only as old as she feels."

The tremor in her voice made Liss feel like a worm. Riven with guilt, one part of her wanted nothing more than to take back what she'd said. Another part was desperate enough to play any card she was dealt. She squared her shoulders and hardened her heart.

"I'm sorry I said that, Mom, but look at the facts. Hadley Spinner is the oldest of the Pilgrims and he's fifteen or twenty years your junior. Most of the others are considerably younger than that. On physical strength alone, you and Daddy would be outmatched."

Violet's recovery was so fast that it made Liss's head spin. "Nice try."

"I beg your pardon?"

"I know I can pull this off. This old girl still has a few tricks left in her."

Liss rolled her eyes. "Will you stop and think this through? You can't just go barging in with no plan."

"I don't see why not." Vi started toward the door. "I'm very good at improvising."

As Liss watched her mother's progress, her gaze also encompassed the view through the plate-glass display window.

"Mom, wait. Look." She pointed. "There in the town square."

Since Vi already had the door partway open, they both stepped out onto the porch. It was chilly, but not unbearably so, and Liss was too interested in the scene in front of her to go back inside for a jacket. A solitary picket marched along the paths. She couldn't tell which Pilgrim he was, but she could see that he kept turning his head so that he was always looking right back at her. It wasn't just the cooler air that made her shiver. She had the uneasy sense that he was only there to keep an eye on the Emporium.

"He was there earlier," Vi said. "He's nothing to be concerned about."

"He's staring right at us, Mom. He probably saw you come in and he definitely knows you're standing here now. If you show up at Pilgrim Farm, claiming we're estranged, he'll know it's a lie."

Violet said a word Liss had never expected to hear coming out of her mother's mouth.

"Mom!"

"Well," Vi said with a philosophical shrug, "unless you want to stage a knock-down, drag-out fight just to impress him, I guess I'll just have to think of some other way to help you identify the murderer."

Despite Liss's earlier inclination, this now struck her as a very bad idea, especially if meddling in the case ended up putting her mother in danger.

"Forget it, Mom. I'm not going to try to solve Jasper's murder and neither are you. We're done." She meant every word. "It's too risky."

"Oh, Liss." Vi wagged a finger at her. "You and I both know that you won't be able to help yourself. You want to discover the truth and you won't back down until you do."

"How can you possibly be so certain of that?" She told

herself that giving up was the sensible thing to do. The police, officers *trained* to solve crimes and paid to take risks, should be the ones responsible for figuring out who killed Jasper Spinner.

"I know," Vi said, "because the apple didn't fall far from the tree. You may not want to believe this, but I'm going to repeat what I said to you earlier. You and I are a lot alike. That's probably the reason we keep bumping heads." She glanced at her watch. "I need to go vote. I told your father I'd meet him at the polls at one."

And with that, she was off the porch and headed across the town square toward the municipal building.

"You're wrong," Liss muttered under her breath.

She watched as Vi's path crossed that of the picketing Pilgrim and winced when her mother waggled her fingers at him in a cheery little wave.

"No, Mom. No way. We couldn't be more different if we tried."

Chapter Nine

Liss was in the stockroom a few hours later when she heard the bell over the shop door jingle. "Be out in a minute!" she called.

"It's only me, honey." That was her father's voice, and by the time Liss had finished taping a shipping carton closed, he'd made his way back to her.

"Well, this is a lovely surprise." Stepping around various packing materials, she gave him a hug. "What brings you back downtown? I hear you came in to vote earlier this afternoon."

"I just wanted to see you . . . and this."

He turned so that he was looking into Moosetookalook Scottish Emporium, the store he'd once owned and managed with his sister, Margaret. With a sense of surprise, Liss realized this was the first time he'd come into the Emporium since his return to Maine.

Although there was no particular reason why it should, that knowledge made Liss nervous. What if he didn't approve of the changes she'd made?

As he turned to survey the stockroom shelves and worktable with sharp-eyed interest, Liss's discomfort increased. She didn't realize she was holding her breath until he spoke. "You've done a good job here, Liss."

"Thank you. I try."

"You succeed."

"Walk-in traffic has declined since your day."

"That's true everywhere. Internet shopping was an idea in its infancy back then. You've built up both the mail-order and the online business. I bet your bottom line is far better than mine ever was. And I like your selection of gift items."

"You've barely had time to do more than glance at them."

"I've browsed on your Web site."

She didn't know what to say to that. She knew her parents owned at least one tablet but she'd never seen either of them do anything on it but read books. They loved being able to enlarge the font to avoid eyestrain.

"Don't let me interrupt you." Mac gestured to the neatly lined up items ready to be boxed for shipment and the stack of packing slips next to them. "We can talk while you work if that won't distract you too much."

"Talk away."

Liss reached for a flattened cardboard box of the correct size to hold a stuffed Loch Ness Monster, folded the sides into shape and taped them, added bubble wrap and the toy Nessie, topped it off with more bubble wrap pulled off a huge roll of the stuff that sat on the shelf behind her, and tucked the packing slip in before she folded down the final flaps and sealed the package. The mailing label was already printed and ready to be stuck on. Once she'd done that, she added the box to the pile waiting to be taken to the post office.

"Very efficient," her father said.

"So what brings you here?" Liss reached for the next

item to be shipped, a Christmas ornament in the shape of a Scottish dancer.

Instead of answering, Mac came around the worktable and pulled off a length of bubble wrap, ready to pass it to her as needed. She smiled up at him, but shook her head. "You'll break my rhythm if you try to help." She plucked several items off the to-be-packed pile, collected their paperwork, and handed everything to her father. "Here, wrap your own."

The table was long enough to allow two people to work at the same time, assuming that both of them knew what they were doing. Mac MacCrimmon was no amateur. "Just like riding a bike," he said after a few minutes. "The muscle memory comes right back."

They worked in companionable silence for a short time. Liss knew her father had something on his mind and suspected it had to do with her mother, but she was in no hurry to hear what he had to say. After a while, though, the lack of conversation began to bother her.

"So," she said. "What's new?"

"I hear you put the kibosh on Vi's brilliant scheme to clear Margaret of suspicion."

A great swath of bubble wrap in her hands, Liss paused to stare at him. "She told you?"

"Of course she did. We don't keep secrets from each other."

Liss wondered what he called it when Vi made plans for both of them without consulting him until they were complete, but she decided not to ask.

"It would never have worked," Mac went on. "Our chances of convincing the Pills that we were serious about joining up were nil to start with. Hadley Spinner may be obnoxious, but he's not stupid."

"You know him?"

Mac shrugged. "Only what I've heard. Your mother and I were already in Arizona by the time he turned up here. Still, it's pretty obvious he's no dope. It takes smarts and hard work to survive a subsistence-level existence for so many years."

Liss thought about that as she resumed wrapping a china cat wearing a Balmoral cap and a tartan sash. Her father boxed up a tin of canned haggis. Given the address—a college fraternity house—she had a feeling the haggis had been ordered as a gag gift. The pun did not escape her notice.

"Well," she said as she smoothed the label into place, "I'm glad I was able to talk some sense into her. I don't know what I would have done if Mom had insisted on going through with her plan to infiltrate the New Age Pilgrims. I know she thought it was a great idea, but it had disaster written all over it."

"She's at loose ends," Mac said. "That's why she's so determined to . . . help."

"How is that possible? She's been connecting with old friends and checking out possibilities for a permanent place to live." The retirement community currently being constructed on the outskirts of Moosetookalook was the lead contender. "And she had all the Halloween plans to oversee."

They reached for more bubble wrap at the same time, bumped hands, and laughed. "Ladies first," Mac said.

Another short silence fell.

"Life here is very different from what we were used to in Arizona."

"I can imagine."

"Can you? You're used to a quiet lifestyle. Where we were living, there was always something going on. To tell you the truth, there were way too many things to keep us busy."

"You didn't have to do them all."

"That's so, and I actually enjoyed shuffleboard at first. I even won a couple of tournaments. But you wouldn't believe how cutthroat some of those teams are." Although he was shaking his head, the expression on his face suggested that he had fond memories of the sport. "In the end, that took all the fun out of it for me. Now, your mother, she had a great time from the moment she retired from teaching. She took all kinds of classes—yoga, belly dancing, even—"

"*Belly* dancing? *My* mother?"

Mac chuckled. "Your mother. But one by one, those things started to pale, and so did the sameness of the weather. We both missed the changing seasons. I know you find this hard to believe, but we even missed those mornings that are well below freezing. And then there were all the rules and regulations in the community where we lived. Your mother wasn't allowed to hang clothes outside to dry in the sun and fresh air—too unsightly. Our lawn had to look just like all our neighbors' lawns. And, horror of horrors, I wasn't permitted to play my bagpipes in a residential area. I had to go to a nearby park to practice and even there people complained about the noise pollution."

He smiled again as he told the tale, but Liss didn't smile back. She'd been under the impression that he'd played in the park by choice, so that he'd have an audience. It broke her heart that people had tried to prevent him from enjoying his favorite pastime.

"It's too bad you couldn't soundproof a room, the way you did here."

"I'd have done that in a minute if there hadn't been

rules against that, too. They weren't very big on DIY projects where we lived." He shrugged. "It doesn't matter. In the end, everything worked out for the best. Once we started thinking about relocating, we realized we'd just as soon move all the way back to a place where we could do as we damned well pleased." Mac slapped package tape onto a box with a bit more force than necessary, then looked sheepish. "No harm done. It doesn't contain anything breakable."

Liss couldn't resist teasing him. "No delicate bisque figurines? No china teacup decorated with a clan crest?"

"Just a ladies' tartan sash."

"You know, you may not have as much freedom as you'd like if you settle in that new retirement community."

"That thought has already crossed my mind. Your mother's, too. One thing's certain, though, even if it hasn't been all sunshine and roses. We made the right choice when we decided to come home to Moosetookalook." At her questioning look, he elaborated. "Too many of our old friends from Maine are either dead or living elsewhere now. And Vi misses having a wide circle of acquaintances to hang out with. Used to be she could walk down to the clubhouse and she'd be sure to run into someone she knew. There were lots of stores nearby, too. You know how much your mother loves to shop, even though she never buys all that much."

Her hands once more busy with the packing, taping, and labeling, Liss didn't look up. "I'd think Mom would be able to find clubs to join. There are plenty of them around. Look how many organizations Margaret has become a member of since she retired."

"That's part of the problem. Vi doesn't want to be perceived as her sister-in-law's shadow. If Margaret already belongs to a group, Vi deliberately avoids it."

"That's ridiculous."

Mac shrugged.

When the obvious finally struck her, Liss sent her father a considering look. "Let me get this straight. Mom doesn't want to be Margaret's shadow, but she doesn't mind being mine?"

He chuckled. "That's about the size of it."

"And that's why she's been pushing me to get involved in investigating a murder and letting her help me? She's bored because she has too much time on her hands?"

"It's not just that. She admires you, honey. She's proud of what you've accomplished, not just here in the shop, but in what you give back to the community."

Liss stopped what she was doing to stare at him in disbelief. "She's never said so."

"Vi's not one to lavish praise."

"No kidding. She's always been much better at expressing *dis*approval."

Mac sighed deeply before he spoke. "You never did try to understand her."

Liss could sense her father's disappointment as a palpable force. It left her feeling guilty and irritable in equal parts.

"I don't want to quarrel with you about this. Can we just drop the subject?"

"That's probably best."

They finished dealing with the orders without saying another word to each other, but the silence was not uncomfortable. As she always had as a child, Liss found her father's presence calming. It had been her mother who made her crazy.

"Thanks for your help," she said when the last of the boxes was stacked for the trip to the post office.

"Anytime. And I mean that. If you need a stock boy, I'm available."

They had swiveled around on their stools so that they were face-to-face. "Don't tell me you need something to keep you busy, too?"

"Oh, I can always amuse myself. A good book passes the time remarkably well. But have you considered that *you* might occasionally need to take time for something other than work?"

Liss reacted to this statement with a puzzled frown. "I have lots of interests that have nothing to do with the Emporium. Or with meddling in police business."

Mac broke eye contact to stare off into the middle distance. "I was thinking that one of these days before too much longer you might want to try being a stay-at-home mom."

"That's the last thing I'd want. I don't want to be a mom at all!"

When she saw the pained expression on her father's face, Liss regretted her lack of tact, but what she'd blurted out was nothing but the truth. Touching his arm, she spoke in a gentler voice.

"Dan and I decided some time ago that we don't want to have children. I'm sorry if that disappoints you, but—"

"Sometimes couples change their minds."

"We haven't and we won't. We know how we feel about this."

The sadness in his eyes made her chest tighten. She felt tears well up and surreptitiously wiped them away.

"I was looking forward to having grandchildren someday," Mac said. "I'd be a great grandpa."

"Yes, you would have been," Liss said, "but I'd have been a terrible mother." She reached across the space between them to clasp his hand in hers. "I'm sorry, Daddy, but that's the way is has to be."

Mac gave a curt nod and managed a weak smile. "We

raised you to make your own decisions. I can hardly criticize you for doing just that."

That evening over supper, Liss brought Dan up to speed on the events of the day. She left out her father's thwarted desire to become a grandparent but repeated what he'd told her concerning Violet's need for projects to occupy her time.

"Any ideas?" Dan asked between bites of mashed potato.

"I could put her to work in the shop." Liss cut a sliver of meat off her pork chop before looking up in time to catch the gleam of amusement in her husband's eyes. "What?"

"She'd rearrange everything and you'd be at each other's throats within a week," he predicted.

"Less than that. You're right. I need to think of something else, something that will keep her out of my hair *and* out of trouble."

Eating occupied them both for the next few minutes. That and warding off Lumpkin's unending attempts to cadge some of the pork for himself. He started by tapping Liss's thigh with one velvet paw, switched to using his claws, and finally escalated to the point where he tried to climb into her lap. She pushed him gently away and told him to stay down, not that giving orders to a cat ever had any effect.

"Why not send your mother to the library?" Dan suggested when Lumpkin's attention shifted to him. "Tell her you need to know everyone's history with Spinner. You were away when he first arrived in the area and your folks had already left, but there should be some references to the Pilgrims in back issues of local newspapers."

Liss paused, a glass of water halfway to her mouth. "You were here. What do you remember?"

"Not much. He didn't stand out so much back then. Bought a farm. Stayed out there."

"Bought it from whom?"

"No idea, but there should be a record of the sale at the town office."

"That's something else Mom can check on. I like this plan." Some of the tension that had been building throughout the day finally begin to ease.

"Well, there you go. There's plenty to keep Violet busy. And here's another thought. Maybe she can cozy up to one of the lavender ladies. She could hire one of them to clean her place. Or, if you think they might refuse to work for anyone related to the Ruskins, maybe Vi could pay a visit to one of their current clients on the same day the cleaning lady is due."

"Do you know anyone who uses them?"

"No, but it can't be too hard to find that out. Ask our know-it-all librarian or the ever-well-informed postmaster. Or Patsy, for that matter."

"I guess I could do that."

At her hesitant tone of voice, Dan gave her a sharp look. "Now you're looking down in the mouth again. Why? Didn't I just solve your biggest problem?"

"You did. It's just that while I was listening to your ideas I realized that I don't want to assign any of those tasks to my mother. I want to handle them myself."

"Then you should split the list between you," said the ever-practical Dan, "and maybe do one or two things together, so that Vi doesn't figure out that you're keeping the best jobs for yourself."

*   *   *

Vi was thrilled by her daughter's suggestion that the two of them question Stu Burroughs about his alibi for the time of the murder, his history with Hadley Spinner, and whatever else he might know about the New Age Pilgrims. Her face lit up like a little kid on the way to visit a toy store and she was the first one through the door of the ski shop.

Stu sold much more than ski apparel and equipment. He also stocked snowmobile gear, biking accessories, and snowshoes. As a result, about a third of the space in the store was taken up with shelves piled high with goods that would not have looked out of place in a hardware store. A significant portion of the rest was given over to clothing racks, while what remained offered various pieces of sports equipment.

Stu himself was a dedicated snowmobiler, a hobby that required less physical exertion than the others, but he was knowledgeable about everything he carried and had established a reputation for fair dealing that extended far beyond Moosetookalook. People on their way to ski areas farther north often detoured to the sleepy little Carrabassett County village just to see what new items he had in stock.

There were no customers in the shop when Liss and her mother burst in. They found Stu behind the sales counter, leafing through print supply catalogs. He gave them each a curt nod of greeting, his eyes already narrowing in suspicion.

"Liss. Vi. How can I help you?"

Liss had intended to do the questioning herself, but she didn't interrupt when her mother took the lead.

"We're here to help you, Stu." Vi went right up to the counter and reached across it to grab hold of his hands. "I don't have to tell you how badly this police investigation is hurting business in Moosetookalook, not to mention what could happen if they fix their sights on you."

Stu looked slightly shell-shocked by Vi's direct approach and rapid fire volley of words. His mouth opened and closed a couple of times without any sound coming out. Then he regained his equilibrium and narrowed his eyes even further. "What the hell are you talking about?"

"Why, your grudge against Hadley Spinner, of course."

When Stu jerked his hands free, Liss swore she could see his hackles rising.

"It wasn't Hadley who got killed."

"Well, no, but only because someone mistook his cousin for him. The motives the police are looking into remain the same and you have a doozy."

"I don't know what you're talking about."

"Then why did you quarrel with him on Saturday? And don't tell me it was just because he was demonstrating in the town square." Vi aimed one finger at him in an accusing manner.

He stared at it, mesmerized, while Liss pondered the effectiveness of the technique called "teacher's finger" as a means of prompting confessions. It could be a powerful weapon, especially when it was combined with a certain look in the eyes and used against someone with a guilty conscience. Even those who were completely innocent quailed before it.

Stu sputtered in indignation and hot color rushed into his face, but he managed to avoid incriminating himself. Deciding that it was time to bring in the reserves, Liss stepped up to the counter. In this scenario, she was to play the part of the "good cop" and soften Stu up for her mother's questions.

"She's right, Stu. The police have blinders on. They're

convinced someone from town killed Jasper Spinner so they're digging into everyone's past. How can we point them in another direction if we don't know what's behind their suspicions?"

Stu slammed his fist down on the countertop with a thump so loud it made both women jump. He uttered a colorful oath.

Undaunted, Vi leaned in. "What do they have on you, Stu?"

"Bad enough I have to put up with being interrogated by the cops," he grumbled. "Nothing says I have to bare my soul to a couple of snoopy broads."

"You think so? You wouldn't be this nervous about it if there wasn't something in your past to link you to the New Age Pilgrims."

Throwing both arms up into the air, he tried turning his back on them, but unless he tossed them out of the store, Liss wasn't about to give up on him. He was a friend. She wanted to help him, even if that meant exposing him to a little tough love.

"Stu, please. We're on your side."

He swung around to glare at her. "Are you? Or are you just looking for someone other than your aunt to sic the cops on?"

Liss and her mother exchanged a glance. Liss would have expected him to mention Joe, too. And Dan. It struck her as odd that he didn't. By now everyone in town must have heard about the altercation with Hadley Spinner at Pilgrim Farm.

"I'll be honest with you, Stu," Vi said. "We are worried about Margaret. But we don't want you to be arrested, either."

"*Somebody* killed Jasper," Stu said. "That means somebody's going to be thrown in jail, probably sooner rather than later."

Liss nodded. "But not you. Let us help you prove it."

Stu huffed out an exasperated breath. "You're not going to quit, are you? You're just going to keep nagging me until you find out what you want to know."

"That's about the size of it," Vi said.

Stu's brows beetled in thought. He scratched his chin. He shifted his not inconsiderable weight from one foot to the other. Finally he hoisted his bulk onto the stool behind the counter and met Liss's gaze squarely.

"Okay, here's the thing. There's nothing in my past that makes me a suspect. Nothing. Got that? It's all because of that shouting match I had with Spinner the day his cousin was stabbed. Afterward, I came back here, closed up shop, went up to my apartment, and got stinking drunk. I didn't hear about the body till the next day."

He looked from Liss to her mother, expectant. His face fell when he didn't find what he was looking for in their expressions.

"Geez, don't you get it? I can't prove I was upstairs, alone, when Spinner was killed. If the cops can't pin it on Margaret, they're going to think I worked up enough Dutch courage to sneak out there and stab him."

"I'm sure someone would have noticed you crossing the town square," Vi said in a soothing voice. "You're . . . uh . . . hard to miss."

"I'm a tub of lard in living color." Stu flung both arms wide to better display that day's outfit—a hot pink, long-sleeved shirt worn with a purple bow tie.

When he tangled with Hadley Spinner on Saturday, Liss recalled, he'd been wearing a chartreuse windbreaker. "Good point," she murmured.

"Nobody's come forward to say that they saw me. Nobody's going to, because I didn't set foot outside the rest of that day. But the absence of a witness doesn't prove I'm innocent. Worse, as far as I can tell, nobody saw anyone else acting suspiciously right before or right after the murder, either."

That was the crux of the matter, Liss supposed. The reason the police suspected everyone who'd been in town that day was because they had no eyewitness and no evidence that allowed them to single out one suspect among the many.

"It's too bad you didn't look out your windows," Vi said. "You must have a great view of the entire town square from upstairs."

"Why would I want to do that? I was trying to ignore the whole ugly scene."

That sounds familiar, Liss thought. Then the proverbial light bulb went off above her head. How could she have been so dense? She and Dan and Stu might have had good reasons to avoid watching what the demonstrators were doing, but surely other people had been curious.

"Are you *sure* there was no history between you?" Vi asked, oblivious to her daughter's epiphany. "I hear you were mighty ticked off at Spinner."

Stu's lips flattened into a thin, stubborn line. His relief was palpable when the door opened and a customer came in. "We're done here. Don't let the door hit you in the butt on the way out."

Not wishing to cost Stu a sale, they returned to the Emporium, where Mac was minding the store. Liss was pleasantly surprised to see that she, too, had several customers . . . until it dawned on her that they hadn't come in to look for Scottish-themed gifts. They were gawkers, drawn to Moosetookalook by the news that there had been a grisly murder in the center of town.

Catching her mother's sleeve, Liss steered Vi into the stockroom and closed the door. "The windows," she said. "I forgot all about the windows until you mentioned them to Stu."

"What about them?" Vi spoke absently, already busily poking around in Liss's supplies, rearranging and straightening as she went.

Liss suppressed the urge to tell her mother to cut it out and tried to stick to the point. "At this time of year, with no leaves on the trees, the upper floors of every building around the town square have an excellent view of everything that goes on there. If someone looked out at the right time, he or she could have seen the killer moving toward the playground or running away from it."

"Wouldn't they already have reported what they saw to the police?" Vi, her interest piqued, stopped fussing with the rolls of package tape stored on an upper shelf.

"Not if they don't realize its significance. I'm not at all convinced that the police did a thorough job of canvassing the neighborhood. Gordon never really followed up with questions about what I might have seen. He was too interested in interrogating Dan."

"But you didn't see anything."

"What if I had and it slipped my mind? All Gordon did was verify that I was at work on the day of the murder and that I didn't see anything suspicious around that time. I told him the same story I told Sherri, but you'd think he'd want to ask follow-up questions in the hope of jogging my memory. If the interviews the police conducted with other people who aren't suspects were as routine, it's entirely possible that they didn't get every detail. Even if they were told something significant, they might not have realized its importance. The state police don't know what's normal and what isn't in this town. It would be easy for them to miss the relevance of a casual reference."

"You're right," her mother agreed. "People often notice trivial things, but if those things don't appear to be connected, and if no one presses them to remember what they were, it might never occur to them to tell the police or anyone else."

"Exactly."

Now that she thought about it, Liss realized she was herself a perfect example of that tendency. She'd heard someone banging on the front door of the Emporium when she was in the stockroom. It had never occurred to her to mention that to anyone. It probably wasn't important, but what if it *was?*

"We need to talk to everyone who lives or works in any of the buildings facing the town square." She reached for a notepad and sketched a rough map. When it was finished, she handed it to her mother. "We'll ask them about everyone they remember seeing and when."

Vi's eyes were bright with the fervor of someone newly introduced to an exciting sport. For the next hour, she and Liss dedicated themselves to making a list of questions. Near the top was, "Did you see someone on the porch of the Emporium, trying and failing to get inside?"

"Dividing up the neighborhood will allow us to canvass it in the most effective manner," Vi pointed out.

"Okay," Liss agreed. "You turn right out the door and I'll go left."

She'd start by talking to Maud, and to the couple who rented the apartment above Carrabassett County Wood Crafts. The post office was only open until noon on Saturdays, but there was an upstairs unit in that building, too. Liss doubted that the museum had enjoyed much business, thanks to the rally, but that just meant that the docent was more likely to have been rubbernecking from inside the building. And if Angie or her son had taken a break from working in Angie's Books to go upstairs to their living quarters, who knew what one of them might have seen?

"Why don't we meet at the municipal building?" she suggested. "I'll question Dolores Mayfield at the library while you speak to Francine Noyes."

Officially, the town office wasn't open on Saturdays, but it was a good bet that someone had been on hand to keep an eye on the demonstration. If that person had not been Francine, the town clerk, she would know which member of the town select board had been there.

The sound of raised voices from the shop interrupted the planning session. Liss exchanged a worried look with her mother before she hurried out of the stockroom.

Gordon Tandy and Mac MacCrimmon stood toe to toe. That in itself wouldn't have been so alarming if Gordon hadn't been backed up by two uniformed officers. A hint of relief showed in his otherwise stony expression when he turned toward her, but that did nothing to soften the effect of his next words.

"Tell your father to back off, Liss," Gordon said. "We have a search warrant for Margaret's apartment."

Chapter Ten

"Now just a darned minute!" Mac MacCrimmon's shoulders hunched aggressively as he started to follow the state police detective and the two troopers.

"It won't help to argue with them," Liss said as the officers started up the stairs. "Let me go make sure Margaret reads the paperwork before she lets them in. That's about all we can do at this point."

"What do they think they're going to find?" Mac demanded.

"They already have the murder weapon." As soon as Vi's words were out, the color receded from her face. "Oh, dear."

"Oh, dear?" But before her mother could explain, Liss realized what must be going through Vi's mind. As the one person besides the murderer and the police to have seen the knife used to kill Jasper Spinner, she knew what it looked like. "Let me guess. It was an ordinary kitchen knife."

Vi grimaced. "I didn't see much more than the handle, but I think it was a boning knife. It looked like part of a set."

Liss sprinted for the stairs. The police were already knocking, which sparked an answering spate of frantic barking from inside the apartment.

"Hush up, you two," Margaret called to the two Scotties. A moment later, she opened the door. "Hello, Gordon. Gentlemen. What can I do for you?"

Although Liss took the stairs two at a time, the three officers were already inside by the time she reached the landing. Margaret held the search warrant, her face as pale as Vi's had been and her hands trembling a bit as she read it. When she'd finished, she passed the paperwork to her niece without comment.

The warrant didn't specify what it was that the police were looking for, but the mere fact that it had been issued meant that there was probable cause to think that Margaret was hiding something. Gordon and his henchmen had been granted the right to riffle through any and all of her possessions, an invasion of privacy that was almost as hard on an innocent person as it would be on someone who'd committed a crime.

"They aren't going to find anything." Liss slipped one arm around her aunt's waist in a show of solidarity.

"Of course not. There's nothing to find." But she couldn't conceal her anxiety. She kept her hands clasped in front of her to control the tremors.

Standing together in the middle of the living room, they watched the searchers. With the two Scotties trotting along at his heels, Gordon headed straight for the kitchen. Not a good sign, Liss thought. She put her mouth close to Margaret's ear.

"Are you missing any knives?"

Margaret sucked in a sharp breath and turned wide, frightened eyes on her niece.

Liss's heart beat a little faster. "Tell me," she whispered.

"I only noticed this morning. I hardly ever roast anything just for myself, so I only use my carving knives once in a blue moon. Most of the time my knife rack just sits there on the counter, gathering dust. When I need to slice something, I pull a paring knife or a serrated bread knife out of the cutlery drawer."

"And this morning?" Liss continued to keep her voice low, even though all three officers had by now left the living room.

"I was going to toast an English muffin for breakfast and the split-with-a-fork technique didn't work and I was closer to the knife rack than the cutlery drawer, so I reached for the paring knife that's part of the set and that's when I noticed the empty space. My boning knife is missing."

"Damn."

"That's what he was killed with, isn't it?"

"I think so. But how on earth did the killer get hold of it?"

Margaret's forehead creased as she concentrated. "Well, I did take the dogs for that walk on Saturday."

Liss nodded. "I saw you when you went into the square." They'd used the outside stairs both going and coming, instead of the flight that came out behind the sales counter inside the Emporium. "Was the door still locked when you got back?"

"It was still *un*locked." Margaret made a "What can I say?" gesture with both hands. "I didn't intend to be gone long, and you were right downstairs in the shop. It wasn't as if I was worried about being robbed."

Liss bit back a groan. Even in a tiny, close-knit community like Moosetookalook, it was a good idea to take precautions. There were always strangers in town, and a few of the locals weren't all that trustworthy either. For the most part, she and Dan locked both the front and back doors at their place, even with Dan spending most of every day in the workshop in their backyard.

"Did you notice anyone hanging around when you got back?"

"Not a soul, but there were plenty of people in the town square." She sent Liss a quizzical look. "Do you remember having a customer come in around the time I would have returned? I thought I heard someone pounding on the shop door just as I was herding the dogs inside, but then I decided that I must have imagined it, because I knew it wasn't yet closing time."

"I locked up early and worked in the stockroom for the rest of the afternoon. I heard it, too, but I didn't bother to go see who was there." She wished now that she hadn't ignored the knocking.

"Mrs. Boyd?" Gordon called from the kitchen.

After exchanging a worried glance, Margaret and Liss followed the sound of his voice. As Liss had feared, he was bagging Margaret's knife rack as evidence. Her heart sank when she saw that it appeared to be remarkably dust-free.

"I'll be taking this with me," he said. "I'll give you a receipt."

The two Scotties sat at his feet, watching his every move with intense interest. One look at their bright-eyed, attentive faces must have been enough to convince him that he'd be wasting his time trying to shoo them away. To give herself time to think, Liss bent to stroke Dandy's head. She had no idea what to say, or even if she should say anything.

Acknowledging Gordon's announcement with the briefest of nods, Margaret walked past him to a wall hook where two leashes had been hung. She took them down and clipped them to the Scotties' collars. "I think it might be best if we waited downstairs while you complete your search." Her voice broke on the last word and she had to clear her throat. "I'll be in the Emporium if you need me."

"But, Margaret—"

"Come along, Liss." She used the same tone she did when giving commands to Dandy and Dondi. "Let the police do their jobs."

Controlled by their leashes, the Scotties had no choice but to allow Margaret to lead them away, but Liss could and did stay behind. She glared at Gordon. "You've no call to treat my aunt like a criminal."

For a moment she thought his stone-faced expression might crack, but only the gruffness of his voice hinted that he might not be as unaffected as he seemed. "We can't play favorites, Liss. We have to go where the evidence takes us."

"Oh, for heaven's sake! You know Margaret couldn't kill a fly."

His silence spoke volumes.

With one final fulminating look, Liss swept out of the kitchen in high dudgeon. She was on the landing when Gordon called her name. A moment later, he came out of the apartment after her, closing the door behind him.

"What? Don't tell me you're going to share information with a civilian?"

"I'm going to give this particular civilian a piece of advice."

"You've already warned me not to meddle."

"For all the good *that* did."

"Well, spit it out then. What do you want to tell me?" In such close quarters, she felt overwhelmed by his greater size. She didn't like that sensation one little bit.

"Get Margaret a lawyer. A good one. Someone who's won criminal cases. And for God's sake, make sure she does whatever he suggests."

With that, he went back into the apartment, presumably to search for more evidence to use to convict Liss's aunt of murdering Jasper Spinner. He shut the door gently, but Liss still winced. There was an awful finality about that soft thump.

Leaving Mac and Margaret to contact a lawyer, Liss and Vi went ahead with their plan to talk to everyone who had an upstairs window overlooking the town square. Discouragement dogged Liss's steps by the time she reached her last stop, Moosetookalook Public Library. She'd struck out everywhere else. Dolores Mayfield, town librarian and dedicated snoop and gossip, was her last hope.

The library was located on the upper floor of the municipal building. It had regular hours, but only twenty of them a week. Patrons had to plan their visits for one of the afternoons or the one evening it was open. Liss knew Dolores was often at work at other times, too, but she had a strict policy of not letting anyone else inside. Fortunately for Liss, Wednesday was one of the afternoons when the library was open. Even better, no one was there except Dolores when she arrived.

The librarian sat behind her high, oversized desk, keeping an eagle eye on the door. Liss got the distinct impression that Dolores had been waiting for her to arrive.

Well, of course she was, Liss thought. *She's probably been watching me go door to door, making my way from the Emporium to the municipal building.*

The bank of tall windows behind Dolores's desk gave her an excellent view of the town square, as well as of almost every building around its perimeter. At some point, to conserve energy, a few of the windows had been made smaller by the addition of wooden insets and insulation, but Dolores got around that problem by standing on the little step stool she used to reach books on the highest shelves. All in all, she didn't miss much that could be seen from her vantage point.

In the past, Liss had resented being the object of Dolores's scrutiny, and she'd taken the precaution of keeping her bedroom curtains drawn on the one evening the library was open. On this occasion, she was grateful for the librarian's nosiness, especially if it led to the identification of a killer.

"I need your help, Dolores."

"Looks like someone does. Those state troopers were in your place for a real long time. What did they want?"

"They're still investigating the murder." Liss hoped Dolores would leave it at that, but she didn't count on it.

The librarian sent her a *look,* the kind that traveled from narrowed steel gray eyes through thick-lensed glasses and down a long, thin nose to drill into Liss's forehead. She could almost feel it penetrate and dig deeper, searching for more dirt to excavate.

"I'm trying to get a handle on what went down Saturday afternoon. I don't suppose you were still here by the time the body was discovered, but I was wondering if you'd noticed anything . . . peculiar earlier in the day."

Liss skirted a long worktable and approached the checkout desk. Dolores's stare never wavered, making Liss feel like a pinned butterfly, but she didn't stop until she was standing right in front of the librarian. Positioning both palms flat on the highly polished wooden surface of the desk, she leaned in.

"You know what they're saying around town. And you know that the police have it wrong. Help me figure out what really happened."

Dolores made a sound that was half laugh and half snort. "I hear a lot of things. Maybe you should tell me what you *think* I know."

So much for flattery! She should have remembered that Dolores believed in the barter system. Give a little. Get a little.

"The police searched Margaret's apartment. They think the murder weapon belonged to her."

"Did it?"

"Maybe. But she left the place unlocked while she was out walking the dogs on Saturday. Anyone could have gone in while she was away and taken a kitchen knife."

"Why would they, though? Unless they *wanted* your aunt to be blamed for Jasper Spinner's death." Dolores's lips pursed as she considered that possibility. "Seems pretty preposterous on the surface, but who knows? People do a lot of crazy things."

"You didn't happen to notice anyone hanging around the Emporium, either pounding on the door or sneaking around to the side where the stairs are?"

"Can't say as I did." Her eyes narrowed again. "What about you? I hear you were in the stockroom all afternoon. Your side door is situated right underneath the outside entrance to Margaret's place."

"I was doing my best to ignore the outside world. I even had earbuds in."

A hint of sympathy lurked in Dolores's expression but her words were harsh. "You have only yourself to blame then. No good ever comes from hiding yourself away."

"What can I say? I wasn't exactly thrilled about everything that was going on that day."

"Demonstrations." Dolores shook her head. "A lot of foolishness."

"I don't suppose you were still here when my mother found the body?"

There was genuine regret in Dolores's voice when she admitted that she'd gone home as soon as she closed the library at four. "All that hooting and hollering gave me a headache," she added.

Liss walked to the bank of windows and looked out. As she'd expected, the merry-go-round was in plain sight. There was an apple tree planted near it. In spring or summer, the foliage would have obstructed Dolores's view, but with all the leaves gone there was nothing in the way. Shifting her gaze across the town square, toward the shops on the opposite side, Liss confirmed that they were also easy to see. If only Dolores had been looking out at the right moment, she'd have seen the person who took Margaret's knife.

She turned back to the librarian. "Who do you think killed Jasper Spinner?"

Dolores, who was still watching her like a hawk, shrugged.

"No idea, although it seems to me that there were a good many people who must have thought about killing *Hadley*. It's a pity, whoever did the deed got the wrong man."

"What do you know about the New Age Pilgrims?" Liss had planned to research the group's history but hadn't yet had the opportunity. "Do you have a file on them?" She held up a hand to stop Dolores's sharp retort. "Foolish question! Of course you do. May I check it out, please?"

Mollified, Dolores led the way to the row of vertical file cabinets against one wall. The old card catalog was long gone, replaced by modern technology, but Dolores stubbornly continued clipping articles of local interest from newspapers—or, in this day and age, printing them from the online edition—and placing them in file folders arranged by subject. She hauled out the one labeled "New Age Pilgrims" and handed it over.

Liss opened it and frowned. "There isn't much here."

In addition to a couple of articles, the file contained nothing more than a pamphlet and a copy of the flyer that had been circulated before the demonstration, the one that listed an incorrect phone number for the Emporium.

"I haven't added the stories on the demonstration or the murder yet."

"That's okay. I saw those for myself." None of them had given any background on Spinner or his people.

"The Pilgrims haven't been mentioned much in the news until recently," Dolores said. "They've always kept a low profile. You never even heard anything about their beliefs until this latest dustup. I always figured they were conservative in their thinking, but I didn't have them pegged as out-and-out bigots."

"The way the women dress didn't give you a clue?"

Dolores chuckled. "Yes, and no. You're too young to remember what hippies looked like. Besides, that lavender's a real pretty shade. I remember thinking on Saturday, watching one of them walk across the town square, that I wouldn't mind having a dress in that color myself."

"Do you know if Spinner is ordained?" Liss asked, flipping quickly through the articles.

"Want me to find out?"

"Please. I'm not sure it matters, but you never know."

Dolores glanced pointedly at her watch, indicating that it was almost closing time. Since she'd been in the library longer than she'd expected, Liss was surprised that her mother hadn't trotted up the stairs to join them. She hoped that meant she'd had better luck than her daughter.

Liss already had her hand on the doorknob when something Dolores had said belatedly registered. "What was that about one of the lavender ladies being in the town square on Saturday?"

Her impatience evident, Dolores glanced up from her computer keyboard to scowl at Liss. "Haven't you left yet?"

"Dolores, you said something about admiring the color of that lavender dress . . . on Saturday. But there were no Pilgrim women participating in the demonstration. Spinner was probably afraid they'd be contaminated by the presence of all those strange men he brought in to join the picketing."

"They *are* allowed off the farm," Dolores objected. "I've seen them in the supermarket and at yard sales."

"But you know about the rules when they clean house for someone, right? How no male persons are allowed to be at home while they're there?"

"What's your point?" Dolores shut down the computer and grabbed a sweater off the back of her chair before joining Liss at the door. Pointedly, she held it open, at the same time reaching for the light switch.

"My point is that the field of suspects has just doubled. I thought that only the men from Pilgrim Farm were there when Jasper Spinner was murdered, but you saw one of the women—just one, right?"

Dolores looked thoughtful as she locked the door. "I think there was only one, but since they all look alike, I can't say for certain."

Liss mulled that over as they descended the wide staircase side by side. "So you couldn't identify her? Not even to tell if she was young or old?"

Dolores shook her head. "Sorry. I didn't get so much as a glimpse of her face. I can't even tell you her hair color. She was wearing one of those sunbonnets they favor when it's bright out."

A sunbonnet? The ways of the Pills just got weirder and weirder.

Just as they reached the foot of the stairs, Liss caught sight of her mother. She was leaving the town office. Signaling Vi to stay where she was, Liss followed Dolores toward the back door that led into the parking lot.

"How late in the day was it when you saw that woman?"

They were passing the police department by the time Dolores answered. "Sorry, Liss. I don't remember, but if you're thinking she could have killed Spinner, you're barking up the wrong tree."

"I don't see why. Surely not everyone at Pilgrim Farm loved their leader."

"But that's just it, isn't it? Any of the New Age Pilgrims would have been able to tell the difference between Hadley and Jasper, no matter how much alike they looked. They'd never have mistaken one for the other."

Vi and Liss waited to compare notes until that evening, when Liss's parents and her aunt were invited to a strategy session in the Ruskins' living room. No one had arrested Margaret yet, but the lawyer she'd hired had warned her that she should be prepared for that eventuality. This news put everyone in a somber frame of mind. Even the Scotties, curled up beside Margaret's chair, seemed subdued. Lumpkin and Glenora, each of whom had claimed a lap, ignored the two dogs.

"It *has* to have been someone from the New Age Pilgrims," Liss insisted from her perch on the sofa. "The people who had to put up with Hadley Spinner on a daily basis would have had the most reason to hate him."

"Spinner?" Dan sat beside her, close enough to be even more comfort to her than the purring cat on her lap. "Or his cousin? Because if they lived in such close quarters for years, surely they'd know the difference."

"Not necessarily." Vi, too restless to sit, circled the room as she spoke, now and then pausing to rearrange a knickknack or check a surface for dust. "The killer stabbed him in the back. Maybe he never got a good look at his face."

"He or she," Liss said, trying to ignore what her mother was doing. "Dolores saw at least one of the Pilgrim women at the demonstration. That seems strange to me. Given Hadley Spinner's chauvinist attitude, I would have expected him to forbid them to be there."

"Doesn't make sense," her father muttered. "Some things are okay for the women to do and some things aren't? Either you trust your wife or you don't."

"Said like a man who's been married a long, long time," Margaret teased him.

He grinned at his sister across the space between their chairs and then sent an affectionate smile winging toward his wife. "True enough."

Vi, her attention focused on Liss, didn't notice her husband's look. "I don't think I've yet caught sight of any of the women in this sect myself. Long skirts, right?" At Liss's nod, she asked, "How did you tell me they wear their hair?"

"Braids. Or twisted up in a bun. They don't seem to cut it short. But Dolores said this one was wearing a sunbonnet."

Margaret's eyebrows shot up at that.

"Shades of the pioneers," she said with a chuckle. "Or maybe *Little House on the Prairie*."

Vi came up behind her husband's chair and braced her elbows on its high back. "A hat like that would do a good job of hiding someone's face."

"What are you getting at, hon?" Mac twisted around so he could meet her eyes.

Instead of answering, she backed up and began to fish in the pocket of her jeans. "I think I—yes, here it is, right where I put it on Saturday." She produced an ordinary-looking bobby pin, holding it on the palm of her hand so that it caught the light from a nearby lamp. "These come in different colors. The woman who used this one was a blonde."

"Now I'm the one who's not sure what you're getting at," Dan said.

"I stepped on this just before I found the body." Vi gave a theatrical shudder, remembering that grisly discovery. "When I heard it crunch under my foot, I bent down to see what it was. I'd just picked it up when I noticed what I thought was someone who'd passed out on the merry-go-round. When I went to take a closer look, I stuck the bobby pin in my pocket without thinking, and when I realized he was dead . . . well, you can imagine. This little souvenir went right out of my mind. I didn't remember I had it until just now when Liss was talking about the lavender lady Dolores saw. Not many women pin their hair up these days, and this was awfully close to the scene of the crime."

"There was at least one blond Pilgrim," Liss said. "One of the younger women. I noticed her because she smiled when Sherri told Spinner he couldn't speak for everyone in the group. She intended to question each of them separately." Dan's attack on Spinner had put the kibosh on that plan.

"Well, then," said Liss's mother, "we need to find out more about her."

"Vi. Liss. It's kind of you to be concerned," Margaret

said, "but please let the police handle this. They may be suspicious of me right now, but—"

"They're more than suspicious, Margaret. They're just itching to throw you in jail."

Vi's blunt words produced a flurry of protest, but when the furor died down a little, Liss was forced to accept that her mother was right. "It won't hurt to do a little investigating on our own. At the very least, I'd like to put names to the faces out at Pilgrim Farm. And there's another idea I'd like to follow through on, and that's to talk to one of the women who does housekeeping here in town."

"I have some of that information already." Vi produced a folded piece of paper from another pocket. "Francine was very helpful. Unofficially, of course."

Dan and Mac exchanged a look that made Liss laugh. "Don't discount gossip," she scolded them. "Sometimes it's the best source of information there is."

"If you really think that bobby pin is evidence, you should turn it over to the police," Dan said.

"He's right," Liss said. "Give it to Gordon and tell him where you found it." At Vi's disgruntled look she added, "It couldn't hurt."

"Nor will it do any good. These jeans were in the load of laundry I did on Monday. If there were fingerprints on the bobby pin, they'll have been washed away."

"Give it to him anyway. Now, let's have a look at that list."

It contained sixteen names. The first fourteen were grouped in couples.

"That last one is a child," Vi said, "Kimmy Miller, and this Chloe Spinner is Jasper's widow. The names marked with an asterisk are women who clean houses for local people."

"All tidily married couples," Liss murmured. "Hadley Spinner's wife is named Miranda." She had an asterisk by her name.

Dan leaned closer to get a better look at the list. "Both Chloe and Miranda would have been called Mistress Spinner out at the farm. Must have been confusing."

"Yes." She ran her finger down the rest of the names. "I wonder which one is our smiling blonde."

Margaret took possession of the page and scanned it. "I know a little about a few of these people. Susan spoke of Diana, George, and Connie."

Connie Gerard's name was marked with an asterisk. Diana Collins's was not. Such mundane names, Liss thought. She'd have expected the Pilgrims to change them to something Biblical—Esther and Esau and Rachel, perhaps. Or, remembering what Dolores had said, maybe Moonbeam, Sunshine, and Cloud.

"How long ago was it that Susan died, Margaret? I don't think you've said."

"Twelve years. Twelve years almost to the day."

"That's not going to look good to the police." Vi's voice was sharply critical.

"What are you talking about?" Liss asked.

"Didn't you look at that folder you brought home from the library?"

Belatedly, Liss realized that as soon as her mother had handed over Francine's list, she'd shifted her attention to the contents of Dolores's file. "I haven't had time."

"There are several clippings. One is Susan Spinner's obituary. Susan *Spinner*," she repeated. "Susan was Jasper's first wife. Wasn't she, Margaret?"

"Yes, she was, but—"

"It was *twelve years ago*," Liss interrupted. She'd already been through that issue with her aunt. "If Margaret had wanted revenge on Jasper, she'd have done away with him long before this."

"I'm not the one you need to convince." Vi glanced at the bobby pin she still held and then shifted her gaze to Margaret's pale gray locks. "It isn't just blondes who use light-colored bobby pins," she remarked. "Lucky for you that you wear your hair short."

Chapter Eleven

After Liss's parents and aunt left, Liss turned her attention to the items in the New Age Pilgrims file. She already knew that, unlike most churches, even small, off-the-wall sects, the New Age Pilgrims did not have a social media presence as a group. Only Hadley Spinner had online accounts, the ones he'd used to spread the word about the boycott and the demonstration. Neither he nor the Pilgrims had a Web page. Now she found something even more peculiar. It appeared that their worship services were private affairs. Outsiders were not welcome to join them.

"They won't get many new recruits that way," she muttered.

She was talking to herself. The cats had disappeared and Dan had fallen asleep in his recliner, an open book still gripped in one hand. She glanced at the clock on the cable box, astonished to see how late it was, but she wanted to finish going through Dolores's clippings before she called it a night, in particular the ones that covered Susan Spinner's death twelve years earlier.

Neither the news stories nor Susan's obituary provided more than the sketchiest of details. She'd "died suddenly" and was survived by her husband. No parents, siblings, or children were listed. No mention was made of her membership in any organizations, not even her church. Funeral services had been private. The photographs accompanying the first report of a body found in a farm pond showed police milling around the water. None of the Pilgrims were visible. Liss wondered if they'd had any particular reason to hide their faces or if it was just that they were camera shy. There was no picture of Susan with her obituary either.

Last of all, Liss came to the pamphlet. She picked it up gingerly, prepared for it to be venomous, and she was not far wrong. After admonishing the reader to follow the straight and narrow path or risk spending eternity paying for the sins of the flesh, the author provided a list of Bible verses. Liss didn't take the time to look them up. She could guess which ones they were and had little tolerance for threats of fire and brimstone, especially when taken out of context and quoted by people who appeared to despise anyone who wasn't just like them.

After tucking Francine's list inside so she'd be able to find it again, Liss closed the folder and set it on the coffee table. "Sufficient to the day," she murmured. Wasn't that a Bible verse, too?

Yawning, she woke Dan and headed to bed. Tomorrow was time enough to decide what to do next.

In the morning, Liss made three phone calls. The first was to the town office. Once she was armed with additional information supplied by Francine, she phoned Audrey Greenwood. According to Francine, Audrey used the services of the New Age Pilgrims to clean both her house and Moosetookalook Small Animal Clinic. Liss was in luck. Two of the lavender ladies were scheduled to work for Audrey that very day. The third phone call was to Mac MacCrimmon, to ask him to mind the store while she paid a neighborly visit to Lumpkin and Glenora's doctor.

The clinic was only a short distance from the town square. Liss walked, enjoying the crisp morning air and noticing, as she rarely took time to, the change in the season. She could smell fragrant smoke, since several families preferred to use their fireplaces or woodstoves when they could. Both stove wood and wood pellets were plentiful and relatively inexpensive in Maine; oil, gas, and electricity? Not so much.

That it would soon be Thanksgiving amazed her. Hadn't it just been Halloween?

In recent years, she and Dan had celebrated with the Ruskins. This year, with her parents living in Moosetookalook, she supposed her mother would expect them to come to dinner at the house on Ledge Lake. Margaret, too, assuming she wasn't in jail.

She walked faster. At the clinic, the barking of a half-dozen dogs made conversation difficult, but Audrey was perfectly willing to answer Liss's questions. She'd always been blunt-spoken. Before she prescribed expensive treatments or performed surgeries, she made certain that pet owners knew what the odds of success would be.

"I have no complaints about the job they do cleaning," she told Liss as she swapped out food and water bowls in the cages. "I think the clothes they wear to do it are a little strange, but each to her own."

A rangy, athletic-looking forty-something, Audrey was a couple of inches taller than Liss's five-foot-nine and had a long, narrow face that matched her build. She wore her blunt-cut blond hair tucked behind her ears and had never felt the need to wear makeup. As for clothing, Liss had rarely seen her in anything fancier than jeans and a sweatshirt.

"Do the Pilgrim women always work in pairs?" she asked.

"Ordinarily, they do, but today only one lavender lady showed up. She's tackling the house first. You can go on in if you want. I have to finish up here and then I have vaccinations scheduled."

Liss rehearsed her pitch on the short walk between the clinic and the pretty little cape with dormers where Audrey lived. She intended to lie and say she was interested in having her house cleaned once a week, that it had gotten to be too much for her to handle, what with working fulltime and all. She smiled to herself at that thought. Lately her father had put in more hours at the Emporium than she had.

Liss changed her mind about what approach to take when she recognized the young woman pushing Audrey's vacuum cleaner around the living room. It was the blonde with the braids, the one who'd smiled when she'd heard Sherri contradict Hadley Spinner. The one she suspected, on the evidence of that bobby pin, of being in the town square on the day Jasper Spinner was murdered.

"Excuse me," Liss called, raising her voice to be heard above the racket.

The woman gave a start, turned wide, frightened blue eyes Liss's way, and hastily hit the power button. She didn't seem to know what to do next. Shoulders slumped, she folded her hands in front of her and lowered her gaze to a carpet that still sported clumps of dog and cat fur and the remains of a potato chip.

"Do you recognize me?" Liss asked. "I was at Pilgrim

Farm the other day with my husband and the chief of police."

The woman nodded but did not speak.

Start slowly, Liss warned herself. *Don't spook her.* "Will you talk with me for a few minutes?"

She sent a furtive glance Liss's way but managed to avoid meeting her eyes. The silence continued.

"You *can't* be afraid of me." But when Liss moved closer, the other woman retreated a few steps. "Seriously?"

She advanced again. This time the Pilgrim kept backing up until she bumped into Audrey's end table. Finding herself trapped, she at last lifted her head to give Liss her first good look at the other woman's face. No, she wasn't afraid. She wasn't on the verge of flight. But she was definitely wary.

"Let's sit down, shall we?" People were supposed to seem less threatening when they were seated. Liss suited action to words by settling into one of Audrey's Danish modern chairs. It smelled strongly of dog.

After a moment, the blonde perched on the far side of the matching couch. As if the movement was habitual, she placed both hands in her lap, loosely folded together, but this time she did not duck her head. Her gaze remained fixed on Liss's face.

"I'm Liss Ruskin." When this didn't elicit any response, she added, "And you are?"

"Anna."

"Anna what?"

"Anna Knapp."

Liss grinned at her. "I half expected you to say it was Spinner."

"We are all his spiritual children."

Liss blinked at her in surprise. "Uh, okay. So, is it all

right if you talk to me a little? I'm curious about the New Age Pilgrims."

"What do you want to know?"

Liss heard an undercurrent of suspicion in the simple question and warned herself to proceed with caution. Instead of asking Anna how long she had been a member, she tried a different tack. "Are your worship services open to the public?" She already knew the answer, but she was curious to hear what Anna would say.

"We pray in private."

"But you hold some kind of religious ceremonies, right?"

Anna shook her head. "We pray in private."

"Are you saying that there is no organized ritual at Pilgrim Farm? I thought Hadley Spinner was a preacher."

"We gather together to hear his words of wisdom."

Oh, brother! Liss thought. The more Anna talked, the more she sounded like someone who'd been brainwashed. Or did she mean hypnotized? Could mass hypnosis be more than just a plot device in a B movie? For once, Liss thought carefully before she spoke.

"There were Bible verses on some of the signs at the protest. Do you have organized Bible study?"

Anna's frown was three parts confusion and one part irritation. "I do not know what you mean."

"Do you have a Bible? Do you read it for yourself?"

"Mr. Spinner has charge of the Bible."

"Just one copy?"

"It is kept on a purpose-built table, open to the page he chooses, so that we may read the day's text whenever it pleases us."

Both fascinated and repelled by this glimpse into Spinner's domination over his followers, Liss pondered what to ask next. Things were even stranger out at Pilgrim Farm than she'd imagined. After a moment, she went with the question she'd put off asking earlier. "How long have you lived at Pilgrim Farm?"

"Three glorious years." Anna's smile was beatific.

"How did you even hear about the group? I mean, it isn't as if they advertise for converts, and if they don't allow strangers to visit, and don't hold regular worship services, let alone any that are open to the public, then I'm surprised they haven't gone the way of the Shakers long before this."

A faraway look came into Anna's eyes. "I was guided to this place. Mr. Skinner found me when I was lost."

"Do you think you could be a little more specific?" Liss couldn't quite keep the sarcasm out of her voice.

Hearing it, Anna snapped out of her reverie. For the first time, the look she gave Liss was more than cursory. Her eyes narrowed, as if she didn't like what she saw. "What do you really want to know? And why?"

"I simply like to know *something* about a person I might employ. I'm looking for a cleaning lady." The lie came effortlessly. Liss added an encouraging smile. "So, tell me about yourself, Anna. Are you from around here?"

"No."

Liss put Anna's age at no more than twenty-five. Subtracting "three glorious years" took her back to twenty-one or twenty-two. Those were impressionable ages . . . and just about when one usually graduated from college.

"Were you a student at Fallstown?"

That seemed like a reasonable assumption. The University of Maine system had a branch there, less than a half hour's drive from Moosetookalook. When Liss spotted the merest flicker of response from Anna—the nervous twitch of the muscle just under her right eye—she felt certain she'd hit on the truth.

Anna did not confirm it aloud. She said only, "I sought answers in all the wrong ways until Mr. Spinner saved me."

"Drugs?" Liss stopped herself just short of adding "Sex, and rock and roll." Impatient as she was for answers, she didn't want to put words into the other woman's mouth. To judge by the responses Anna had given so far, that young woman was adept at parroting back other people's opinions.

"I was tempted from the righteous path."

"Are you on the righteous path now?"

A serene smile accompanied Anna's answer. "I am."

"And is marriage to a member of the New Age Pilgrims part of your redemption?"

The smile abruptly disappeared. "A woman needs a man to guide her. Mr. Spinner gave me Mr. Knapp."

"Is that what you call your husband? Doesn't he have a first name?"

Liss was beginning to lose patience. How could any normal young woman in this day and age be so complaisant about an arranged marriage and the loss of her individuality? She recalled Joe saying that the Pills advocated "the old ways," but this was going too far.

"Charles," Anna said. "His name is Charles Knapp."

"Is he the man who put a hand on your arm to restrain you when my husband and the chief of police came out to the farm?"

Anna frowned but did not answer.

Liss leaned forward until they were almost touching and waited for the other woman to meet her eyes before she asked her next question. "What was your maiden name?"

"What I was called before no longer matters."

"Are you sure about that?"

The bright blue eyes bored into her with laser intensity. "You took *your* husband's name."

"That doesn't mean I've forgotten my own, or that I don't continue to use it in my business. It's MacCrimmon. I take great pride in my Scottish heritage."

Anna's eyes widened slightly. "You own the shop in town."

"I do."

Liss was surprised Anna hadn't already made the connection, given the New Age Pilgrims' campaign to ruin her business and the fact that she clearly knew Liss was married to a Ruskin. She studied the other woman, trying to make sense of her story.

"So," she began again, "you married a stranger. Did Hadley Spinner perform the wedding ceremony?"

Anna nodded.

"The usual one?" Liss asked. "Love, honor, and obey and all that?"

Another nod.

"How about 'be fruitful and multiply' or did that not apply?"

Anna's face flamed. "We do not engage in physical congress."

Why the hell not? Liss wanted to ask. What was the point in arranging marriages for his flock if they were going to live apart? She frowned as another contradiction struck her. If nobody at Pilgrim Farm had sex, where had that little girl come from?

With more pressing matters to ask about, Liss didn't delve into details about the child's history. She took a moment to regroup, and then got to the point. "You were in the town square on Saturday. How is it that you were allowed to join the men?"

Anna's head shot up. For once, her face revealed more than she intended. Liss recognized shock and then saw a flash of fear before Anna was able to control her reaction.

"There is no point in denying it," Liss said when Anna once more presented her with a bland countenance. "You were seen."

"That is impossible. I was not there."

"Who was, then? One of you went into town. The style and color of your clothes are unmistakable." After a short silence, she switched gears. "If you wanted to come into Moosetookalook, how would you get here? Are there cars available at Pilgrim Farm? Horses? Bikes?"

At the mention of a bicycle as a means of transportation, a muscle in Anna's jaw twitched. Liss tried to imagine it. She'd have had a long, tiring ride, especially when hampered by an ankle-length skirt. Only someone in good physical condition would have attempted it. Even then, she'd have to have had a good reason to make the effort. Had Anna, or whoever had come into town, been obeying Hadley Spinner's orders? Or had she acted in spite of them?

"You dropped a bobby pin near where Jasper was murdered," Liss said.

This accusation startled Anna and briefly brought a stricken look into her eyes, but she kept her lips lightly pressed together, refusing to incriminate herself or anyone else.

"I'm not sure how that could have happened," Liss mused aloud. "Considering that you were wearing a scarf over your hair and all."

At this point in a poorly scripted television cop show, Anna would have conveniently fallen into the conversational trap Liss had set, protesting that it was a sunbonnet, not a scarf. Or maybe she'd have pointed out that she wore braids and had required no bobby pins. Instead, Anna continued to sit on the couch, looking like the statue of "speak no evil" as she waited for Liss to try another gambit.

"Fine. You weren't there. The woman in lavender was seen some time before the murder anyway. She isn't a suspect. But maybe something she did or said had a bearing on what happened later. It could be important, Anna. Surely you don't want an innocent person to be arrested for Jasper's murder."

Bolting to her feet, Anna reached for the vacuum cleaner. "I must finish my work."

"According to Ms. Greenwood, you usually clean in pairs. Where's your partner?"

"Mistress Spinner is indisposed."

"Which Mistress Spinner? Miranda or Chloe?" Liss left her chair and managed to close the distance between them in time to observe Anna's start of surprise. She hadn't expected Liss to know their first names.

"Chloe," she blurted out. "She just lost her husband. She is in mourning."

"She . . . loved him?"

Anna shrugged. "She owed him her respect. I must get back to work." She turned on the Hoover, counting on the roar to drown out any further questions.

Liss reached around her and shut it off again. This close to Anna, she realized that lavender wasn't just the color of her clothing. She wore the scent as well.

"Anna, listen to me. If you want to leave Pilgrim Farm you have only to say so. You can't be forced to stay there against your will."

The Pilgrim woman's eyes brimmed with tears. "Please, I must finish my work. Mr. Knapp will return for me soon and I have a great deal left to do."

Although Liss heard the desperation in her voice, she couldn't tell if it was caused by fear of the other Pilgrims, or a sense of misguided loyalty, or a reaction to her own dogged perseverance. With a sinking heart, she accepted that, no matter which it was, nothing she could say now would convince Anna to change her mind.

As soon as Liss stepped away from her, Anna resumed her vacuuming. She did not so much as glance her way again.

Frustrated by her inability to talk sense into the other woman, Liss barely refrained from slamming the door behind her as she left the house. If she'd encountered Charles Knapp waiting outside, she'd have been sorely tempted to punch him right in the nose. As it was, it took her the entire walk back to the Emporium to calm down.

When she reached the shop, she went straight into her father's arms. "I've been so lucky," she whispered when he returned her hug. "You and Mother raised me to be my own person and taught me to be choosy enough not to marry a man unless he could love me just the way I am."

"That's the way it should be in a marriage," Mac MacCrimmon said. "You love the other person, warts and all."

Later that day, when her father had gone home and Liss was behind the sales counter checking the computer for new orders, her mother swept into the Emporium.

"We need to break into the Pilgrims' compound," she announced.

Liss stared at her. Then her gaze shifted to the window and her view of the solitary picket who was marching up and down in the town square with his sign.

"Liss, did you hear what I said?"

Still distracted, she said, "It's more like a commune than a compound. As far as I could see, it's a working farm."

Vi huffed out an exasperated breath. "Are the Pilgrims armed?"

The question focused Liss's attention on her mother once more, and on the innocuous-looking tote bag she carried slung over one arm. Did it still contain that ridiculous but deadly pink gun?

Liss cleared her throat. "I didn't see any weapons when I was out there with Sherri and Dan. I didn't see anything to indicate that they're an anti-government or pro-militia group either. They aren't living completely off the grid. They're just . . . weird."

"Too bad," Vi said. "If they were breaking the law, they could be arrested and questioned and who knows what would come out."

She scooped up the dust rag and the can of lemon-scented furniture polish Liss had abandoned on a nearby shelf and went to work shining a wooden plaque, one of a series Liss had purchased because of the Scottish-themed slogans painted on them.

"Something to shift suspicion away from Margaret would be nice," Liss agreed, but her mother's industrious cleaning brought a frown to her face. The plaques hadn't been *that* dusty.

"Are the lavender ladies allowed to keep the money they earn cleaning houses?" Vi moved on to a higher shelf laden with glassware. "If not, that's slave labor, or enforced servitude, or something like that."

Liss almost cracked a smile. It appeared that her mother's grasp of legal matters was even more tenuous than her own. "You'll have to ask Sherri. Or better yet, ask Dolores Mayfield to research the topic, but I suspect the Pills see it as volunteering, and that's something people ordinarily applaud."

"Volunteering," Vi scoffed. Then she froze, dust rag

raised, as if struck by a thought. "Volunteering," she repeated, more slowly this time.

"Mom?"

Bright-eyed behind her glasses, Vi abandoned her cleaning to approach the sales counter. "Margaret belongs to all sorts of organizations here in Carrabassett County. At least one of them must be raising money for something. I could go out to Pilgrim Farm—it has to be me because they know who you are—to solicit a contribution. Or maybe I could tell them I was *looking* for volunteers for, well, *whatever* community event is coming up next."

Liss hated to douse her mother's enthusiasm, but the last thing she wanted was for Vi to go into that nest of vipers on her own.

"Since the town discontinued its Twelve Days of Christmas Shopping events, there's nothing going on in Moosetookalook until the annual March Madness Mud Season Sale, unless you count Joe's Thanksgiving special at The Spruces. Somehow, I don't think soliciting help with that would be well received at Pilgrim Farm."

"There is no need for your sass, missy. Perhaps it would be best if I made something up."

"Mom, any variation of this plan of yours is a *bad* idea. And it could be dangerous."

"Hah! If they didn't already know what you look like, you'd be raring to act on this idea yourself. You're just put out because I get to do it."

"Do what, exactly?" Liss planted her elbows on the counter and leaned across until she and her mother were nearly nose to nose. "Suppose you do drive out there and tell them some cock-and-bull story about a fictitious event—what then? You won't get any takers. They'll send you packing and you'll be none the wiser for having wasted your afternoon."

"You can't be sure about that. Besides, I've been think-ing about it and I'm pretty sure I'm already acquainted with Miranda Spinner. That's not a common first name, you know."

"When did you meet Miranda?"

"I'm not *sure* I did. Can you describe her for me?"

Liss called up the image in her mind, discounted the cos-tume, and frowned a little as she tried to remember details. "I'd say she's somewhere in her early fifties, or else she's younger than that but looks older. She's got that beaten-down-by-life look, but she's sturdily built. She wears old-fashioned rimless glasses, round in shape, and she has a snub nose." She shook her head. "Sorry. That's all I can recall."

"The snub nose clinches it. She was Miranda Harrison before she married, a local girl from Lower Mooseside. In fact, if Pilgrim Farm is where I think it is, her father must have been the one who sold that property to Hadley Spin-ner. My goodness. I can't imagine why I didn't realize that sooner."

"How did you come to know Miranda?" Liss asked. "She's a lot younger than you are."

"That's exactly how I came in contact with her way back when. I was her seventh grade teacher. I can't claim to remember every student I ever taught, but I always tried to help the ones with low self-esteem think better of them-selves. I truly believe that I guided a few of them to a more positive outlook on life." She sighed. "Some were so des-perate for attention that it nearly broke my heart."

"And Miranda was one of those?"

"I'm afraid so. At thirteen, she was a great lump of a girl, and her looks were not improved by the addition of glasses and braces. She was teased unmercifully by the other children. She hated school—with good reason, I suppose. She had no interest in history, which was my passion. Try as I might to engage her attention, she spent most of her time in my class doodling on her notebook cover. Little hearts with initials in them, as I recall. But that's not the most significant thing I know about Miranda. She had a younger sister. I had *her* in my class a few years later."

"Why is that significant?" But even as Liss asked the question, she caught her mother's drift. "You don't mean—?"

"Oh, but I do. Miranda Harrison's younger sister was named Susan."

Chapter Twelve

As soon as Liss closed up the Emporium for the day, she and Vi went upstairs to talk to Margaret. It was with a certain reluctance that Liss rapped on the apartment door. If Vi was right about Susan and Miranda being sisters, then there was no way that Margaret hadn't known of their relationship. She must also have known that Susan was Hadley Spinner's sister-in-law. Why hadn't she mentioned that, if not to the police, then to her family?

The usual barking preceded the sound of locks clicking open. Margaret peered out through a crack but she kept the chain on. "Oh, Liss. Vi. I was just going to lie down and take a little nap. If you could come back later, that—"

"Not a chance," Vi said. "We've figured out a few things and now you're going to fill in the missing pieces."

Without making further objections, Margaret closed the door, took the chain off, and opened it again to let them in. "I'll just make some—"

"No tea!" Liss was all too familiar with this delaying tactic. She caught her aunt's arm and steered her firmly toward the living room sofa. "Let's just sit down and get this over with."

The two Scotties danced around her ankles, threatening to trip her up at any moment, but Liss managed to get both her aunt and her mother settled before slipping out of the room to fetch one of the lined legal pads Margaret always kept in a kitchen drawer. Margaret was a list maker, just as Liss was. Armed with the tablet and a felt-tip pen, she returned to the living room and perched on the ottoman facing the sofa Vi and Margaret now shared. From the expression on Margaret's face, Vi had already read her the riot act for her failure to share everything she knew about Susan.

"I can't imagine why everyone thinks that's so important after all this time," Margaret said as Liss took the cap off the pen. "Susan's been gone for a dozen years. Nothing to do with her can possibly have any bearing on the present day."

"Except that Susan left family behind," Vi argued. "Her husband, now dead. And her sister. Or had you forgotten about Miranda?"

"I haven't forgotten, but I don't see how she's relevant."

"She's married to the head honcho."

"Which makes me feel very sorry for her, but it still doesn't explain why—"

"Margaret," Liss interrupted, "let's go about this in a sensible fashion. Any little detail could turn out to be important, so if we start at the beginning and fill all of them in, we should be able to tell what's significant and what isn't."

Margaret eyed the pen and paper. "What do you have in mind?"

"A time line." She wrote down a date, the year she'd left Moosetookalook for college and her parents had moved to Arizona. Twenty years ago. That hardly seemed possible.

"You need to start earlier," Margaret said. "A lot earlier. Go back another . . . twenty-four years, more or less."

"What happened then?" Vi looked as puzzled as Liss felt.

"That's when Stu moved to Moosetookalook and opened up the ski shop."

"Oh, I remember that." Vi chuckled. "Not only was he from away, but he made quite a splash by buying one of the white clapboard Victorian houses on the square and painting the shutters purple. Then he put that sign with the life-sized skier on the roof of the front porch."

For Liss, Stu and the ski shop had always been part of the everyday scene in Moosetookalook, but she could imagine the uproar his arrival must have caused. Back then, most of the businesses that now housed shops and apartments had still been single-family homes.

"Well, that's the thing," Margaret said. "Stu wasn't exactly from away. His mother was a Harrison from Lower Mooseside. Miranda is his niece."

"Huh," Liss said, startled. That Stu had a family connection to the Pilgrims was the last thing she'd expected to hear.

Vi sent her sister-in-law a thoughtful look. "If the police think you killed Jasper because of Susan, then they have just as much reason to think Stu did, and for the same reason."

"That about sums it up, but I still think it's a foolish notion. Susan's death was just too long ago to have any bearing on what's happening now."

"So you keep saying." Vi didn't sound convinced.

"Let's get back to the time line." Liss hastily wrote in the approximate date Stu had set up shop and moved her pen down on the page to the next empty line. "Hadley Spinner arrived fifteen years ago, right?"

Margaret nodded. "Hadley, Jasper, George Gerard, and

Charles Knapp. Old Man Harrison sold them his farm and died soon after. The next thing you know, Miranda and Susan up and married Hadley and Jasper."

"Fast forward three years." Liss made a notation. "Susan wants to leave. Did she say why?"

Margaret shook her head. "She was never very specific. Back then, she and her sister often came into town, and they wore normal clothing. They didn't wear makeup, but then neither do a lot of rural Maine women."

"Who else was living at Pilgrim Farm by then?" Vi asked.

"And was it called Pilgrim Farm?" Liss put in. "Were they the New Age Pilgrims from the start?"

Brow furrowed, Margaret had to think about that last question for a moment. "I'm not certain how soon they established themselves as an organized group. Lower Mooseside is in the middle of nowhere. No one would have noticed what was going on out there unless they did something to call attention to themselves. I do remember that Hadley Spinner, when he deigned to show his face, was quite the charismatic figure. All the girls were sighing over him and wondering how plain, dull Miranda managed to catch him."

Liss's face twisted into a moue of distaste at the thought of lusting after Hadley Spinner. "I suppose he might pass as good-looking if he were fifteen years younger and didn't have that awful beard, but I didn't sense an iota of charisma in him."

"You had to be there," Margaret said. "Think of rock stars. All those girls screaming and swooning. Then ten, fifteen, twenty years later, some of them still have that . . . something. In others, the magic has just faded away."

"I'll take your word for it." She studied her time line.

"Twelve years ago, Susan wanted to leave, changed her mind, and then drowned in the stock pond at the farm. What else was going on at the time? Did she talk about the other Pilgrims?"

"Some. Not a lot. There were more of them by then. George Gerard had married Connie. Charles Knapp was still single."

"So marriage wasn't a requirement?"

Margaret shook her head. "Not that I know of, but there was another couple there by then. Diana was the woman's name, but I don't recall her husband's."

"And three more couples have joined up since."

"Unless there were some who came and left again," Vi said.

"Nobody leaves."

Liss and her mother exchanged a worried glance at Margaret's morose tone of voice.

"How would you know?" Liss asked. "You just reminded us how remote the location is."

"That's what Susan told me. Nobody was supposed to leave, ever. Hadley Spinner demanded a lifetime commitment."

The next day, Friday, Liss opened the Emporium at the usual hour. Ten minutes later, her parents walked in.

"Mac's going to work for you," Vi announced. "You and I are going on a field trip."

"We talked about this yesterday, Mom. It's too risky for either of us to go out to Pilgrim Farm."

Her mother's response was a vigorous shake of the head. "Nonsense. Take another look at that Pilgrim marching back and forth in the town square with his ridiculous sign. That's Hadley Spinner himself. That means that this is the perfect time to pay a visit to his wife."

As Liss drove them toward Lower Mooseside, she still had her doubts. Her hands gripped the steering wheel much too tightly and her misgivings hovered over her head like a rain cloud. Spinner might be the alpha dog, but the other men in his pack could be just as vicious. She must have been crazy to let her mother talk her into this.

Then again, their excuse for a visit—Vi's desire to reconnect with an old student—might just be simple and direct enough to convince the Pilgrims that it was sincere. It was probably worth a shot.

As seemed to be the pattern, Liss saw no one about when she pulled into the dooryard at Pilgrim Farm and parked. The stillness made her uneasy, but she hoped it meant that all menfolk were out working in the fields, or doing whatever it was they did on the farm, and would never know that strangers had trespassed on their land. She got out of the car and followed her mother through the door to the ell, but she was unable to stop herself from scanning her surroundings for hidden dangers.

No one leapt out at them when they entered a perfectly ordinary Maine building. The ell was a sort of shed attached to the house on one side and the barn on the other. Firewood for the coming winter was stacked against the back wall. In a corner, unless Liss was much mistaken, that door with the quarter moon cut into it opened into an indoor outhouse.

Vi knocked on the door just to their right as they entered the ell. A few minutes later, it was flung open to reveal Miranda Spinner. She squinted at them for a moment before recognition dawned on her plain, pale face.

"Mrs. MacCrimmon," she murmured. There was a note of awe in her voice.

"Hello, Miranda. It's nice to see you again. I hope you don't mind my stopping by, but I'm always curious about my former students. May we come in?" Since Vi was already through the door and into the kitchen, there wasn't much Miranda could do to keep her out.

It was a pleasant room, if somewhat old-fashioned. A long table with benches on either side suggested that meals were taken here rather than in a dining room. An enormous wood-burning cookstove took up most of the rest of the space. Delicious aromas filled the air. A pot of stew simmered on a back burner and bread dough was rising in a bowl on the shelf above. The cloth over the top was already bowed upward.

"Come through." Miranda sounded unhappy but resigned. "We're working in the parlor."

Liss and her mother exchanged a glance. So much for talking to Miranda alone.

They followed their hostess along a short hallway, past the entrance to stairs that turned sharply upward, and into a large, comfortable room with a fireplace that, like the kitchen stove, radiated heat. The Pilgrim women sat in a circle, industriously plying their needles.

"Oh, my goodness!" Vi exclaimed. "It's a quilting bee. What lovely work."

"Needful," Miranda said. "Cold weather's coming."

"And the gentlemen?" Liss asked. "What do they work at while you keep busy inside?"

It was Anna Knapp who answered her. "They're all at the wood lot. It takes many cords of wood to cook our meals and keep us warm though the winter."

Liss breathed a silent sigh of relief. Free of interruption by their husbands, it might be possible to start a dialogue with these women.

Vi beamed indiscriminately at them all. "Hello. So nice to meet you. I'm Violet MacCrimmon and this is my daughter, Amaryllis Ruskin. And you are?"

Liss winced at her mother's use of her full name, but no one in this group seemed to think it was odd that she'd been named after a flower. She couldn't tell if there were any Buttercups or Rosebuds among the lavender ladies. Miranda introduced her companions as Mistress Spinner, Mistress Collins, Mistress Gerard, Mistress Knapp, Mistress Miller, Mistress Fontaine, and Mistress Callahan.

She thought she remembered a Laurel from the list the town clerk had drawn up for her mother. Yes—Laurel Miller. Mistress Miller was a buxom young woman with rosy cheeks and a dimple in her chin. The child, Kimmy, was her daughter, but Liss saw no sign of the little girl. Maybe it was nap time, or maybe they just locked her up somewhere to keep her out of the way. Considering the bars on the windows of the women's dormitory, that was certainly possible.

The other Mistress Spinner, Chloe, was younger than Liss expected, given that her late husband had been in his fifties. While Vi chattered at Miranda, Liss maneuvered herself into position behind the widow and complimented her on her handiwork.

"I wish I could sew," she confided—a blatant lie, but in a good cause. "I'm all thumbs when it comes to handling a needle and thread. I can't even fix a snagged hem." That much was the truth.

Chloe kept her eyes fixed on the fabric in front of her and did not respond. Anna Knapp, who sat next to her, managed a covert glance in Liss's direction but gave no other sign that she was interested in their visitor. Liss wondered if she'd concealed their earlier encounter from her friends.

"Everyone should be taught wifely skills at an early age," said the woman Miranda had identified as Mistress Collins.

She had to be Diana, Liss thought, the lavender lady who, along with Connie Gerard and Miranda Spinner, had been at Pilgrim Farm when Susan was alive. Liss wished her aunt had been able to remember more about the other woman, but it *had* been a dozen years. All Margaret had been able to recall was that either Connie or Diana had been sympathetic to Susan's desire to leave and the other had argued against it.

Diana Collins had a starchy look to her, even though the floor-length dress she wore was soft from repeated washings. She was an angular woman with a thin face and sharply defined features. Liss would not have chosen her to confide in, but that did not mean Susan had found her unsympathetic. Appearances were often deceiving.

It was even more difficult for Liss to form an impression of Connie Gerard, who kept her head down and contributed nothing to the conversation. At the first opportunity, she excused herself to visit what she called "the necessary" and did not return.

After some initial awkwardness, most of the women seemed pleased to have company. Liss let her mother take the lead in the conversation. She'd never thought of Vi as a domestic goddess, but girls had been required to take classes in home economics back in the day. Vi knew far more housekeeping tips, cooking secrets, and needlework terms than her daughter ever would.

"I was so sorry to hear about Susan's death," Vi said after ten minutes of inconsequential chitchat. "So sad to go so young."

A deafening silence fell over the entire group.

"That happened a long time ago." Miranda's voice was sharp. "It's best forgotten."

"But she was your sister. And you both stayed on here

after your father sold the farm." Vi's tone became arch. "I imagine there's a romantic story there, what with both you and Susan finding true love among the Pilgrims."

"It was a practical matter," Miranda said. "Neither of us wanted to leave our home."

Well, that was honest enough, Liss thought.

Gamely, Vi soldiered on. "And my condolences to you, Chloe, on the loss of your husband. Your former brother-in-law, was he not, Miranda?"

Chloe kept her head down. She might as well have been deaf.

Miranda was made of sterner stuff. "Delightful as this has been, Mrs. MacCrimmon, the men will be returning soon for their lunch. I'd advise you to leave before they arrive."

This unsubtle hint, combined with Miranda's firm grip on Vi's arm, propelled Liss's mother out into the dooryard. Liss trailed behind, amused in spite of herself. There had been more than one occasion in the past when she'd been tempted to use a similar technique to get her mother to stop nagging.

Once they'd been evicted, Miranda stood in the doorway, feet braced wide apart and arms folded over her chest, blocking the entrance to the ell. "Mr. Spinner prefers that we keep to ourselves," she announced. "There's no point in you coming back here again."

"She'd have made a good teacher," Liss remarked as they walked back to the car.

Her mother's response was a snort of laughter.

They were nearly back in Moosetookalook, mercifully driving on a straight stretch of road, when a pale face topped with a mop of disheveled hair suddenly appeared in Liss's rearview mirror. Her hands jerked on the steering wheel and she barely managed to keep control of the car. Her heart was still racing when her mother realized they were not alone and twisted as far around as her seat belt would allow to see who was there.

"We appear to have a stowaway," Vi said in a laconic tone of voice. If she was rattled, it wasn't obvious.

Liss tried to mimic her air of calm. "I can see that." A second glance in the mirror put a name to their uninvited passenger.

"Please don't make me go back," Connie Gerard whispered.

"We wouldn't think of it," Vi said, "but you'd better scrunch down again until after we pull the car into Liss's garage. You don't want Hadley Spinner to catch sight of you."

With a whimper, Connie sank out of sight.

"Mom," Liss asked in a low voice, "are you sure that's the best plan?"

"Do you have a better one?"

"We could take Connie straight to the police station. Sherri will know where the nearest women's shelter is located." There was a parking lot behind the municipal building and a back entrance. Spinner wouldn't see Connie getting out of the car and hurrying inside.

"That won't do."

"As soon as Hadley Spinner hears she's missing and is told about the visit we paid to Pilgrim Farm, he'll know exactly where to look for her."

"We have time. He's not going to stop picketing and go home for hours yet."

"Mom—"

"Don't argue with your mother." Vi was adamant. "We'll

go to your house, where we three can talk in private. After that, we'll decide what's best to do. "

Liss gave in. She could always phone Sherri and ask her to join them.

There was no direct entrance to Liss's house from the garage, but it did have a back door. From there, it was only a few steps to the small porch that led into Liss's kitchen. Their exit into the backyard went smoothly until Dan chose that moment to emerge from his workshop. Connie froze, a deer-in-the-headlights look in her eyes. For a moment, Liss was afraid that she might bolt and end up running straight into Hadley Spinner's line of sight.

"Go on in." Liss tossed her house keys to Vi and shooed the two women in that direction before making a beeline for her husband. "Don't say a word," she warned him as she steered him back into the shop and closed the door behind them.

Sawdust hung in the air, along with the smell of polyurethane. There wasn't a lot of room to move around, what with saws and worktables and walls lined with storage racks, but Liss needed only enough space to stand face-to-face with her husband. She placed her hands lightly on his forearms and waited until their eyes locked.

"It would be really really helpful if you didn't come into the house for the next hour or so."

"I was about to take a lunch break."

"Why don't you go to Patsy's? Treat yourself to something hot."

"Fine, but first tell me who that woman is and what she's doing here."

"It's complicated."

"Isn't it always?"

"I don't know any details yet. That's why Mom and I

need some time alone with her." She released Dan and turned to leave, but he caught up with her before she could go two steps.

"What *do* you know?"

"Dan—"

"We don't keep secrets from each other—remember?"

She braced herself for fallout, but she stopped trying to evade his questions. "Mom and I went out to Pilgrim Farm because Spinner was accounted for. He's today's one-man picket line." She'd caught a glimpse of him just before she turned into her driveway. "Connie hid in the car before we left. It's obvious she wants our help, but she's a little gun-shy. She'll be more at ease if there are only other women in the house."

"I don't like this, Liss."

"It will be okay. You'll see. Just let us talk to her and then we'll call Sherri in."

"You're sure Spinner didn't spot her?"

"Positive."

He didn't look happy about the situation, but he promised to give them time alone with Connie. "Just be careful," he warned. "Lock the door after you go inside. Spinner's already got a grudge against us. It wouldn't take much to send him over the edge."

"The longer he stays away from Pilgrim Farm, the longer we'll have before he finds out that one of his flock has flown the coop." She met Dan's worried gaze. "I'll get her away from here as soon as I can. I promise. But I want to hear what she has to say first."

Dan's arm went around her and she rested her head against his chest. "Here's hoping she'll know something that will help the police find Jasper's killer." He kissed the tip of her nose before releasing her. "For luck."

Liss slipped out of the workshop and trotted across a small expanse of grass. In the kitchen, she found Connie and Vi at the table with cups of tea in front of them, but Connie wasn't drinking hers. She was sobbing uncontrollably while Vi patted her shoulder and murmured words of comfort.

The tears continued for the next quarter of an hour, until Liss was sorely tempted to administer that time-honored cure for hysteria, the slap to the face.

"Connie, you have to calm down. You'll make yourself sick if you keep this up." It was only the twentieth repetition of words to that effect. It didn't work any better than it had the last nineteen times.

"I think I know what might work," Vi said. "Come with me, Connie. No, Liss. You stay here."

Connie was weaving a bit as they headed into the hallway that led to the living room and the front door. When Liss heard them climb the stairs to the second floor, she got up and busied herself clearing away the teacups and starting a pot of coffee. Even if no one else wanted any, *she* was in desperate need of a jolt of caffeine to stimulate her brain cells. She had no idea what her mother was up to, but at this point she welcomed anything that would put an end to Connie's pitiful weeping.

When they returned, Connie's eyes were dry and she was smiling. Well, why not? For the first time in years, she was wearing something other than Pilgrim-sanctioned attire. Liss's sweatpants were a little snug on her but one of her sweatshirts—moss green in color with flowers on the front—fit perfectly. Then Liss noticed what else had changed.

"You cut your hair," she blurted.

At Pilgrim Farm those gray-streaked brown locks had

been pulled back into a tight bun. Now they were short and sassy, framing her face in a way that flattered her features.

"Your mother did it. She . . . freed me."

Vi looked smug.

"I suppose you have questions," Connie said, taking a seat, "but if it's Jasper's death you want to know about, I'm not sure how much help I can be. I never left the farm that day."

"Someone did. She was seen in town." Liss filled three mugs with coffee and carried them to the table.

The bewildered expression on Connie's face convinced Liss that she didn't have a clue who it might have been. "Only the men were permitted to take part in the demonstration."

"You didn't notice that one of the other women was missing for a while?"

"We all had chores that kept us busy."

Liss let that aspect of the mystery go . . . for the moment. "When Jasper didn't come home with the other men, didn't anyone think that was strange?"

"He usually came in last. It was his responsibility to do the final check on the livestock and make certain the perimeter was secure."

"You make Pilgrim Farm sound like an armed camp."

When Connie didn't respond to that comment, Liss felt a chill streak up her spine.

She cleared her throat. "I don't know how many vehicles you have, but to transport eight men you'd need more than one. Didn't the others who shared a ride with Jasper wonder where he was?"

Connie shook her head. "Most of the men rode in the back of the truck. Jasper took the old Beetle. It barely runs, but it would have gotten him there and back again."

Riding in an open truck bed was not the safest way to travel. Liss wasn't even sure it was legal, but that was beside the point. "So no one had any idea that there was anything wrong until the police arrived to notify Miranda that Hadley had been murdered and they discovered that he was alive and Jasper was missing?"

Connie's mug landed with a thump on the table, sloshing coffee over the side. Her face drained of color. "I don't understand. Are you telling me that they thought the murdered man was Hadley?"

"You didn't know?"

Connie shook her head, a lost look in her eyes.

"Connie. Connie!" Liss waited until the other woman focused on her once more. "This is important. It's likely Jasper was killed because someone mistook him for Hadley. Who would want Hadley dead?"

"Anyone who knew him!" She clapped both hands over her mouth. Above them, wide, terrified eyes stared at Liss and her mother.

"Why do you say that?" Vi asked in a coaxing tone of voice.

"He . . . he . . . oh, I can't explain it. You wouldn't understand."

"Try us," Liss suggested. "Go back to the beginning. How did you end up married to George?"

"We met at the Common Ground Fair."

Liss nodded encouragement. The annual event featured crafters, livestock, and old-time fair attractions—no Ferris wheels or bumper cars need apply.

"I was into all that back-to-the-land stuff. I'd even taught myself how to weave. When George described the lifestyle at Pilgrim Farm, it sounded ideal, and when I met Mr. Spinner—Hadley—I thought I'd died and gone to Heaven."

Liss stared at her, convinced that she was serious but unable to believe that anyone could be taken in by such a blowhard.

"Oh, I know what you're thinking." A faint smile made the corners of Connie's mouth turn up. "Look at him now. But back then he was a different man. He was . . . inspirational. His enthusiasm carried you along, even if you weren't too certain what it was he was talking about. When he suggested George and I marry, it seemed like the most natural thing in the world to agree. I wasn't giving up my freedom. I was becoming part of a greater whole."

"Didn't the small-mindedness turn you off? The man's a bigot."

"His preaching was more inclusive back then. The change to what he's like now came gradually." She gave a short, humorless laugh. "So gradually that we didn't notice, not at first. Not for a long time. The rules got stricter. Mr. Spinner's suspicion of outsiders grew stronger. The New Age Pilgrims had been set up as a religion for the tax advantages, but there was never much preaching, not at the beginning. Then Mr. Spinner started reading the Bible and picking out verses that went along with what he wanted us to believe. He had his own interpretation of them, and that's the one we had to accept. That's when I started to get worried. And just lately, there have been numerous occasions when he's spouted opinions that make no sense. That's what makes me wonder if he could be suffering from some sort of mental disorder."

"Is anyone else worried about the same thing?" Liss asked.

"If they are, they haven't dared speak of it. Over the last year or so, Mr. Spinner's control over every aspect of our lives has gotten tighter and tighter. Early on, I welcomed having someone else make decisions for me. I liked that there were rules. I felt looked after. Loved. But lately . . ."

As her voice trailed off, an aura of despair seemed to settle over her. A single tear rolled down one cheek.

"You've been afraid," Vi said in her most sympathetic voice, one Liss had rarely heard from her mother, "but today you took the risk and ran away. Why?"

"It was what you said to Mistress Spinner. About Susan."

When she fell silent again, Liss moved to kneel beside Connie's chair. She took both of her hands in her own. "My aunt, Margaret Boyd, was Susan's friend. She told us that Susan spoke of you, and also of Diana and George. Were you the one who encouraged her to leave?"

Looking more sunk in misery than ever, Connie nodded. "She tried to leave and she died."

Liss felt her stomach muscles clench. "Died how?"

"Drowned."

"Did she . . . have help?"

"She took her own life," Connie whispered. "Mr. Spinner said the devil tempted her, first to run away and then to do herself harm."

Even twelve years ago, Hadley Spinner had been twisting Scripture to his own ends. The paranoia and the vindictiveness might be more recent manifestations of his ego, but it sounded to Liss as if the man's personality had always been warped. Whatever charisma he'd possessed hadn't been the harmless, crush-on-a-rock-star variety. He'd deliberately set out to create his own little kingdom full of devoted subjects.

Liss hardly considered herself an expert on mesmerism or brainwashing or Stockholm syndrome, but she'd bet good money that Spinner was. Combine that with a natural talent for manipulating others and he'd have all the tools he needed to convince his followers to let him make all their decisions for them, especially if they came from troubled backgrounds, or had issues with self-esteem, or, like Connie, had already been trying to escape from the modern world.

She squeezed Connie's hands. "Do you believe that? That Susan took her own life rather than simply walk away from life at Pilgrim Farm?"

"It's hard to leave when you have nowhere to go."

"Susan had people willing to help her. She could have left. What pulled her back?"

Connie fell silent.

"She was afraid of Hadley Spinner, wasn't she? Afraid of what he'd do if he caught up with her." And in a sudden burst of certainty, Liss added, "Afraid of what he might do to those who helped her?"

"He took her back," Connie whispered.

"And what happens if Spinner finds you here?" Vi asked.

Connie's voice shook as she answered, but she sounded certain that she spoke the truth. "He'll take me back."

"And then? Would you be . . . punished?"

Connie began to weep again, quietly this time. Her answer came out in fits and starts mingled with tears. "It's the shame I wouldn't be able to bear. The shunning. I think I might end up killing myself, just as Susan did."

A thunderous knocking at the front door interrupted them before either Liss or Vi could react to Connie's admission. Vi's hand went to her heart. Connie blanched. Liss was halfway to her feet when the second barrage began, this time accompanied by a shouted demand.

"Come out, Mistress Gerard!" Hadley Spinner bellowed. "I am here to take you home."

Chapter Thirteen

"Is the door locked?" Vi whispered.

Momentarily stunned into silence, Liss could only nod. How did Spinner know Connie was with them?

The scrape of a chair being pushed away from the table jerked her attention back to her guest. Connie was already on her feet. "I have to obey. It will be worse for everyone if I don't. You don't deserve his wrath for helping me."

By the time she stopped speaking, her voice was shaking so badly that her final words were difficult to understand, but Liss caught the gist of what she was saying and was appalled.

"Don't go. He can't force you to return."

Now that Connie's tears had all been spent, she seemed to have gained a new strength of purpose, but it was directed in what Liss considered to be the entirely wrong direction. She'd reached the entrance to the hall when the rattle of Dan's key at the back door made all three women jump.

He burst into the room, the expression on his face so fierce that even Liss felt a moment's anxiety. Connie shrieked and brought up her arms to protect her face, giving Vi the chance to catch up with her. She was too petite to forcibly restrain the other woman, but she could slip past Connie to block her path to the hallway.

Dan tucked the cell phone he carried in one hand back into his pocket before turning to lock the door behind him. Then, ignoring everyone else, he went straight to Liss's side and placed both hands on her upper arms, holding her a little apart, as if to assure himself she was unharmed. The touch of his fingers, even through layers of cloth, instantly made her feel more secure.

"I called Sherri," he said. "She should be here any minute."

"How did you—?"

"I've been keeping an eye on Spinner since you left the workshop. A couple of minutes ago, he got a phone call."

"*Spinner* has a cell phone? So much for living by that 'old things are best' rule."

"Focus, Liss. Someone tipped him off about your visit to Pilgrim Farm and the fact that one of the lavender ladies was missing. It didn't take him long to put two and two together."

Out of the corner of her eye, she saw her mother urge Connie to sit, but the other woman looked ready to bolt at the drop of a hat. She plucked at her borrowed clothing and fussed with her shorn locks, clearly regretting these acts of rebellion.

The pounding at the front door had let up just after Dan's arrival, but it now resumed with greater force.

"How strong is that wood?" Liss asked.

"Strong enough." The lines around Dan's molasses-colored eyes crinkled as he flashed her a quick grin. "Aren't you glad you married a master carpenter?"

At the sound of glass shattering, they broke apart.

Liss gasped as her mother reached for her tote bag and calmly pulled out the pink gun. "Put that away!"

Vi huffed out an exasperated breath. She returned the weapon to the tote, but she kept the bag close at hand.

"Stay here," Dan ordered, and started toward the front of the house.

"Not a chance." She was right at his heels when he reached the living room.

It was a window that had been broken. Spinner had thrust one hand through the jagged hole and was fumbling for the catch, trying to open it.

"Get off my porch, Spinner," Dan shouted. "You're the one who's trespassing now."

The hand abruptly withdrew, leaving behind a smear of blood that made Liss's stomach twist. Then she got her first good look at Hadley Spinner's face. With a gasp of alarm, she recoiled.

His eyes were wide and wild. Spittle clung to the corners of his mouth. His beard was snarled, and the hair on his head stood up in tufts, as if he'd been tugging on it. He looked demented and his words made him seem even more so.

"Send her out!" Spinner bellowed. "You've no call to keep that woman against her will!"

"Your grasp on reality is slipping, Spinner," Dan said. "You're the one she's trying to escape."

"Lies! All lies!" He took a threatening step toward the window, making Liss fear that he meant to throw himself through it.

When Dan tensed in preparation for advancing on the intruder, Liss grabbed his arm in an attempt to hold him back. She was in favor of defending their home, but she was not at all certain he could win a fistfight with a madman.

Before anyone could make another move, two uniformed officers, one in the blue of the local police department and the other wearing a deputy sheriff's brown, appeared at the foot of the porch steps.

"That's enough, Mr. Spinner," Sherri said. "You're already in enough trouble."

With excruciating slowness, Spinner turned away from the window.

Ignoring the broken glass that crunched under her feet, Liss stepped closer, anxious not to miss anything. Sherri stood with her hands on hips—the right one close enough to her holster to draw her gun. She was armed with a Taser, too, and pepper spray. She could make use of whatever degree of force the situation called for.

The deputy beside her was her husband and if the fierce scowl on Pete Campbell's face was anything to go by, he'd tackle Spinner in a heartbeat if he tried anything funny. The Pilgrim leader was burly and hardened by farm work, but Pete had the build of a linebacker and was not only younger but had kept himself in shape by competing in the highland games.

Spinner drew himself up to his full height, towering over Sherri as she approached him, but he was wily enough to know that the odds were against him. He abandoned the tactic of shouting belligerently and instead asked a question in a voice that sounded nearly normal. "Is there a problem, Officer?"

Even viewed from the back, even with his hair wild and his clothes disheveled, Spinner's body language sent the message that here was a man who was humble yet compelling. A hint of that charisma everyone kept talking about came through, muted and dulled by age and by Liss's awareness of the kind of man he really was, but still surprisingly po-

tent. If he'd been thirty years younger and hadn't just tried
to break into her house, she might almost believe him capable of sweet-talking Sherri into letting him off with a
warning.

"Turn around and put your hands behind your back,"
the chief of police ordered.

Pete backed up Sherri's authority by giving Spinner a little shove when he was slow to obey. The clink of the handcuffs as he snapped them closed had Liss breathing easier,
but her relief was short-lived.

Since Spinner was once more facing the window, she
found herself staring directly into eyes that blazed with ha-
tred. She hastily backed away. Dan did the same, slinging
a protective arm around her shoulders as he did so.

It should have calmed her to watch Pete lead Spinner
away. Instead the sight brought home to her just how
much danger they'd been in. They might not be out of the
woods yet. Spinner had followers. And what would happen when he got out of jail?

Sherri leaned in to examine the damage to the window-
pane. Peering through the hole, she called out to them,
"Everyone okay?"

Liss nodded. Dan muttered something profane.

"Uh-huh. I don't think I'll quote you on that. Do you
want to press charges?"

"Damned straight I do." Dan vibrated with barely suppressed anger.

Turning in his arms, Liss brought one hand up to his
cheek. "That might make things worse."

He sent her an incredulous look.

"He didn't insist that you be arrested for attacking
him," Liss reminded him, "but he could change his
mind."

"Liss—"

Her fingers moved to his lips. "No. Listen to me. We need to think about Connie's safety, too."

"She's safest with him in jail."

"And when he gets out?"

"Uh, guys?" Sherri still stood on the other side of the window. "You want to let me in? I need to take statements from you two and anyone else in the house. I have a feeling that there's a lot about this situation that I don't know."

"Can you still lock him up if I don't press charges?" Dan asked.

"Sure. For a little while. Disturbing the peace will work. I can throw in vandalism for good measure."

Liss managed a faint smile. "Sounds like a plan to me. I'll get the door."

Once Sherri had made arrangements for Pete to take Spinner to the county jail in Fallstown, she came inside and was introduced to Connie Gerard. The runaway Pilgrim listened without comment while Liss, Dan, and Vi brought Sherri up to speed on the reason Spinner had been trying to break into the house.

"I take it you don't want to return to Pilgrim Farm?" Sherri asked.

Connie answered with a vigorous negative shake of her head.

"Okay, then. Hadley Spinner can't make you do anything you don't want to do. Neither can anyone else."

"Hadley's the one she's afraid of," Vi put in. She'd been surprisingly quiet, remaining seated at the kitchen table with Connie. The pink gun was nowhere in sight.

"At a guess, it'll be Monday before a judge sets bail.

You don't need to worry about him over the weekend, but what about your husband?"

Connie stared down at her clasped hands and said nothing.

"Connie?" Liss prompted her. "Will George come looking for you?"

"I don't know." The words were so softly spoken that Liss had to lean in close in order to catch them.

"Was he with the rest of the men who were working in the woodlot?" Wherever that was, Liss didn't imagine that it was too far from the house. Miranda had probably sent word to them as soon as she realized that Connie was gone.

Again, Connie shook her head. "Mr. Spinner sent George to the hotel."

"Picket number two," Sherri murmured. "There's usually a man in front of the entrance to The Spruces at the same times when someone is demonstrating in the town square. Does George have a cell phone?"

"No. Only Mr. Spinner is permitted one."

"How nice for him." Vi's sarcastic comment amused her daughter, even though this was no laughing matter.

"What is Spinner afraid of?" Liss asked Connie. "What does he think you're going to tell us?"

Startled, Connie's head shot up. Her wide-set brown eyes met Liss's blue-green gaze. "You're mistaken. I can't hurt him or anyone else. I don't know anything."

"You may know more than you think you do," Sherri said.

Even with all four of them lobbing questions at her, Connie couldn't come up with one shred of evidence against the founder of the New Age Pilgrims. She appeared to know nothing more than she'd already told Liss and Vi. About the murder, she knew even less.

"Jasper was stabbed to death? I thought someone shot him." Connie's face pruned up in what appeared to be her struggle to make sense of what she was hearing. "How could anyone confuse Jasper and Hadley if they were close enough to use a knife?"

"Same beard. Same clothing." Liss didn't think it was a stretch for someone to be confused. "And he was stabbed in the back."

"Even so," Connie insisted, "the two men were very different."

"Only, I think, to people who lived and worked with them both on a daily basis." Sherri didn't sound pleased by that conclusion.

Neither was Liss. If the other Pilgrims were ruled out, then someone from town had to be the murderer. Someone who *could* mistake one for the other. Someone who did not know either man well enough to tell them apart.

Sherri closed her notebook and glanced at each of them in turn. "Since Connie isn't going back to Pilgrim Farm, she needs a safe place to stay."

"What about the women's shelter down to Fallstown? Or do you have to be battered by your spouse to qualify to hide out there?" If Connie was to be believed, Spinner might play mind games with his followers, but he did not resort to corporal punishment.

Before Sherri could answer, Vi cut in. "Don't be absurd, Liss. Connie will come home with me. Mac and I have a lovely guest room all set up." She placed one hand over Connie's. "You'll like it on the water. It's remote and quiet."

Ledge Lake was also a long way from town and very isolated at this time of year. With most of the other camps closed up until spring, Liss's parents had no close neighbors to rely on in an emergency. "Are you sure about this, Mom?"

"We'll be fine. No one will think to look for Connie at our place, and once she has new clothes and puts on a little makeup, her own husband won't be able to recognize her."

Connie looked intrigued by the notion.

"Now, since you picked me up this morning," Vi continued, "I think it would be best if Dan took your car to drive us out there. Connie can duck down in the back seat, as she did earlier, until we're clear of the village, just in case someone else is watching."

Violet MacCrimmon was a force of nature once she got an idea into her head. No one argued with her for long. Within a quarter of an hour, she and Connie and Dan left for Ledge Lake.

Sherri lingered, the furrow in her brow suggesting that she had something on her mind.

"You may as well spit it out." Liss poured two fresh cups of coffee and carried them to the table, along with a package of ginger snaps.

"Things do not look good for Margaret." Sherri sipped at her coffee and ate one of the cookies. "You understand that I'm not supposed to tell you any of this?"

Liss nodded and waited while her friend fought a brief battle with herself. Sherri risked losing her job if she shared too much information.

"They found one of Margaret's fingerprints on the murder weapon."

"Only Margaret's?"

"I know what you're going to say. It was her knife, so of course her fingerprints would be on it, and of course the real killer would have worn gloves."

"Well, duh."

"But that fingerprint was enough for the police to get their search warrant. The murder weapon was definitely part of the set they found in Margaret's kitchen."

"Someone came in while she was out with the dogs and stole it."

"There's no proof of that."

"But why would Margaret kill either Hadley or Jasper? The only possible motive is a tad dated—twelve years and change."

Sherri leaned across the table, her eyes betraying just how worried she was. "Liss, someone saw Margaret *confront* one of the Spinners in the town square during the demonstration."

"So she took the dogs for a walk and encountered him. They had words. No big deal."

Sherri shook her head. "It was described as a heated argument."

Clenching both hands around her coffee mug, Liss stared at the rapidly cooling liquid and tried to marshal an argument. This was not good, but she was sure there was an explanation that didn't involve her aunt wielding a boning knife.

"Who was it that saw Margaret?"

"That I don't know, but whoever it was, he or she was apparently close enough to the two of them to hear how angry Margaret sounded."

Liss made an impatient gesture. "I can see Margaret quarreling with Hadley—"

"Or Jasper."

"Or Jasper, but there is no way she went back to her place afterward, grabbed one of her own knives, lurked in the town square until she saw an opportunity, and then stabbed him in the back."

"I don't believe it happened that way, either, but the district attorney may."

"Don't the police have any other suspects?"

"Not good ones, and you aren't going to like pinning the crime on one of them any better."

Liss sighed. "They're looking at the people who clashed with Hadley Spinner shortly before Jasper was murdered."

"That's right," Sherri said. "So take your pick—if not Margaret, then you're left with Stu Burroughs . . . or with Dan."

When Sherri had gone, Liss spent a few minutes clearing the table and then set off for the Emporium, where her father had ended up holding the fort for the entire day. From his cheerful greeting, she surmised that he had not noticed the activity at her house. She debated how much to tell him and decided to ease into the subject.

"I feel guilty imposing on you to work like this," Liss said. "You're supposed to be retired."

Her father shrugged and continued closing out the cash register. "To tell you the truth, I'm getting a kick out of it. It's just like old times. Besides, I scored a real triumph this afternoon. I sold that hideously overpriced crystal Loch Ness Monster you've had in stock for at least five years."

Liss's eyes widened. That purchase had been one of her most expensive mistakes. She'd thought she'd be stuck with it forever. "I'm impressed, Dad. You can work for me anytime."

"Any day but tomorrow." He mimed playing the bagpipe, then chuckled at her blank look. "Parade in Falls-town? Veterans Day? Any of that ring a bell?"

Liss felt even worse than she had at the start of their conversation. She'd completely forgotten that her father had rejoined his old bagpipe band after moving back to Maine. "That sounds like fun. I wish I could come and cheer you on, but—"

"—somebody's got to mind the store. No problem."

She turned the sign on the door from OPEN to CLOSED, glancing out at the town square as she did so. People were walking there, but none of them carried signs warning prospective customers away from Moosetookalook Scottish Emporium or Carrabassett County Wood Crafts. She secured the dead bolt and turned back to her father.

"Mom and I had an interesting day. . . ."

When Mac MacCrimmon left for home a short time later, sending Liss a wave as he pulled out of the driveway between the Emporium and Stu's Ski Shop, he had been forewarned about the guest his wife had invited to stay with them and had heard the highlights of Hadley Spinner's reaction to Connie's departure from Pilgrim Farm. He was not a happy camper, but Liss felt certain her mother would convince him to let the lavender lady stay. He rarely quarreled with her. When he did, she usually won the argument.

Liss continued to have mixed feelings about Connie's hiding place. Spinner obviously had a temper. She wasn't sure about the others at the farm, but the thought of six burly men descending on the camp at Ledge Lake was enough to make her break out in a sweat. She checked the locks one last time before heading for the stairs that led up to her aunt's apartment.

Once she'd run the usual gamut of excited dogs and of-

fers of tea, Liss persuaded Margaret to sit down and answer a few more questions. They pulled out adjacent
stools at the island in the middle of the kitchen and settled
in for a heart-to-heart talk. Liss spoke first.

"You didn't tell me you argued with Hadley Spinner on
the day of the demonstration." She could not quite keep
the accusing tone out of her voice.

"I didn't."

"You were seen."

"I mean it wasn't Hadley I had words with. It was
Jasper."

"All the more reason why you should have mentioned
your quarrel. Did you tell the police about it?"

"They didn't ask and I didn't volunteer the information. Of course, at that point, Gordon Tandy was still letting everyone believe that Hadley was the one who'd been
killed, so it didn't seem relevant."

"And if he had asked you about Jasper?"

Margaret shrugged. "I'd have mentioned that we had
words. Probably. It wasn't a big deal. I was angry that the
Pilgrims and their newfound pals were preventing me
from taking the dogs for their usual walk in the town
square." She reached down to tickle Dondi behind one ear.
"Then I decided that I wasn't going to let a bunch of ya-
hoos interfere with my routine and we went over there
anyway. I had no intention of speaking to any of the
demonstrators, but Jasper planted himself in front of me,
waving his sign around and scaring the Scotties."

As if Dandy knew they were talking about her and her
brother, she stood on her hind legs and waved her front
paws in the air. Liss rewarded her performance with one of
the dog yummies Margaret kept in a small ceramic dish on
the island.

"He wasn't the one with the 'prevert' sign, was he?" She gave a second treat to Dondi, even though he'd done nothing more adorable than sit beside her stool and look cute.

"No. This one had Bible verses. Hypocrite. The man didn't have a religious bone in his body. He just liked having an excuse to tell his wife that she was inferior to him because God made Eve from Adam's rib."

Liss could imagine what long-term exposure to such a mindset would do to a person. Like most women, she'd had men try to make her think less of herself just because she was female, but until she encountered the Pilgrims, she'd never truly appreciated how completely cowed a woman could become if she allowed herself to be controlled by a domineering man. Hadley Spinner undoubtedly preached that male supremacy was the natural order of things.

"Did Susan believe that?" she asked her aunt.

"I don't know. What I do know is that when she first met Jasper she was flattered by the attentions of an attractive older man. He wasn't bad looking before he grew that ghastly beard. And you have to understand the circumstances. Susan's father died right after he sold the family home to Hadley. Once Miranda decided to marry him, Susan didn't feel she had many choices. She didn't want to stick around as a third wheel. Oh, I know you'll say that she could have left and started fresh somewhere else, but she'd never been out of Carrabassett County. The world beyond scared her. When Jasper set himself to courting her, she thought marrying him would be the ideal solution. She'd get to stay in her home, but she'd have a husband of her own rather than being Hadley and Miranda's dependent. Sadly, marriage is the height of ambition for some girls, even these days."

"Obviously things didn't work out quite as she'd hoped."

Even after so many years, Margaret still grieved for her friend. Liss could see the sadness and the regret in her aunt's eyes. "Poor kid," Margaret murmured. "She didn't have a clue what she was getting into. Of course, Hadley's opinions weren't quite as peculiar to start with. Those took time to develop. But even at the start, he was an odd duck. What sense did it make for four men from away to move to the middle of nowhere and take up farming on a piece of land that hadn't produced a decent crop in decades?"

Liss had no answer for her, so she asked another question of her own. "What did Susan tell you about Connie Gerard?"

Margaret toyed with the revolving tray that held a sugar bowl, a set of salt and pepper shakers shaped like lobsters, and a seven-day pill case. "Why are you interested in Connie?"

"She's left the New Age Pilgrims." Liss provided her aunt with a short version of the day's adventures.

Too restless to remain still, Margaret slid off the stool and walked to the windowsill where she grew a few herbs for teas and to use in cooking. She plucked several leaves from one of them—some kind of mint by the smell that drifted Liss's way—and held it to her nose, as if she hoped the scent would soothe her. More effective was the way both Scotties trotted over to her to bump their heads against her legs until she squatted down to cuddle them.

"It was a long time ago," she said from her crouch. "I don't see how anything Susan told me can be relevant now."

"I don't know how it can be, either, but if the only association you've had with the Pilgrims goes back to the time you spent with her, then there must be a connection. Think about it, Margaret. Someone deliberately came into your apartment, took one of your knives, and used it to kill a man. Whoever did that *wanted* you to be blamed. Unless someone else has a huge grudge against you, it must have been one of the people in town that day."

"That makes no sense. The only Pilgrim I clashed with was Jasper, and he certainly didn't murder himself."

"But in the past you accused all of them of causing Susan's death. Maybe someone took that personally." She paused, thinking about what she'd just said. "There was a Pilgrim woman in town that day. I thought it was Anna, the lavender lady who cleans for Audrey Greenwood, but she denied it. Now I'm wondering if it could have been Connie."

At times, sitting in Liss's kitchen, she hadn't seemed quite sane. She'd burst into tears far too easily. She'd answered some questions, but she'd been downright evasive when it came to others. She had clearly been the victim of psychological abuse, but that didn't mean she couldn't commit a crime. Liss heartily wished that she'd insisted on sending Connie to the local women's shelter. She didn't think her parents were in any danger from their house guest, but she'd have felt a lot better if Connie was staying somewhere else.

"I suppose," Margaret said, "that if Connie was in town last Saturday, she could have killed Jasper, but why would she? And why would she use my knife to commit the crime? I've never even met the woman."

"Connie and Susan were friends. She told me that she knew you tried to help her, but what if she thinks you didn't do enough? Maybe she's held you responsible all this time for Susan's decision to kill herself."

Margaret had gone pale, but she recovered quickly.

"Liss, all that happened a dozen years ago! And even if my friendship with Susan somehow gave Connie, or anyone else, a twisted reason to implicate me, why kill Jasper at the demonstration? If she wanted to punish him for his part in what happened to Susan, surely she'd have found an opportunity to do so long before this."

"Unless, despite everyone's claim that the other Pilgrims could tell Jasper and Hadley apart, she *did* mistake one for the other."

Margaret threw both hands up in the air. "And why, pray tell, would she want to kill *Hadley?*"

"Because she was fed up with his bullying? Because she wanted to escape? Maybe she hid in the back of my car because she's terrified that he's figured that out."

"It's a nice theory, Liss, but it's full of holes. I suppose I can accept that she might have wanted to kill Hadley. Who didn't? But why go out of her way to make me look guilty? There's no earthly reason why she'd steal one of my knives to use in the crime."

"Well, *someone* set you up. Think back, Margaret. The key must be out at Pilgrim Farm. Anything else makes even less sense. Did you ever go out there back when you were friends with Susan?"

"Only once. I didn't like what I saw. It still baffles me why an otherwise intelligent woman would submit to being treated that way. The women were *allowed* to do housekeeping and sewing and cooking and the like, but other than when they were hanging out the washing, they scarcely got a breath of fresh air. Outdoor work was for the menfolk. I sometimes thought that was what bothered Susan most, that she only left the house when she was sent out to earn money by cleaning for other people."

"If her movements were that restricted, how did you two ever strike up a friendship?"

"How do you think? I hired her to clean the apartment."

"I thought the lavender ladies always worked in pairs."

"Not in the old days when there were fewer Pilgrims. To tell you the truth, I have a feeling that rule was put in place *because* I befriended Susan. I knew who she was before that, of course, since she and her sister were local girls."

"What about the other Pilgrims? Did Susan ever say where they came from?"

Margaret frowned, trying to remember. After a moment, she rummaged in a drawer for a notepad and pencil and returned with them to the kitchen island. Liss scooted her stool closer so she could see what her aunt was writing.

"Right from the start, they were almost all couples out there. Two by two, like the animals on Noah's Ark." Margaret's mouth puckered into a moue of distaste. "That never made any sense to me, especially after Susan told me that the women all slept in the house while the men bunked in another building."

"Makes you wonder how they ended up with a child."

Holding her pencil in midair, Margaret's hand froze. "There's a *child* out there?"

"Only one that I saw. She's named Kimmy and belongs to Laurel Miller."

"Solomon Miller. *That's* the husband's name." She'd written "Hadley and Miranda Spinner" and "Jasper and Susan Spinner" on the first two lines and now added "Solomon and Laurel Miller" on a third.

"Jasper remarried. His widow's name is Chloe."

Margaret added her to the list. "The other people Susan talked about were Connie and George Gerard and Diana . . .

Carter? No, Collins. I don't remember her husband's name."
She added them to her list. "I think that's everyone who was
at Pilgrim Farm twelve years ago."

"What about Charles Knapp? I thought Hadley, Jasper,
George, and Charles were the original four who founded
the group."

"I'd forgotten about Charles." She added his name. "He
was the exception to the rule. He was still single. Susan told
me that he fell in love with a Moosetookalook girl, but her
family broke it up. She was smart, whoever she was, to let
wiser heads prevail."

Mary Ruskin, Liss thought, but she didn't enlighten her
aunt. Mary's past was not her secret to share.

"I suppose he's married by now," Margaret said.

"His wife is that Anna I told you about, the one who
cleans for Audrey." Liss repeated what Anna had told her
about meeting Charles and marrying him, even though he
was still a virtual stranger.

Margaret's expression was grim as she wrote down
Anna's name. "Foolish, foolish girl. I can't help but feel sorry
for her. Who else is out there?"

"Polly Callahan and Denise Fontaine are the other
women Mom and I met at Pilgrim Farm this morning. I
don't know their husbands' names."

Margaret added them to her list and tallied up the en-
tries. "It looks like we've identified all eight couples, but
what good does that do us? I don't buy your theory about
blaming me for Susan's death and I can't think of any
other reason why one of them would try to frame me for
murder. I've never even met most of them."

Liss toyed with the pencil Margaret had abandoned.
"Why embrace this . . . lifestyle in the first place? I guess I
can understand why Miranda and Susan married Hadley

and Jasper after they bought the family farm, but why did the others join them? Where did they come from?"

"And were they couples before they arrived at Pilgrim Farm, or did Spinner insist they marry in order to stay?"

The idea of Hadley Spinner as matchmaker made Liss shudder. It wasn't that arranged marriages were unheard of. She knew of a case or two where the children of the rich and famous had married to combine their families' fortunes and things hadn't turned out too badly, but she couldn't think of a single reason why any sensible woman would agree to wed a stranger when all she'd get out of it was a hardscrabble life on a farm in rural Maine.

"You know," Margaret said. "If it hadn't been for the odd clothing and the fact that they established themselves as a religious group, I'd never have thought twice about how peculiar the New Age Pilgrims are. It was flat-out nosiness that made me offer Susan that first cup of tea when she came to work for me. The sympathy only developed after she trusted me enough to share confidences."

"Did you deliberately try to persuade her to assert herself?"

Margaret shrugged. "I just told her what I thought. As far as I could tell, she was already coming around to my point of view. It was obvious that she'd been brainwashed. She described Spinner's effect on her. When he spoke, she said she believed every word that came out of his mouth, but when she was away from his influence, away from Pilgrim Farm, doubt started to creep in."

"Brainwashing? You really think that's how he controls everyone?"

"I do. After Susan died, I did some reading about cults and why they appeal to people. It's a complex subject, but the forcefulness of the leader seems to be the key. It doesn't appear to matter if that leader is a terrible, wrong-headed person. Someone who is charismatic enough, and convinced that he's in the right, is likely to attract a devoted following. Once they are persuaded that he can do no wrong, it is almost impossible to get them to listen to any other opinion."

Chapter Fourteen

Liss passed an unquiet evening and a restless night after she left Margaret's apartment. Dan was filling in at the hotel, so she was alone until after midnight. She jumped at every odd sound, until even the two cats were giving her a wide berth.

The possibility that Connie had killed Jasper nagged at her, but her aunt was right. That theory made no more sense than thinking Margaret was guilty. There was no reason to rush out to Ledge Lake to confront the Pilgrim woman, but Liss did phone her mother twice during the evening. Both times, Vi reported that Connie was asleep.

"Let her be," she insisted. "Talk to her when she's rested."

The next day was Saturday. Just one week had passed since the demonstration . . . and the murder. As Liss walked to the Emporium, she scanned the town square, relieved when she saw not a single picket sign. With Hadley Spinner in jail, someone might show up to take his place, but it was equally possible that the protest would fall apart without its leader.

This proved to be the case, and Liss's day passed uneventfully.

She had time to brood.

As soon as she closed up shop, she made a quick stop at home before heading for her parents' cottage. It didn't bother her that Dan opted to watch a football game on television rather than pay a visit to his mother-in-law. She didn't need backup. She was just going to have a little chat with Connie Gerard.

The moment she walked in the door, she spotted Connie through the big windows that overlooked the lake. She was bundled up in a wool coat and sat, shoulders hunched, in one of the Adirondack chairs on the deck, a shadowy figure illuminated only by what light spilled out from the living room.

"How's she doing?" Liss asked.

"She's settling in," Vi said, "and I think she's beginning to feel safe. It helped that Sherri came out earlier today and assured her that Spinner is still in jail."

"Sherri was here?"

Liss was not surprised that her friend had talked to Connie, but she was a little miffed that she hadn't stopped by the Emporium afterward to fill her in on that conversation. As chief of police, Sherri had no obligation to keep the general public informed. In fact, the responsibilities of her job usually inclined her to be closemouthed about the situation with everyone . . . but that didn't ordinarily stop her from using Liss as a sounding board.

"I think that's why Connie's so quiet now," Vi continued. "Sherri asked her a lot of questions. Some of them seemed to confuse her."

"So nothing new?"

"Only that Benny Callahan is the Pilgrim who can't spell."

Liss ran an imaginary finger down the list in her head. She'd met Benny's wife, Polly Callahan, but try as she might, to call up an image, nothing emerged but the blurry memory of a nondescript woman in a floor-length lavender dress.

"Do you think Connie will open up to me?"

Vi shrugged. "All I can tell you is that the motherly approach didn't work."

"The . . . motherly approach?" Liss couldn't help but sound skeptical. "What, exactly, would that be?"

"You know. Interest. Support. Sympathy and . . ." Her voice trailed off as she listened to her own words. "Oh, well, I can see now why that would fail. I haven't had any practice, have I?"

Liss marveled at the self-deprecating tone in her mother's voice. Could it be that Vi was more aware of her failings than Liss had realized? She hesitated to say anything, lest it be misinterpreted, but she suddenly found herself in a more cheerful frame of mind. Maybe there was hope for their mother-daughter relationship after all.

"On the other hand," Vi said, sounding a trifle defensive, "I was a pretty good teacher. I know how to deal with recalcitrant teenagers."

"Connie's not that young."

"She's closer to your age than mine. She was in her early twenties when she married George Gerard. Go talk to her. With luck, you'll get better results than I did. If we're going to prove that Margaret is innocent, we need to know everything Connie does about the people at Pilgrim Farm."

Liss had taken a step toward the deck when she realized that she hadn't heard a peep out of her father. "Wait a minute. Where's Dad?"

"He's not home yet," Vi said. "He was invited to a party after the parade with some of his old bagpiping pals. I don't expect to see him for quite a while yet."

So it's just the three of us, Liss thought as she slid the

glass door open and stepped outside. After the warmth of the interior, it seemed doubly cold on the deck and she was glad she hadn't removed her jacket or gloves. Late afternoon in Maine in mid-November, even when the day had been sunny, got downright nippy as soon as the sun set. Since twilight was already past and the moon had not yet risen, she moved cautiously across the wooden planks to make sure she didn't bump into any of the deck chairs or occasional tables.

Connie must have heard her approaching, but she didn't look up. Liss sat down in another of the Adirondack chairs. She squirmed a bit, trying to get comfortable. No cushions softened the hard wood and her legs were just the wrong length. To avoid ending up tipped back at an awkward angle, she perched on the front edge of the seat. Connie remained silent during these maneuvers. Liss gave her a few more seconds to say something, but by then it was obvious she didn't intend to open the conversation.

"I hear Chief Campbell talked to you today."

Liss's eyes had begun to adjust to the low level of light. She could see that Connie didn't shift her gaze from the blackness of lake and sky.

"She did."

"I hope that didn't upset you too much."

"I'll get over it."

Impatience, Liss's besetting sin, quickly vanquished her resolve to be subtle. "I don't get it, Connie. You seem to be an intelligent woman. How on earth did you end up at Pilgrim Farm?"

Connie's head turned in Liss's direction. Her words came out in a rush. "I was lonely. I thought nobody cared if I lived or died. I'd been drinking. A lot. I met George in a bar. He *wasn't* drinking."

No, Liss thought. *He was recruiting.*

"We talked. He told me about this wonderful place where he was living and invited me to come see for myself. It sounded like heaven." She gave a short, rueful laugh. "I was so grateful for the attention. So anxious for acceptance. It never dawned on me that Mr. Spinner was taking advantage of my insecurities. When he suggested that George and I marry, I didn't think twice about it, I just said yes. It wasn't until after the ceremony that I discovered I'd also vowed to follow all the passages in the Bible that require women to be subservient to men."

"I expect at least some of those were quoted out of context."

"They could have been. I had no way of knowing. I didn't have a religious upbringing and when Mr. Spinner insisted that he was the only one qualified to interpret the word of God, it didn't seem worth the effort to argue with him."

Since they appeared to be in agreement about what a mistake that had been, Liss moved on to another question. "How many Pilgrims were there when you joined them?" She wasn't certain this mattered, but the more she learned about the New Age Pilgrims, the better.

Connie didn't reply at once. When she did, she used her fingers to count. "Mr. Spinner," she said, "Mistress Spinner. The other Mr. Spinner. The other Mistress Spinner. Mr. Gerard and Mr. Knapp."

"Hadley, Miranda, Jasper, Susan, George, and Charles?"

"Yes."

"When did the others arrive?"

Connie shrugged. "Every once in a while one of the men would bring in someone new. They were all losers, just as I had been. A few of them stuck around, mostly because they didn't have anyplace better to go. Neither did I." Bitterness underscored the admission.

Liss tried to probe more deeply into their background, but Connie denied any knowledge of their lives before they came to Pilgrim Farm.

"We abandoned the past in exchange for a fresh start," she insisted. "If we once had relatives or other close ties, we never spoke of them."

"What about Chloe?" Aside from Anna, she was the most recent addition to their ranks. "Where did Jasper find her?"

She expected to hear more of the same, but Connie surprised her. "She was a student at the University of Maine's Fallstown branch. There was a time when Mr. Spinner would go down there and stand outside the student center and sermonize. Most of the students made fun of him, but every once in a while one would stop and listen to what he was saying. Chloe wasn't happy in college. She was going to drop out. Marrying Jasper gave her a purpose in life."

Liss sent Connie a sharp look, thinking she'd heard an undercurrent of sarcasm in that comment, but the other woman's face was in shadow. She found herself wishing that she knew more about the effects of brainwashing. Connie continued to refer to Hadley as Mr. Spinner, although she was less consistent when talking about the others. That form of address must have been drummed into her. Now and again, she showed herself to be a rebel, but just now her entire body drooped, as if all the energy, or perhaps all the hope, had drained out of her. If she was offered the chance to go back, would she take it? Liss didn't risk asking. Instead she broached another subject.

"Can we talk about your marriage?"

Even Connie's shrug was listless.

"I'm a little confused. If he's your husband, why don't

you share a room? For that matter, why don't you have your own house? Surely there's room at Pilgrim Farm to build a separate cottage for each couple."

"That's not the way we do things."

We, not *they.* That was not a good sign. "Why not?"

"Mr. Spinner says sex is only necessary for procreation and we don't need to procreate right now. We never have, according to him."

Although Liss couldn't see Connie's features, she got the distinct impression that the other woman was smiling. "Did you . . . mind?"

Connie's reply was sharp and unequivocal. "No."

"But you and George, you . . . get along okay? He doesn't . . . mistreat you or anything?"

"We like each other." Connie voice went back to sounding dull and uninflected. "We always have." She paused before she added, "I feel bad for him sometimes."

"Why's that?"

This time Connie was silent for so long that Liss thought she didn't intend to answer. She gave a little start when the other woman resumed speaking. What came as an even greater surprise was that Connie's words came out strong, steady, and underscored with sadness.

"He tries so hard to live up to Mr. Spinner's teachings, but there are some things he can't change. At least he has a sense of humor about it. He thought it was pretty funny when Benny made the prevert sign and then boasted about painting that word on the door of the coffee shop. George could have told him the right way to spell it, but he didn't."

"Why did he think that was so funny?" Liss asked in confusion. "Did George *want* Benny to be arrested?"

Connie shifted in her chair until her entire body was

turned in Liss's direction. She reached out with one gloved hand to touch her arm.

"Promise me that you won't tell Mr. Spinner."

"Believe me, the last thing I want to do is talk to Hadley Spinner. If I never lay eyes on that man again, it will be too soon."

Connie spoke in a whisper, even though there was no one else around to hear her. "George has a . . . special friendship with Solomon Miller."

Liss recalled that Solomon was Laurel's husband but the significance of Connie's phrasing wasn't lost on her. It just took a moment to sink in. "Do you mean they're lovers?"

She nodded. "They have been for years."

"But I thought Hadley Spinner was dead set against same-sex relationships."

"Oh, he is. But he doesn't know about them. They've been careful to keep their relationship a deep, dark secret. I'm the only one George has ever told and it took him years before he dared confide in me."

"I suppose having a child with his wife made it easier to deceive everyone. Solomon is Kimmy's father, right?"

Connie gave a snort of laughter. "Who knows? But I can tell you one thing. It didn't go over well with Mr. Spinner when Laurel fell pregnant. He insisted that she give birth at the farm with only Mistress Spinner in attendance. He said she had to be made to suffer for the sin of Eve."

"That's monstrous!" Men like Hadley Spinner deserved to be locked up. If it was up to her, she'd put him in solitary confinement and throw away the key to his cell.

Connie abruptly heaved herself out of the chair and headed for the sliding glass door. She was inside before Liss could get to her feet and had disappeared up the stairs by the time Liss reached her mother's living room.

"Leave her be," Vi said. "You've upset her."

"She was in a sorry state long before I came along. I just wish I knew what to make of her."

"Connie suffered long-term psychological abuse. No one can recover from that overnight."

Was that it? Or was Connie conning them? Liss honestly couldn't decide, although if her mother was right, that poor woman deserved sympathy and support, not suspicion.

"Can you persuade her to get professional help?"

"Let's wait a bit longer before calling in a shrink," Vi said. "She's making progress."

Liss didn't argue, but she knew she wouldn't rest easily until she knew what had pushed Connie into leaving Pilgrim Farm . . . and whether or not it was connected to the murder of Jasper Spinner.

Between the end of leaf-peeper season and the uptick in pre-Christmas shopping right after Thanksgiving, Moosetookalook Scottish Emporium was open on Sundays "by chance or appointment." That being the case, Liss didn't rush to get to work the next day. It was after nine before she set out, taking the time to appreciate the cloudless blue sky and the warmth of the sun on her face as she strolled at a leisurely pace toward the shop. At the corner, when she paused before crossing the street, the sound of raised voices broke the peaceful quiet of the morning. They were coming from Stu's Ski Shop.

She intended to walk on past without even looking in through Stu's front window. It was none of her business if he chose to quarrel with someone on such a beautiful day. She changed her mind when she recognized the vehicle parked at the curb. It was Gordon Tandy's unmarked car and right behind it was a state police cruiser. The uniformed trooper sitting inside gave her a hard stare before redirecting his attention to Stu's front door.

Liss followed the direction of his gaze just as it was flung open. Stu was still inside, but he was yelling loudly enough to be heard on the far side of the town square. Liss was only a few feet away and couldn't miss hearing even if she wanted to.

"You're out of your mind if you think I'd do such a thing!" Stu bellowed. "I've known Margaret Boyd since you were still pooping in your diapers."

Gordon's broad back filled the opening. He wasn't exactly in retreat, but he wasn't throwing Stu down and cuffing him either.

"I'm not saying that I think you would do that, but you were seen at the front of the shop and then going around to the side. You've got to admit the timing's suspicious."

"I was trying to get Liss's attention, not her aunt's. I've already told you that I banged on her door. It was locked. When no one answered, I went around back to see if she was in the stockroom."

"Why?" Gordon asked.

Liss took a few steps closer. She wanted to hear that answer, too.

Stu's voice dropped to a mumble. He hated having to confess to a weakness. "I'd had a few drinks. I get maudlin when I drink. Sometimes it helps to talk to someone. Liss is a good listener."

"Oh, Stu," Liss murmured. She'd never thought twice about providing him with a shoulder to cry on. That's what old friends did. She covered the distance to the porch of the ski shop in a rush.

Gordon heard her coming and turned. He looked annoyed until he recognized her. "Can you verify that?"

"What? Someone pounding on the door of the shop? Yes, but I ignored it and I have no idea what time it was."

"And? You told me you were in the stockroom. Did Stu talk to you?" He sounded disapproving, as if he thought she'd deliberately neglected to mention the encounter.

"I had earbuds in and was busy packing orders. "If anyone came to the back door, I wasn't aware of it."

She sent an apologetic glance Stu's way, but he was pre-occupied with glaring at Gordon. The expression "hopping mad" took on new meaning as she watched him bounce on the balls of his feet, his face turning redder and redder as his hands curled into fists.

"What's going on?" Liss asked. "Why are you giving Stu a hard time?"

Gordon didn't answer her. No surprise there. Instead he addressed Stu. "Anything else you want to tell me? Anything you might have seen? Because if no one went up there while she was gone, then Margaret Boyd is in deep trouble."

"Either arrest me or get out of my shop," Stu shouted. "I've got nothing more to say to you."

When Gordon left, Stu slammed the door behind him but he didn't lock it and the OPEN sign remained in place. Left standing on the porch, Liss watched Gordon speak with the uniformed officer and then get into his own car. Only after they'd both driven away did she let herself into the ski shop.

"So?"

"Give me a minute." Stu's voice was low and gravelly, as close to a growl as Liss had ever heard it. "I'm still pissed."

"As in drunk or as in angry?"

The question, as she'd intended, made Stu laugh in spite of himself. "Come on back," he invited her. "We'll talk."

His office was a cubbyhole with barely enough room for the standard pieces of furniture. Stu settled into the swivel chair behind his desk while Liss perched on one corner of that sturdy wooden object.

"I repeat . . . so? Obviously, you've moved up a notch or two on Gordon's suspect list. Why?"

"He's got some cockamamie idea that I saw Margaret leave with the dogs and decided that it was a perfect opportunity to sneak into her place, steal a knife, and use it to stab Spinner."

"That's crazy."

"That's what I said, but he claims someone saw me knock on the door of the Emporium and then sneak around to the back."

Liss wondered who had come forward. Certainly no one she or Vi had questioned had admitted to seeing anyone on her porch. Still, she was glad to finally know who it had been.

"I heard the knocking, but you couldn't have tried very hard to get my attention at the back door. I was right there. I'd have heard you if you'd made a racket."

"I was going to bang on that door, but when I looked inside, I saw that you were wearing earbuds. It was obvious you didn't want to be interrupted, so I left. I didn't go back the way I'd come. I just cut across the driveway and into my place through the back door. I had a couple more beers and then I fell asleep. I never set foot in the town square again after my quarrel with Hadley, and I certainly didn't kill Jasper Spinner."

"They think he was mistaken for Hadley."

"I wouldn't have killed him, either. I wouldn't have minded beating the crap out of him, but stab him in the back? No way."

"I believe you," Liss said. She was certain he'd told her the truth, too, but she could understand why the police had their doubts. Gordon must know Stu had gone off the rails once before and ended up in jail. Drunk driving was a serious offense, but he'd cleaned up his act since then and he'd never been accused of anything worse.

A little while later, when Liss crossed the short distance between Stu's office and her stockroom, she tried to envision what the police thought had happened on the day of the murder. Even if Stu had seen Margaret leave with the dogs, why would he try to get into the building by way of the Emporium's front door? That made no sense. Neither did a scenario where he'd creep into her unlocked apartment to steal a knife to use to kill Spinner. The pieces didn't fit. Even if, by some wild stretch of the imagination, he had decided to kill Hadley Spinner, he'd never have tried to frame Margaret. Those two had been neighbors for decades and had always gotten along.

Liss tried to tell herself that she was glad that Gordon now appeared to be open to the possibility that Margaret had been set up. Unfortunately, pegging Stu as his main suspect was almost as bad. The police needed to consider other alternatives . . . and so did she.

Instead of turning the CLOSED sign to OPEN when she entered the Emporium, she called in reinforcements.

Sunday was not one of the days that the library was open. At first, Dolores Mayfield was adamant that she could not invite Liss in on a Sunday morning.

"Sure you can," Liss insisted over the phone. "You're queen of your domain. You can do anything you want."

She braced herself for an argument, but the intrepid Moosetookalook librarian surprised her.

"I *was* planning to contact you later today. I suppose there's no reason we can't meet at the library. Can you be there at eleven?"

Liss readily agreed. Instead of opening the Emporium, she spent the time until then making more notes to herself about what she already knew and what she suspected.

At five minutes past eleven, Liss and Dolores were seated opposite one another at one of the long library tables. Dolores's smirk suggested that she was well pleased with herself even before she handed over the printouts she'd made. They were copies of newspaper articles, vital records, and other documents. There was so much material that Liss couldn't immediately take all of it in.

"Can you give me the abridged version?"

"Certainly." Puffed up with her own self-importance, the librarian started by delivering a little lecture. "I want you to understand that all of this comes from perfectly legitimate, perfectly legal sources."

"Of course." Dolores had always boasted that she had better contacts than most branches of law enforcement. Liss had never seen any reason to doubt it.

"First of all, it looks like Hadley Spinner really is a preacher. He has a diploma from one of those online colleges."

"So he's authorized to perform marriages. That's too bad. It would have saved . . . well, never mind."

"You mean that Mistress Gerard, the one Spinner was carrying on about on Friday, would have an easier time of it if she wasn't really married? I agree, but she can always divorce her husband."

Liss had forgotten that Dolores would have enjoyed a bird's-eye view of Hadley's arrest. She'd obviously overheard whose name he'd been shouting, too. While Liss felt certain that the librarian couldn't know that Vi and Mac were hiding Connie, and preferred to keep it that way, she had no qualms about sharing her suspicions about the runaway Pilgrim.

"Divorce may be a moot point if Connie Gerard is the one who killed Jasper Spinner."

When Dolores's eyebrows arched in a display of skepticism, Liss outlined her reasoning. Explained aloud, her logic sounded lame even to her own ears. By the time she finished laying out her case against Connie, Dolores was shaking her head.

"I didn't find anything in her past to make me think she'd turn violent. You can never know for certain, naturally. Anyone can kill, given the right circumstances."

"Did anyone else strike you as a viable suspect?"

"In the murder? No. But I found plenty of evidence that the Pilgrims weren't averse to committing lesser crimes. Hadley and Jasper Spinner first met George Gerard and Charles Knapp when all four of them were in jail."

Liss stared at the librarian for a long moment before shaking her head to clear it. "I don't know why that should surprise me. Hadley Spinner has con man written all over him."

"Oh, that's not why he was arrested. He was picked up for being drunk and disorderly. Jasper, too."

"And the others?"

"The cops got George for picking pockets and Charles was charged with furnishing liquor to a minor. They all went to court the same day and they all got off with slaps on the wrist."

Dolores riffled through the printouts until she found the one of the applicable newspaper account. Liss had to squint to read the tiny print. It was a long article, since the four men she was interested in hadn't been the only ones in court that day.

"When did this take place?" she asked. "The date is too smudged for me to read it."

"Almost two decades ago. By the time the four of them arrived here, they'd known each other for several years."

"But *why* did they come here? That's been bothering me. They bought a farm that was barely sustaining itself. If you're going to live off the land, shouldn't you pick a place with more potential for producing good crops?"

"Miranda must have been part of the deal. The ink was barely dry on the deed and her father hadn't been dead a week before she married Hadley." Dolores shrugged. "Don't look at me for a better explanation. All I know is that those four men came here, bought a worthless piece of land, and invented a religion that put the male of the species at the top of the food chain. Need someone to take care of the house? Find a wife and convince her she's subservient to you for life. Need more farm laborers? Go recruit some with the claim that they'll be saved if only they buckle down and work hard."

"Don't forget that the other men were also rewarded with wives." Liss relayed how Connie, Chloe, and Anna had come to join the New Age Pilgrims. She didn't mention Dan's sister. By some miracle, that incident appeared to have been one of the very few that never became grist for the Moosetookalook rumor mill.

"I've heard of worse behavior against women, but I sure wouldn't turn my back on him," Dolores said. "He's only a few steps away from turning into one of those cult leaders who orders his followers to kill people, or kill themselves. I'm glad he's locked up."

United in their distaste for Hadley Spinner and what he

had created, Liss shared a rare moment of complete accord with the older woman before she focused her attention on the pages in front of her. The text she skimmed confirmed her earlier conclusion about the Pilgrims—they'd all been at low points in their lives when they met Hadley Spinner.

"A lot of these folks seem to have ended up substituting one kind of dependency for another," she observed.

"People with low self-esteem make easy targets," Dolores agreed.

"So they do. But wouldn't you think at least one of them would have smartened up after spending a little time at Pilgrim Farm?"

"One did. She ended up dead."

"Susan." Liss frowned. "Since it was her home before Hadley came, she probably had more reasons to stay than most. Doesn't it seem odd to you that she'd be the one to rebel?"

"Not really. She just had that much longer to get fed up with Jasper's high-handedness. I'll tell you one thing. If Roger ever tried to send me out to clean houses, it would be his clock that got cleaned."

Liss had to smile at that. Roger "Moose" Mayfield, for all his faults, was devoted to his prickly wife. He'd never dream of trying to make her do anything she didn't want to do.

Although Liss continued to go through the printouts, a new train of thought kept distracting her from what she was reading. If Susan had reached the point where she wanted to leave the only home she'd ever known, maybe other longtime Pilgrims had gotten sick of Hadley's lording it over them, too. What if one of the three men who'd started out with Hadley Spinner had come to resent his leadership? She remembered the way Jasper had looked

when Sherri stood up to Hadley. It was as if he was glad to
see his cousin get his comeuppance. What if George and
Charles had felt the same way?

"They met in jail," she murmured. "Dolores, did any of
them have criminal records before that?"

"Nothing major. Petty theft. Bar fights. OUI and driving
after a license was suspended. Why? What are you thinking?"

"Jasper looked . . . pleased when Sherri talked back to
Hadley."

"That would be on the day Dan lit into him?"

Liss felt her face grow warm. Of course Dolores would
have heard about that incident. The whole town had.

"That's neither here nor there. What I'm wondering is if
there was a rebellion in the works. Maybe George or
Charles meant to kill Hadley and murdered Jasper by mistake."

"Any of the Pilgrims should have been able to tell the
two men apart."

Liss was heartily sick of hearing that line of reasoning.
"It was getting dark by the time Jasper was killed and he
was stabbed in the back."

"They were all in the town square that day," Dolores
conceded. "I guess any one of them *could* have done it,
but why try to frame Margaret? Let's face it, Liss. The
killer had no reason to go into her place to look for a
weapon unless implicating her was part of the plan."

Too restless to sit still any longer, Liss pushed away
from the table. "There must be some way to find out
more. I hesitate to go out to Pilgrim Farm again, but
maybe one-on-one—"

She broke off as an idea occurred to her. She had Joe
Ruskin on speed dial and he answered on the first ring.

"Is anyone picketing the hotel today?" she asked. No

one had shown up in the town square since Hadley's arrest, but the hotel had been the original target of the protest, not the downtown businesses.

"There was," Joe said, "but he left about an hour ago. Why?"

Darn, Liss thought. There went her best chance to lob a few questions at another Pilgrim. "Do you know which one it was? Was it the same man who picketed you on Friday?"

"I don't know the guy's name, but I've got his picture on one of my security cameras." There was a pause. "Liss? None of the Pills were out here on Friday."

"Interesting." *More* than interesting. "Thanks, Joe."

After she hung up, Liss relayed what she'd learned to Dolores.

"I can see from your expression that you think something's not right about that. What's bothering you?"

"George Gerard was supposed to have been picketing the hotel all day Friday while Hadley Spinner did his thing in the town square. Why wasn't he there? Where was he?"

Dolores grinned. "Goofing off? When the cat's away . . ."

Liss shook her head. "I think there's more to it than that, and good old George just went to the top of my suspect list."

"Why?"

"Because it was his wife who decamped on Friday, and as far as I can tell, he hasn't tried to find her."

"Maybe he doesn't care that she's gone. Or, consider this: the New Age Pilgrims may be in total disarray. For the first time in fifteen years, they don't have someone there to tell them what to do." Dolores fixed Liss with a stern look. "You could take advantage of the situation. Get yourself out there and question the Pills."

"That's pretty much the same reasoning I used when my

mother and I paid a visit to Miranda, but because of that visit, I'd be even less welcome there now. Besides, Sherri will kill me if I go out to Pilgrim Farm on my own." And Gordon, if he heard about it, would probably lock her up for life.

"But you'll never get a better opportunity," Dolores insisted. "It's go today or don't go at all, because odds are good that Hadley Spinner will be out on bail sometime tomorrow."

Chapter Fifteen

Pilgrim Farm was in chaos when Liss pulled into the dooryard. She was once again reminded of chickens. These still had their heads. They were clucking as they fluttered about, a flock of demented hens, and some of them were pecking at each other.

Dolores, from the passenger seat, swiveled around to take in all the action. She'd solved Liss's dilemma about venturing into enemy territory alone by insisting upon coming with her. Although Liss knew it would have been wiser to bring Sherri, or even Dan, she'd agreed to the plan. She'd been having second thoughts throughout the drive to Little Mooseside.

The thump, as Laurel Miller threw a bulging duffel bag into the trunk of an aged station wagon, caught Liss's attention. When Laurel opened the passenger-side door, Liss saw that Kimmy was already installed in a child seat in the back. Anna was behind the wheel. More amazing still, both women wore blue jeans and sweatshirts. Where, Liss wondered, had those come from? Come to think of it, hadn't someone told her, or at least implied, that the Pilgrims only owned two vehicles, a pickup truck and an old VW bug?

Miranda stood in the doorway to the ell, a furious ex-

pression on her face, but she didn't try to stop the other
women from leaving. The raised voices Liss heard as she
got out of her car came from a quarrel in progress between
Chloe Spinner and one of the Pilgrim men.

"Shut up, George!" Chloe shouted. "I'm done listening
to you!"

George, Liss thought. *Not Mr. Gerard.* Hadley Spinner's control over the little things had slipped badly since
his arrest.

"You need to calm down." George was so wrapped up
in his argument with Chloe that he failed to notice that
there were strangers present. "Mr. Spinner will be back tomorrow and all will be right again."

"Mr. Spinner can go hang," Chloe shot back. "I never
realized until he was gone just how much I hated this
place. It was like waking up and seeing the world around
me for the first time in years. Pilgrim Farm is toxic and I'm
getting out while the getting is good."

She wasn't the only one. A couple, suitcases in hand,
emerged from the barn. Liss identified the woman as Denise,
but she drew a blank on her husband's name.

"You're just scared the cops will come back," George
yelled, pulling Liss's attention back to him. He sounded
worried about that possibility himself.

"Of course I am. You may be okay with going to jail,
but I'm not."

"They've got nothing on us. We're . . . we're transparent."

"How can you believe that? Hadley made us lie for him."

"You—"

"I know about the knife. We all do."

Liss's gasp was loud enough for both Chloe and George
to hear. Chloe's face drained of color when she realized
who Liss was. George was made of sterner stuff.

"You've got no business here." He took a threatening step toward the two women from Moosetookalook.

As a jolt of fear shot through her, Liss considered retreat, but Dolores had her back. Leveling her patented librarian's glare at him, she shouted, "Stop right there."

George glowered, but didn't come any closer. "You're trespassing."

"And your happy little group is falling apart. Why is everyone running away?"

Miranda had crossed the dooryard to stand beside George. "That's none of your business."

The librarian's glare did not work on Hadley Spinner's wife, but Jasper's widow welcomed the chance to air her grievances.

"I'll tell you why." Chloe jerked her head at Miranda. "Her husband is seriously disturbed."

"Be silent, Mistress Spinner."

"Oh, come off it, Miranda! You know it's true."

Chloe turned her back on Hadley's wife to focus on Liss and Dolores. If looks could kill, Chloe would have a knife between her ribs. Fortunately for the younger woman, Miranda simply stood there, her arms folded across her bosom and her back as stiff as a poker. When George tried to place a comforting hand on her arm, she shook him off without sparing him so much as a glance.

Her expression earnest, her voice pleading, as if it was of the utmost importance that she make two strangers understand, Chloe said, "He used to be different. Hadley Spinner was . . . eloquent. It was easy to believe what he told us. And then things changed. Some days he can barely string two coherent words together, and half the time those don't make any sense."

"She doesn't know what she's talking about," Miranda said through clenched teeth.

George sighed deeply. "Yeah, she does."

"Traitor!"

"I'm only telling the truth. You know there's something wrong with him, Miranda. Jasper did, too. That's why—"

"Enough! Mr. Spinner is your friend. Your leader."

"Not so much anymore." As if a dam had broken, George couldn't seem to stop talking, any more than Chloe had been able to. He directed his words at Liss and Dolores. "Hadley Spinner has self-control issues. I expect you've seen that for yourself." As abruptly as it had blossomed, his anger was gone, leaving only sorrow and regret behind.

"That's putting it mildly," Liss murmured.

"He's obsessed with taking revenge on anyone he thinks has slighted him. That's why he went after Joe Ruskin. Nobody can hold a grudge like Hadley Spinner."

"It wasn't the couples issue?" Liss watched George's face as she asked the question and caught the flash of panic in his eyes.

"That was a bonus," Chloe said, apparently unaware that Liss had touched a nerve.

Liss moved on. "Did he also want revenge on Margaret Boyd?"

George's brow furrowed in confusion. "Who is—oh, you mean Susan's friend? That was a long time ago."

"It was," Liss agreed, "but you just said he doesn't let go of grudges and it was one of her knives that was used to kill Jasper."

Although Laurel and Anna had driven away with Kimmy, the rest of the Pilgrims remained, even the couple with the suitcase. Their expressions ranged from confused to worried to terrified.

"Mr. Spinner only carried that knife to protect himself," Miranda stated in a flat voice. "He has enemies."

I know about the knife, Chloe had said. Belatedly, Liss realized that she hadn't meant the one from Margaret's kitchen, after all.

"Let me get this straight. Hadley Spinner took a knife to the demonstration? "

It was Diana who answered. "Connie saw him put it back."

"Mr. Spinner needed it for protection," Miranda insisted. "It wasn't the knife someone used to kill his cousin."

George rounded on her. "I thought Jasper was shot."

"That's what Hadley told us, after the police came," said another of the Pilgrim men.

"He lied." The moment Liss stated that fact, the missing piece of the puzzle fell into place. What must have happened that day in the town square was so clear to her that she was amazed no one had worked it out before. "I don't think Hadley took that knife for protection. He planned to use it to rid himself of a rival. No wonder Connie was worried."

Stricken, George gaped at her. "Is that why Hadley lost his temper with her when she mentioned it? He told her to shut up about it if she knew what was good for her."

"Was Jasper planning a coup?" she asked. "Was he that worried about his cousin's state of mind?"

For a moment, she didn't think anyone would answer her. Then George spoke up.

"He was . . . concerned."

She looked him straight in the eye. "It seems to me Hadley might have suspected that your tribe, led by Jasper Spinner, was about to vote him off the island."

George surprised her yet again by understanding the reference. "Jasper was thinking about it."

Apparently, the Pilgrims had a television stashed some-where. Probably in the men's quarters, Liss thought, so that the poor, weak-minded womenfolk wouldn't be cor-rupted by it.

"You need to go to the police and tell them everything you know," she said aloud. Her gaze paused briefly on each of the Pilgrims. "All of you need to talk to them."

"But we don't know anything for sure," George insisted.

Liss thought otherwise. Connie might have been the only one to see Hadley with a knife, but the rest of them, espe-cially the men, had almost certainly witnessed more than they were aware of during the demonstration. Maybe one of them had even seen Hadley sneak into Margaret's apart-ment. He could easily have done so while Margaret and Jasper were focused on each other.

"You need to leave," George said before she could ask any more questions. He took her arm in an unbreakable grip and steered her toward her car.

"Hey!" Dolores trotted after them. "Unhand her!"

George lowered his voice to keep the others from over-hearing. "Please. Let us handle this ourselves. Miranda's the key, and she'll stick to her guns as long as there are outsiders here. We'll talk this over among ourselves and decide what's best to do."

"You need to act before morning. Chances are good that Hadley will be released on bail."

George went pale beneath his tan. "Believe me, I know that time is of the essence."

Liss stared groggily at the face of the clock, unable to believe that it was nine-fifteen. "Of all the days to over-sleep," she muttered.

Since it was Monday and the Emporium was closed, she hadn't set the alarm, but she was almost always awake by seven. If nothing else got her up, the cats would. They ran on "sun time" and wanted their breakfast at the crack of dawn, no matter how early that was.

It didn't take her long to figure out what had happened. Dan was unaware of her plan to talk to the police first thing in the morning. He'd been helping his father at The Spruces when she arrived home the previous afternoon and hadn't returned until well after midnight. By then, she'd been asleep, and she'd still been sleeping when her considerate husband got up, fed the cats, and closed the bedroom door so that they wouldn't come back in and disturb her rest.

Groaning, she grabbed the first clothes she could lay hands on. She dressed in a rush and barely took the time to run a comb through her night-tangled hair, beset by the feeling that she'd made the wrong decision when she'd agreed to trust George.

What she *should* have done, as soon as she got home from Pilgrim Farm, was call the police. Instead she'd let sentiment sway her. She'd been moved to pity by George's request. How could she not be? The remaining Pilgrims were as much Hadley Spinner's victims as Jasper had been. He'd taken away their freedom to choose. Now that they were finally prepared to think for themselves, didn't they deserve a chance to act on their own?

What she'd willfully ignored was that some of them had been ready to run. Surely they wouldn't all flee? It was only necessary that a few of them testify against Hadley, and Connie was the one who'd seen the knife. Still, she knew she should have phoned Sherri and told her what she'd deduced.

She saw that the lights were on in Dan's workshop when she stumbled into the kitchen in search of coffee. He'd been hard at work while she'd been a lazy slugabed. He'd even taken care of cleaning the litter box. On any other day, she'd be pleased by his thoughtfulness. This morning she couldn't shake the uneasy feeling that she was going to regret those additional hours in the sack.

"Don't be stupid!" she said aloud, startling Glenora into opening one green eye. "Hadley Spinner won't even have had his bail hearing yet, and if it's set high enough, maybe he won't be able to raise the money. You're worrying for nothing."

Cheered by her own words, she filled a go-cup with coffee from the pot Dan had made. She'd heard of cases where family members had to put their houses on the line to get relatives out of jail. Hadley's "family" didn't seem likely to do anything for him. Even Miranda's defense of her husband had not been entirely convincing.

She grabbed a coat and headed for the police station. She felt certain Sherri would be in by now. Heck, she'd probably been at work for a couple of hours already.

Sherri looked up, her expression unrevealing, as Liss entered her office. "I'm glad you stopped by. I was about to call you."

"You may not be so glad to see me after I've confessed." She took a hasty sip of the hot coffee to fortify herself. "Or do you already know about yesterday's visit to Pilgrim Farm?"

The sudden furrowing of Sherri's brow was answer enough.

"Damn. They were going to talk to you. Or tell someone. Maybe Gordon—"

"Why don't you start at the beginning? Why on earth did you go out there alone?"

"I wasn't alone. Dolores was with me."

Sherri rolled her eyes. "Talk."

In a reasonably coherent manner, given that she'd only had a few swallows of coffee to jump-start her brain, Liss described the scene they'd found when they visited the New Age Pilgrims the previous day and recounted the conclusions she'd drawn from what had been said.

"A kitchen knife," Sherri repeated when Liss ran down the list. "That's it?"

"Well . . . yes. But it shows intent, doesn't it? And if Jasper was the leader of a rebellion, that's motive for Hadley to have gotten rid of him. George said he never lets go of a grudge, so if he still resented Margaret's accusations about Susan, there's the reason he decided to use one of her knives instead of the one he brought with him."

"That's pretty iffy logic."

"Maybe, but everyone agrees that Hadley wasn't firing on all cylinders. The thing is, the Pilgrims were supposed to tell someone about that knife before Hadley's bail hearing. If they didn't come to you, they must have called the state police."

"I'm not so sure about that. I'm out of the loop on the murder investigation, but do you remember that I said I was glad you stopped by? That was because I was going to warn you that Hadley is *already* out on bail. His case came up first thing this morning and since he's the owner of record of Pilgrim Farm, he put the deed up to secure the bond. I'm told Miranda picked him up at the courthouse."

The hollow feeling in the pit of Liss's stomach had nothing to do with the fact that she hadn't yet had breakfast. "No one went to the police."

"It doesn't sound like it. If Gordon had heard from them and thought there was more to look into, I'm pretty sure he'd have contacted the D.A. and she'd have tried to convince the judge to set bail a lot higher. She didn't."

Liss polished off her coffee as she tried to process what Hadley's freedom would mean. "Do you think he'll try to find Connie?"

"There were conditions set on his bail. He's not to go near The Spruces or your house or business. He's forbidden to contact Connie or you or Dan or Joe."

Liss mimed wiping sweat from her brow.

"That's no guarantee that he won't ignore the conditions of release."

"Especially if he *is* the one who killed Jasper. Stop rolling your eyes! I'll admit that the fact that he took a knife to the demonstration isn't proof of anything, but shouldn't someone question him about it? I'd like to hear his answer myself. And I'd like a chance to tell George Gerard what I think of him for promising to talk to the police and then wimping out."

Sherri stood, pulling her utility belt out of the drawer where she kept it when she wasn't on patrol. The gun, the Taser, the pepper spray, and the handcuffs should have reassured Liss about her friend's safety, but somehow they didn't.

"You can't go out there alone."

"I'll call for a backup from the sheriff's department, but it'll probably take them a little while to get here."

"You should wait for them."

Sherri's eyebrows shot up. "So now you're an expert on police procedure? Spinner isn't going to give me any trouble. At worst, he'll refuse to answer questions."

"We're talking about the guy who broke my window and tried to take Connie away against her will."

"Did you see him resisting arrest? He may have some

strange beliefs, and maybe he's got a few screws loose, but he's smart enough not to tangle directly with the law."

"Famous last words," Liss muttered, but she was talking to empty air. Sherri had left the building.

By the time Liss walked home and refilled her go-cup, she'd come to a decision. She couldn't let Sherri go out to Pilgrim Farm on her own. Liss knew she probably wouldn't be much help, but until Sherri's backup arrived, she had to be better than nothing. Although Spinner might be angry enough to strike out at one person, even one who was armed, surely he'd think twice about taking on two, especially if he'd realized he could no longer count on the support of the other Pilgrims. They might not have ratted him out, but Liss doubted they'd let him assault a police officer.

The only vehicle in sight when Liss pulled into the dooryard at Pilgrim Farm was the Moosetookalook cruiser. Sherri stood a few feet in front of it, talking to Miranda. She turned at the sound of the approaching car to scowl at Liss, but she didn't immediately order her to turn around and leave.

Liss got out of the car and joined the other two women.

"They've gone," Sherri said. It was cold enough that Liss could see a puff of breath accompany each word. "All of them but Mrs. Spinner here. I was just asking her where her husband is."

"I have no idea," Miranda said.

"You picked him up this morning."

"Of course I did. He is my husband."

"And?"

Miranda sounded exasperated. "We came back here. I told him about the defections. He was not pleased."

That, Liss felt sure, was the understatement of the century.

"I made him eat breakfast. Oatmeal is so strengthening. And then he took the truck and said he had things to attend to."

"Things?" Sherri asked.

"He does not tell me what his plans are. Why should he? My place is to remain here and maintain the house."

"The house he'll lose, along with the land, if he violates the conditions of his release."

For the briefest moment, Liss thought she saw anger flash in Miranda's faded blue eyes. Hadley's wife's lips pursed in disapproval and a faint hint of color came into her cheeks before her usual stoic expression returned.

"Do you know where the others have gone?" Liss asked.

Sherri shot her a quelling glance but didn't interrupt when Miranda answered.

"Scattered to the winds. Just as well," she added, "once George and Solomon made us all privy to their secret."

Sherri looked blank, but Liss understood. "They came out? Good for them."

"Came out, and left together. May they find peace and happiness."

"You . . . don't condemn them?"

"Why should I? We may have cut ourselves off from the world in many ways, but contrary to what some people seem to think, Mr. Spinner does not have the power to control other people's feelings, least of all mine."

He probably believes he does, Liss thought, but she didn't contradict Miranda.

"Was everyone else as accepting?" Connie and Laurel and Anna had already left, but Liss suspected that Laurel already knew where her husband's affections lay. Connie certainly had.

"Benny was confused," Miranda admitted, "but then he never really understood what a 'prevert' was in the first place."

Comprehension at last dawned on Sherri, quickly followed by concern for the two men. "Did you tell your husband about them? That he'd been deceived all these years?"

Liss had been feeling pleased for George and Solomon. Like Miranda, she believed that two people in love deserved the chance to be together. Sherri's questions hit her like a bucket of cold water. Hadley Spinner was not known for his tolerance . . . and he believed in taking revenge against those who challenged his authority.

Miranda didn't answer. Instead, she turned and walked away from them. "I trust you will excuse me. I have things to do, now that I am once again the sole mistress of this house." She closed the ell door behind her with a final-sounding thump.

Liss glanced at Sherri. "Are you going to send out a BOLO for Hadley Spinner?"

"I think I'd better, don't you, before he catches up with any of the runaways? I don't have a reason to arrest him, but I want to keep an eye on him." She got into the cruiser and reached for the radio. "Go home, Liss. I'll handle this."

"I think I should head out to Ledge Lake and talk to my parents first. They need to know what's going on."

"Fine. Just stay out of trouble."

Sherri spoke to the dispatcher at the sheriff's department while Liss walked to her car. In the crisp, clear morning air, her every word carried clearly. Liss heard her friend slam the cruiser door and start the engine a moment before she turned the key in her own ignition. She sat for a moment, letting the heater warm the interior, and watched the other vehicle disappear around the curve of the driveway. She was about to follow Sherri when the passenger-side door abruptly opened and Miranda Spinner slid into the car.

Liss eyed her warily. "What do you want, Miranda?"

"I could hear what you said from inside the ell. If you're going to your parents' house, you need to take me with you."

"Why?"

"I know Connie's there. Where else *could* she be? She left with the two of you. She wouldn't be foolish enough to stay in town. That leaves Mrs. MacCrimmon to give her shelter. I doubt your mother has changed much since I had her as a teacher. She always liked to manage things. It would be only natural for her to take Connie under her wing."`

Miranda's logic worried Liss. "Does Hadley know where Connie's gone?"

"I have no idea, but if I could figure it out, so could he."

Liss hit the gas.

Chapter Sixteen

As she drove toward Ledge Lake, Liss was beset by an ominous sense of déjà vu. An incident in her past had ended at another camp on the lake. She still shuddered at the memory of how scared she'd been and how helpless she'd felt. History couldn't repeat itself . . . could it?

She wished she had someone in the car with her other than Miranda. Gordon would be ideal, or Sherri. Dan would be a steady presence beside her. Even Dolores would do in a pinch. As Liss well knew, the librarian had hidden resources. Her mother? Well, Vi was already at the cottage, and probably her father was, too. Would either of them have a clue how to react if Hadley Spinner showed up?

Although it was both illegal and dangerous to use a cell phone while driving, Liss fished hers out of her pocket and hit Sherri's number on speed dial. When nothing happened, she risked a glance at the screen and saw that she was in a dead zone. She cursed under her breath. That situation wasn't likely to improve until she got to her destination. One of the wealthier summer residents had lobbied hard for a cell tower in the immediate vicinity.

"You said your husband was driving the truck?" she asked her passenger.

"He took it and left me stranded," Miranda answered. "Typical."

Liss kept her eyes peeled for the vehicle. With luck, it would take Spinner a while to find the camp. Vi and Mac were newcomers to the area and they hadn't been living there long. Then she remembered that large, brightly painted sign her mother was so proud of. If Spinner got as far as the camp road, he wouldn't be able to miss seeing it.

"*Would* he go looking for Connie?" she asked. "He can't think any of his former followers will come back to Pilgrim Farm now."

At first she thought Miranda wasn't going to answer her, but after a lengthy silence, she said, "It's that stupid knife. She saw him put it back after the demonstration. He doesn't want her to tell the police about it. It doesn't mean a thing, of course, but he's obsessed with it."

"Did any of the other Pilgrims bother to talk to the police before they left town?"

"They voted against it. Most of them just wanted to get away before Mr. Spinner returned."

That must mean that Hadley thought Connie was the only one who could link him to Jasper's murder. Liss was sure he'd killed his cousin and she was very much afraid that he was now intent upon killing Connie to cover up that crime.

A glance at Miranda's stiff posture and tightly pursed lips persuaded Liss that Miranda was worried about the same thing. She pressed down harder on the gas pedal, despite the fact that she was already speeding.

"Does he have a weapon with him?"

"I doubt it. He's convinced he can compel obedience with his words alone."

Liss had reached the camp road. She slowed only minimally to make the turn and sped up again with a squeal of tires. She drove twice as fast as she normally would and keeping her eyes on the pothole-filled surface ahead meant that she couldn't see Miranda's reaction when she asked, "Did he kill your sister, too, to keep her from leaving?"

"Don't be absurd."

"Your husband killed his cousin and tried to put the blame on my aunt. He's hunting Connie. I don't find the idea absurd at all."

"I kept an eye on him," Miranda murmured. "I did my best."

Liss risked a glance at her passenger. "What are you talking about?"

They were almost at the cottage. Liss hadn't seen hide nor hair of any other vehicle, let alone a truck. She should have been relieved, but Miranda's words fueled her anxiety.

"You kept an eye on him," she repeated. "Good grief! Were you the one in the town square on the day of the demonstration?"

Miranda wasn't a blonde, but with hair that was fading to gray, she might well use blond bobby pins to keep the strands in place.

"Did you *know* he took one of your knives with him that day? Were you worried about what he planned to do?"

Only silence answered her.

"Did you see him sneak into my aunt's apartment?"

Again, silence.

Liss pulled into her parents' parking area. Spinner's truck wasn't there. Neither was her father's car. In the best-case scenario, her parents and Connie had gone out and wouldn't be back for hours.

She scrambled out of the driver's seat, casting wary glances in every direction as she took the path that led to the house. Hadley Spinner could have parked at another of the camps around the lake and walked back. She didn't dare assume she and Miranda had beaten him to his destination.

With the other woman following close behind her, Liss reached the porch, grateful that Vi had given her a spare key for emergencies and that she'd put that key on the same ring with her house and car keys. She unlocked the door and went inside with Miranda right on her heels. Liss was just pulling out her cell phone when the faint sound of Vi's voice reached her from the direction of the master bedroom on the first floor. She couldn't make out her mother's words, but when Connie spoke, every syllable rang out with crystal clarity.

"The landline isn't working," she announced. "He must have cut the cord."

Liss felt all the warmth drain from her body. The sensation left her light-headed. Hadley Spinner *had* gotten to Ledge Lake first. She glanced at Miranda. Friend or foe? The expression on the older woman's face indicated that she was listening intently, but what she intended to do next was anybody's guess.

Liss rarely texted, but she didn't dare take the risk that Spinner would hear her voice. She typed quickly and clumsily, sending word of their situation to Sherri, but she had no guarantee that her friend would read the message in time to send help.

Almost in lockstep, she and Miranda crept up to the door of the bedroom. Liss stopped short and stared. Hadley Spinner was there all right, but he wasn't threatening Connie and Vi. It was Vi who held him at bay. Her little pink gun was aimed right at his heart.

The next little while was filled with purposeful activity. While her mother herded Spinner into the living room, Liss pulled out her cell phone again and this time talked to

Sherri. Assured that the police were on the way, she turned her attention to Miranda.

Hadley's wife was watching her husband the way a mouse keeps an eye on a snake.

"I'd feel safer if we tied him up," Connie said.

Hadley Spinner's smile encompassed all four women. Liss found the sight disconcerting. He seemed to think he still possessed the charisma of his younger days.

"Mistress Spinner, be so good as to tell these poor misguided creatures that I mean them no harm. Their fragile feminine brains seem incapable of grasping my intent."

"Your intent was crystal clear," Vi interrupted. "You broke in. You threatened Connie with a knife." She turned to Liss. "If you go look in the bedroom, you'll find it on the floor. I made him drop it. I'd have shot him without a qualm if he hadn't."

"Let's leave it for the police to find. It's evidence."

The more charges against Spinner the better, Liss thought grimly. He'd already violated the conditions of his release, but no matter how certain she was of his guilt, it was all too possible that there wasn't enough evidence to convict him of murder.

Abruptly, Spinner sat down, nearly missing the chair he'd aimed for. Liss exchanged a worried glance with her mother. Was this some kind of trick?

On closer inspection, the Pilgrim leader didn't look well. Beads of sweat stood out on his forehead and his face looked ruddier than it had been a moment earlier. He bared his teeth and uttered a low, threatening sound that was cut short by a spasm of pain.

"Give me that gun," he said in a harsh whisper. "I will not be threatened by a mere woman."

Without warning, he surged to his feet, lunging at Vi. She backpedaled, but there was a hassock in her way. Before Liss could call out a warning, she slammed into it at knee level. As she lost her balance, the gun flew out of her hands.

Liss dove for it.

Spinner got there first. A gleam of triumph in his eyes, he turned it on her. "Over there," he ordered, gesturing for her to join Connie in front of the sliding glass doors.

"Don't worry," Vi called out as she struggled to her feet. "It isn't loaded."

Liss sent her mother an incredulous look.

"Why would I keep a loaded gun in the house, let alone carry one around with me? It's not safe." She sounded short of breath, but otherwise seemed unhurt, and the look she sent Hadley Spinner was fearless.

With a sound of disgust, he tossed the gun aside. "Mistress Spinner, fetch me the knife."

"Mr. Spinner," Miranda answered, "I have spoken to you before about removing items from my kitchen."

His eyes widened. "You dare to disobey me?" His astonishment was so great that he seemed to forget there were others in the room. He turned away from them to focus on his wife.

"Quickly," Liss whispered to her mother and Connie. "Into the bedroom." If they locked the door, they'd be safe until the police arrived.

Connie moved in the opposite direction, grabbing hold of a lamp that sat on one of Vi's end tables as she went.

"You really have lost your mind this time, Hadley," Miranda said.

While he was distracted, Connie swung the lamp. It connected with Spinner's head with a sickening crack. Dazed and bleeding, he sank slowly to the floor, landing facedown on the carpet.

"Here, use this." Vi unhooked the cord from her phone charger and handed it to Liss. "Tie him up."

She knelt beside the fallen man, but before she could wrench his hands behind his back, Spinner rolled over and began to retch. Liss hastily stood up again and stepped out of the way, fighting a gag reflex of her own.

"Don't worry," Miranda said in a preternaturally calm tone of voice. "He won't hurt you. He won't hurt anyone ever again."

"The oatmeal," Spinner croaked.

"Yes, dear. The oatmeal. Ghastly stuff. I will never eat another bowl of it as long as I live . . . and neither will you."

Liss stared at Miranda Spinner in slowly dawning horror. She looked so harmless in her floor-length lavender dress, her hands primly folded at waist level. Light pouring in through the sliding glass door to the deck glinted on her granny glasses, hiding whatever emotion her eyes might have revealed, but the faint smile curving her lips upward spoke of satisfaction in a job well done.

With Hadley in the hospital and Miranda in jail, both of them facing felony charges, Liss concentrated on running her business. The nine days leading up to Thanksgiving were busy ones as Christmas shopping began in earnest. She worked long hours at the Emporium and saw little of anyone but Dan in her free time. The day Connie moved out of the cottage at Ledge Lake, Liss's father left a message on her answering machine to say that he and her mother would be away for a few days. She assumed they were taking a mini-vacation, although she doubted that Vi needed one to recover from her ordeal. She'd appeared to enjoy every minute of it.

During those nine days, Liss saw almost nothing of

Margaret and only talked to Sherri in fits and starts. Although Gordon, following his usual practice, kept mum about the case, Sherri was able to fill in a few details. Not surprisingly, she reported that both Hadley and Miranda would have to undergo psychological testing before either case went to trial.

On the day before Thanksgiving, Vi phoned the Emporium to announce that they were home again. She took it for granted that she and Mac would celebrate the holiday at Liss's house and wouldn't hear of it when Liss suggested that they join Joe and his family at the hotel. Thanks to the "Thanksgiving Special" every room was booked, but the Ruskins could still gather there for a traditional Thanksgiving dinner.

"Joe and the others have had your company for the last ten years," Vi said. "It's our turn. Now don't you worry about food. I'll cook the turkey here and bake rolls and we'll bring them with us. The gravy, too, and Margaret has already agreed to do the desserts. That leaves you with the side dishes. Mashed potatoes, corn, peas, and some of that instant stuffing. It isn't healthy to make it inside the bird anyway."

Liss gave in.

By the time her parents, her aunt, and the two Scotties arrived the next day, she'd set the dining room table with a tartan tablecloth and had all the prep work done for the side dishes. The cats appeared out of nowhere at the first whiff of roast turkey. Lumpkin wound himself through Mac's legs, trying to trip him as he carried in the box containing a heavy enamel pan surrounded by towels to keep it hot.

The kitchen was already redolent with festive aromas—baked apples, cinnamon, and chocolate—but it was the yeasty smell of the fresh-from-the-oven rolls that Vi brought with her that made Liss's mouth water. It didn't take long to get everything ready to serve. Once Dan had mashed the potatoes, everyone pitched in to carry the platters and serving dishes to the table.

"That's too heavy, Vi," her father said, grabbing the bowl with the stuffing away from his wife.

Momentarily alone in the kitchen with her mother, Liss sent her a questioning look. "Is there something you're not telling me?"

"If you must know, we weren't on vacation last week. I went to Portland to have a pacemaker put in. The surgery was scheduled ages ago."

"And you didn't think you should tell me about it before-hand?"

"Why worry you? It's not as if I had open heart surgery. The procedure went well and now I won't have any more of those dizzy spells." She sent Liss a bright smile and breezed out of the kitchen.

Liss stared after her, speechless. What was there to say? Her mother was never going to change.

When she heard laughter coming from the dining room, she put on her party face and joined the others. She had to smile in earnest when she saw what had amused them. Dandy was sitting on one of the dining room chairs, look-ing for all the world as if she expected to share in the family's Thanksgiving dinner. And there, halfway along the table, unerringly close to the turkey Dan was about to carve, a large yellow paw poked up from between two empty seats. Lumpkin was up to his old tricks.

Margaret collected the dogs and confined them in the downstairs bath. Liss corralled Lumpkin and Glenora and carried them off to the pantry. Except for an occasional yowl from that direction, the humans in the house were able to enjoy their meal without interruption. Everyone was careful to avoid controversial topics and concentrate on counting their blessings. It wasn't until Mac and Dan had adjourned to the living room to watch football that the word *Pilgrim* entered the conversation.

"It still bothers Mac that he was out grocery shopping when Spinner showed up at our place," Vi confided as she picked up the empty gravy boat in one hand and a butter dish in the other and headed for the kitchen. "He seems to think he should have been there to protect me."

"He's not alone." Liss hefted the turkey platter. "Dan has been beating himself up over the fact that he let me sleep in on the day of Spinner's bail hearing. I keep telling him that it probably wouldn't have made any difference."

"It's nice they care about their wives," Margaret said, following them with a stack of dirty dinner plates, "unlike some people I could name."

"The Pilgrim men weren't all bad," Liss objected. "They were duped by a charismatic con man. That reminds me. Sherri found out where George Gerard was on the day Connie left Pilgrim Farm. Remember? He was supposed to be picketing the hotel but he wasn't there. It turns out he was house hunting. He and Solomon have rented a nice little place in Three Cities."

"Connie's gone to Boston," Vi said.

"So," Margaret said, leaving the plates and making a quick return trip to the dining room for water goblets, "are the police going to be able to prove that Miranda poisoned Hadley's oatmeal?"

"Probably. Sherri told me that they think she slipped some herbal concoction into his food before he went out looking for Connie."

"He had it coming."

"Mother!"

"Well, he did."

"He drowned Susan," Margaret said in a subdued voice. "Miranda's lawyer told me that Hadley confessed while he was in the hospital. I guess he thought he was going to die. I'm glad he recovered. He deserves to be locked up for the rest of his life. I don't care if it's prison or a mental hospital, just as long as he never gets out."

"Did you know that Chloe Spinner called the state police?" Liss asked. "Gordon was already on his way to talk to Hadley when Sherri got my text."

"I doubt she could tell them much." Vi scraped leftover vegetables into storage containers while Liss and Margaret went back and forth to finish clearing the dining room table. "I mean, wasn't Connie the only one who actually saw Hadley with a knife? And if Miranda was the lavender lady in the town square, Chloe wasn't there, either."

"I feel sorry for Miranda," Margaret said. "All she ever wanted was to be able to stay on the family farm." She tackled stripping the remaining turkey from the bone and dividing it into three equal portions of leftovers.

"Actually, Chloe knew quite a bit," Liss said. "According to Sherri, she was aware that Jasper was about to make a move to usurp Hadley as leader of the New Age Pilgrims and that he had the support of most of the rest of them. They'd realized that Hadley was out of control. Call it what you like—dementia, megalomania, narcissism, paranoia, or just plain craziness—they were all scared of him. Chloe was a bit confused at first because Hadley lied about the details of the murder. He claimed his cousin had been shot. But once she knew Jasper was killed with a knife, she didn't have a doubt in the world that it was Hadley who murdered him."

"If you hadn't kept going out there, *against all sensible advice,*" Vi said, "Chloe might never have worked up enough courage to talk to the police."

Had that been a compliment? With her mother, it was hard to tell.

"The phrase 'too stupid to live' comes to mind." Margaret smiled as she said it, but her words still stung.

Once the sealed containers of leftovers were safely stored in the refrigerator, out of reach of both dogs and cats, Liss freed the animals. She caught Glenora as she tried to streak out of the pantry, picking her up and cuddling her. "I don't believe I was ever in any danger at Pilgrim Farm. Frankly, the camps on Ledge Lake are more dangerous."

Vi ran water into the sink and added a dollop of dishwashing liquid. While she washed, Margaret dried, leaving Liss to put everything away in the proper cabinets.

"What I still don't get," she said after a moment, "is the rationale behind the New Age Pilgrims. Why start your own religion at all, especially when it doesn't sound as if it was particularly faith-based? The Pilgrims were more like a flock of sheep with Hadley as the sheepdog. He'd bark out commands and they'd follow blindly, even if they were just going around in circles to show off at the county fair."

"Interesting comparison," Margaret said in a dry voice, reaching down to stroke Dandy's soft fur.

Both dogs sat at her feet, watching her every movement with intense interest. They had not yet gotten the message that the food was already put away. Lumpkin, on the counter, was in a stealthy approach pattern to the empty roasting pan. Liss put Glenora down and went to intercept him.

"You know what I mean," she said to her aunt. "I can understand why Miranda and Susan married Hadley and Jasper. They didn't want to leave the only home they'd ever known. That's pitiful but it makes sense. And I can accept that before Hadley went completely around the bend, he was one of those charismatic leaders who draw people to him, people who latch on and become obsessed, the way some fans attach themselves to movie stars. But so much of what he convinced them to do seems irrational."

"The housecleaning?" Margaret grinned.

"No. That actually makes sense. They needed income to keep the farm running. What I don't understand is why he insisted that everyone be married and then kept the couples separated."

"Oh, Connie explained that to me," Vi said, never looking up from the soapsuds. "Hadley was under the misapprehension that wives can't testify against their husbands. He thought it would be safer if the women, being the weaker sex, were prevented by law from harming the rest of the community."

"Are you serious? I'm no lawyer, but it's the rule that a wife couldn't be *forced* to give evidence against her husband?"

"It doesn't surprise me that Hadley was confused. The rest of what Connie told me just confirms it."

"I'll bite," Liss said. "What other cockamamie claims did he make?"

"She said that Hadley established the Pilgrims as a religious group because he believed that members of a congregation couldn't testify against their pastor."

Liss stared at her. "That's ridiculous."

"Maybe so, but apparently the Pilgrims believed what Hadley told them, at least at first. I guess he was pretty convincing. It's only been during the last few years, after his self-control started to slip, that Connie and some of the others realized that the real goal of most of his rules was to keep everyone in line. He liked being the ruler of his own little kingdom. If he decided he hated something, then they all had to hate it."

"Here's another thing I don't understand," Liss said.

"Only one?" Margaret asked, sotto voce.

Liss ignored her. "Back in the beginning, what was he afraid one of his followers might testify to in court?"

Vi chuckled. "Connie told me that, too. It's not such a big deal now that Maine's marijuana laws are changing, but fifteen years ago the crop Hadley harvested at Pilgrim Farm wasn't exactly legal." She took a final swipe at the roasting pan and handed it to Margaret.

In a few more minutes, the cleanup was complete. Margaret suggested they join Mac and Dan.

"I know the Pats aren't playing," she said, "but we should be able to get some idea of the competition New England will be facing for the rest of the season."

"You go on ahead," Vi told her sister-in-law. "We'll be right in."

When she made no move to leave the kitchen, Liss stayed behind, too. An awkward silence fell between them. Liss had a feeling she should say something, but she wasn't sure what. She didn't want to get into another debate over her mother's failure to share information about her health. There was no way she could win that one.

It startled her when Vi flung her arms around her. "I was so proud of you that day," she said, still holding Liss tight. "I should have said so at the time, but between Hadley Spinner and the police, I never had the chance."

Liss rarely heard words of praise from her mother. She was so pleased that she blurted out the first words that came to mind: "I was proud of you, too. We make a good team."

Vi beamed at her. "We do, don't we?"